IMPERFECTIONS

IMPERFECTIONS

bradley somer

NIGHTWOOD EDITIONS

Nightwood Editions
P.O. Box 1779
Gibsons, BC V0N 1V0
Canada
www.nightwoodeditions.com

Author photo: Nenad Maksimovic
Cover photo: Etienne Girardet/fStop/Getty Images
Cover design: Jonathan Taylor, PTI Graphic Design
This book has been produced on 100% post-consumer, recycled, ancient-forest-free paper, processed chlorine-free and printed with vegetable-based dyes.

Nightwood Editions acknowledges financial support from the Government of Canada through the Canada Book Fund and the Canada Council for the Arts, and from the Province of British Columbia through the British Columbia Arts Council and the Book Publisher's Tax Credit.

Canada Council   Conseil des Arts
for the Arts   du Canada

BRITISH COLUMBIA
ARTS COUNCIL
An agency of the Province of British Columbia

Library and Archives Canada Cataloguing in Publication

Somer, Bradley, 1976–
    Imperfections / Bradley Somer.

ISBN 978-0-88971-271-3

    I. Title.

PS8637.O4479I46 2012   C813'.6   C2012-903576-9

for Mrs. Buckingham

CHAPTER 1

Russell, Bob and Derrick

Everyone has heard that old joke at one time or another. We've all heard the one about the guy with no arms and no legs in a bush. His name is Russell. It's really not that funny.

There are several jokes like this, all of them made by people with four limbs, I am sure. They have basically become chicken-crossing-the-road jokes. There is Bob, the guy with no arms and no legs in the water. There is Derrick, the guy with no arms and no legs in the middle of an oil field. I know there are many others.

Here is one maybe you haven't heard. What do you call a guy with no arms and no legs locked in the trunk of a car?

The answer: Richard Trench.

Doesn't make much sense. This joke is more specific to my story. Richard Trench is my name and here I am, reduced to a torso and sandwiched between a spare tire and a gallon of oil glugging around in a red plastic container. Underneath my cheek, leaving an unattractive impression like some chronic skin disease, is a low-grade nylon carpet.

It's the kind of carpet they put in every trunk. The kind that is cut and installed under fluorescent lights in a factory by some guy with large, greasy hands and a bored look on his face. This carpet is black and stinks like gasoline. There is a musty undertone, probably from some variety of mould that grows in the damp, dark nylon and feeds on spilled petrochemicals.

A blanket covers my body. It's the type of blanket that's kept in the trunk for emergencies, like when you come across an accident or get stranded on a winter road and need to survive the night, or when you have to transport a torso. It's not the kind of blanket you would sleep under on a soft bed or even cover your legs with while reading a book in an easy chair. This is a blanket that smells like trunk and is now clotted with blood. Good thing it is the type of blanket you can just throw away.

There is also a shovel, one that bounces against the back of my head whenever we hit a bump. I have been abused to the point where I don't care. I have been sedated to the point where nothing hurts.

I guess what I am saying is things could be worse.

I saw these things in the trunk when they loaded me in. The last thing I saw was a worm's-eye view of two leering faces shadowed by the backlight of a streetlamp and the stars in the night sky. The streetlamp cast a halo around their heads and the stars were nearly blotted out.

"That's it, then?" one of them asked, not looking at the other, eyes fixed on the trunk.

"I suppose," the other replied. "I kind of expected more, really."

The first let a hiss escape.

I guessed it was a laugh.

"What did you expect, that he'd be filled with gold or something?"

"I don't know. Either that or chocolate."

Then one of them lifted his arm, rested it on the trunk for a second before closing it. I tried to say something but my mouth was dry and my vocal chords were crusted. I felt like I had swallowed glue.

There was a creak from the rusty hinges and the slam and click of the latch catching.

I am in the trunk of an '82 Monte Carlo. Maroon. Big eight under the hood with pistons slamming and dirty oil flowing. The kind of engine they don't make anymore. There is the sharp tang of burning antifreeze from the tailpipe, which rattles in its brackets as we power over bumps in a gravel road. There are rust holes above the rear wheel wells and it's bubbling like leprosy underneath the paint.

This is all I can remember. This is what I saw as they took me out of the house on the blanket and carried me like a stretcher down the lawn. It was in the suburbs somewhere. My addled mind reeled with the familiarity of it. The smell of grass in the cool night air. The black and white leaves flicking on and off as they reflected streetlights. Above my head and below the stars, a gentle breeze blew. A dog barked in the distance and, through the bay window across the street, the back of someone's head was framed by the blue glow of a television set.

Had my mother known I would have ended up this way, if she could have seen into the future, her son without the arms and legs she had birthed him with, without the perfect ten fingers and ten toes that every mother counts when she first sees their baby ... if she could have seen her son locked in the trunk of a car, she might have named him Jack. That would have been more in keeping with the joke than Richard Trench; it would have made more sense. Mind you, nothing is making too much sense at the moment. It really hasn't for a while.

The shovel hits me in the back of the head and I try to think of the instant that led me down this path. There had to be one split second where the road forked, where everything turned ninety degrees. In hindsight there is always something you can pick up on, that moment when one reality splits from the next and leads to the point when you look back and think: if I had seen it then ... if only I had seen it, I could have done something differently.

Now, in the stink of the trunk, I think I've figured it out: that specific moment.

It started under the fluorescent lights, while standing on the polished white linoleum tiles in the menswear section of a department store. The store was peppered with mannequins wearing suits and others wearing sweater vests. A muzak version of ABBA's "Gimme! Gimme! Gimme!" played quietly from speakers hidden somewhere in the rows of clothing.

"Hey." Someone was trying to get my attention.

I don't know how many times it had been said, how long this person was trying to get me to notice, so I apologized.

"Sorry, hi."

"Ain't I seen you somewhere before?"

That was it, that second, the moment that led to the trunk. Nothing after that could have changed the outcome. These were the last words before everything went wrong. They seem normal enough really. In my line of work I had heard them so many times I didn't think they would be the point where the world started tilting awkwardly to one side, never to right itself again.

"What's that?" I have learned to feign distraction, it prolongs the moment that, admittedly, brings me some joy. I had been noticed; someone recognized me.

"You look familiar."

I never even considered that those moments would be the bridge from my old life to this one, this new life with four bleeding stumps, lying on a low-grade nylon rug with the typical denizens of a trunk as my only companions: a gallon of oil, a spare tire, a blanket and a shovel.

Oh, there is also the stink of exhaust and gasoline from a rarely tuned engine. I can only imagine the freedom of the clear night breeze passing a short distance away, on the other side of the thin metal trunk, a breeze that sweeps across the car and swirls, invisible in the darkness of our wake, a darkness not quite as complete or oppressive as that of the trunk.

I think we are out of the city now, out of the suburbs. There was some stop and go for a while but now the engine has been running at the same pitch for some time. Outside, I imagine the moon and stars as the only things to light our way as we tear across the empty terrain. Perhaps a coyote watches us pass from a distance, its eyes two spots of light floating in the dark, before it skitters off into the scablands.

It strikes me that I don't know where my limbs are. They aren't in the trunk with me.

Anyway:

"Ain't I seen you somewhere before?"

"What's that?"

"You look familiar."

"I've done some modelling." Smile and wait for the eyebrows to rise in response.

"No kiddin'." A pause. A head cocked to one side in examination. "Yer the tank-top guy, right? The one on the boat."

This is a reference to one shoot I did for Jungo undergarments. That promotion was everywhere. I saw myself on the sides of buses, the backs of newspapers, the billboards near the airport, and even those little advertising slips that fall out from between glossy magazine pages.

The Jungo shoot was about eleven years ago. Those were prime days. The idea for the shoot was that there was this sexy and insanely beautiful guy on a boat (that was me) and he was wearing loose pyjama pants and a white tank top while pulling on a rope to tighten a sail. The boat actually sat on a trailer in the middle of a parking lot. The shot was angled skyward so none of the background, the rusted VW, the graffiti on the building at the end of the lot, the homeless guy sleeping in a puddle of piss near the dumpster, none of that was visible.

The sun was a bank of bright white lights run by a noisy generator. The wind tossing my hair came from a giant fan, towed behind a pickup truck and powered by the same noisy generator. The water droplets on my arms and face were a sticky glycerine solution. The world was in colour but the picture was black and white. It was all completely fabricated and it was the best world to work in.

"That's me, all right. That was a while ago though."

"Yeah, I remember that. Musta been early nineties."

The Jungo shoot was in the mid-nineties, actually. 1994. Grunge was in full swing. Pearl Jam validated plaid jackets and workboots as a statement of individualism that everyone was wearing. *Pulp Fiction* reacquainted us with the genius of John Travolta and, at the time, we were all still blind to the fact that genius is actually all about being in the right place at the right moment. It was the year of the Lorena Bobbitt trial. That year the world learned an important thing: a severed penis could be reattached and still function. That year, Dow Corning was served a class action lawsuit that would eventually be backed by half a million women unhappy with their breast implants. Actually, they weren't just unhappy: their tits were poisoning them.

There was a pause in the conversation.

"You see that mannequin?" I pointed across the menswear floor to a wool trench coat supported perfectly by the slender shoulders of the plastic torso. "That one over there?"

"Yeah."

"That's me."

Wait for it.

"Really?" Comparing eyes flit from plastic to flesh. "The face ain't yours."

"It's my face."

"I don't know. It don't really look like you."

"It is my face," I say. "It's just … stylized. You know? They made the nose sharper."

That mannequin had been cast twelve years ago—I was eighteen. If you have ever shopped that big department store, the one that has Seniors' Day the first Tuesday of every month, you have seen me, too. Sure I have put on a few pounds, fleshed out since they cast that, and my smooth, alabaster belly wouldn't work as well as a washboard now.

It is amazing how easily the body can be compartmentalized. Without even thinking, the eye will deconstruct a face or a body, notice little imperfections in an isolated feature and ignore the whole. It takes the subconscious mind mere seconds to do it. Some believe it is inherent, in our genes. Some say we are looking for physical perfection, good breeding stock.

There is always something wrong.

I think he's hot, but his lips are too thin. I think she's hot but her eyes are too close together, too far apart, different colours, and on and on. I do it myself. Like a mechanic, I can tear down a face or a body and rebuild it, noting everything that needs tweaking or tuning. I am probably more astute than most with such things—being in the business, I look for works of art.

Down the aisle, a clerk is undressing mannequin-me. She has taken off the wool coat. The mannequin-me stands on a display so, to remove the more personal articles, she is forced to mount a chair. She looks me in the eyes. Her hands glide deftly over my smooth, plastic skin as she removes a smart sweater vest. She runs an open palm down my chest and across my abdomen and she shifts her position slightly, rubbing her knees together once, one past the other.

The clerk climbs down from her perch. Her eyes level with the mannequin-me's beltline, she reaches out and pauses. Her cherry red fingernails grasp the fabric on either side of the button. Her tongue breaches her bubble gum lips, a fleshy petal tilting toward the sun. It slides to the corner of her mouth leaving those lips glistening, slick and seductively puckered. She smiles before drawing her hands together, the button slipping out of the buttonhole. The clerk looks up the length of mannequin-me's body. She pinches the zipper and pulls the tab slowly and the pants loosen from mannequin-me's hips.

"Yer nipples that pointy?"

"No. That's stylized too. My nipples are normal."

"Oh."

You have seen me naked. If you have been around when they were changing the mannequins then you have seen me naked. They took a few liberties with the nose, the nipples and the face. Still, that moulded plastic body has caused many a blush on Seniors' Tuesday.

"So, what you been doing lately?"

That hurts. It prompts the words "nothing" and "looking for work."

Lately, I have this feeling of panic.

"Things are still moving along nicely. I've decided to do less modelling and take more of a management role. You can't stay beautiful forever, right?"

Lately, I have this tightness in my chest. Makes it hard to breathe.

It's like I'm trapped in a car that has driven off a bridge and into a lake and the water is slowly leaking in through the cracked windshield. This is okay because there is still lots of air for the moment but the problem is that there is someone else in the car, some big fucker with strong hands around my neck choking the living shit out of me so I can't even enjoy the last, sweet bit of air before the car fills up. I can just feel the water pressing against my skin. I have been trying to get back the five years that saw my career shrivel.

Modelling is a cruel thing. You have passed your prime before you hit thirty. At a time when other people's careers are just blossoming, yours wilts. Your friends, the ones who went the doctor/lawyer/accountant route, have just been promoted. They are married. They have a kid or two. They have just bought a house and a new car. They have retirement savings. They have a dental plan and an expense account. They get paid vacations and flex days.

There are many things that older models wind up doing. We see them every day. Me, however, I would rather be homeless than get a paycheque pointing at green screens for a weather channel or telling people that I lost twenty pounds of unwanted fat on some diet. I would rather die than peddle an orthopaedic shoe or do a commercial spot for all those starving kids in Third World countries. Who has the time to save the whales and polar bears? I have been planning a comeback. I have been working hard toward it. I have a plan and I was about to get it underway.

It worked for John Travolta.

The essence of genius is being in the right place at the right moment.

My agent called me "quixotic."

I have no clue what that means.

"So, what you been doing lately?"

"Things are still moving along nicely. I have decided to do less modelling and take more of a management role. You can't stay beautiful forever, right?"

"No ... you can't stay beautiful forever. It ain't like there's a fountain of youth or nothing to make you immortal." A chuckle. "Right?"

There was something sick in the laugh, something desperate. The words were spoken too quickly, as if trying to convince me of something that wasn't true. This should have been a clue.

"True." I smiled uncertainly.

"The body of work you left behind's admirable, though. In itself it kinda preserves an immortal youth, right? Kinda like a time capsule."

This should have been a clue.

"Oh, you know my work."

Vanity blinds.

CHAPTER 2

Every Tree is Known by Its Fruits

Memories are an unreliable fiction. Different people remember the same things in different ways. Even so, memories construct a core truth for a person no matter how unreliable they are. I remember my birth. Well, I am not sure I really remember it or I have just imagined it so vividly and repeatedly that it became a memory for me.

I remember my mother being beautiful.

Psychologists also say that our response to beauty is something crawling around our subconscious mind, a little goblin working behind the scenes. They say that in the first ten minutes of life, babies can follow the outline of a face and after a few days they can recognize their mother. They say that babies react more favourably, form a stronger bond with people who portray health, people who have symmetrical faces, and all of the other things that form beauty.

My mother was definitely beautiful.

Things I don't remember about my birth are the ejection from a warm, wet world into a cool, dry one. I don't remember the suffocation of muscles contracting around my body. I don't remember the dark giving way to harsh banks of white lights. I also don't remember how to breathe fluids and I don't remember my umbilical cord being cut.

What I do remember is the comparative absence of smell. Absence is the wrong word. There was a smell there; the smell was clean, sterilized to the point of being a simulacrum for the absence of smell. It was that sterilized smell coupled with my mother's face that led to an association between the two that I carry with me to this day.

"Congratulations," said the nurse, her features covered by a surgical mask. She was talking to my parents but looking at me. "You are the proud parents of a perfect, beautiful baby boy."

Ten toes, ten fingers, two arms, two legs, everything was there.

My mother smiled. Beaming at my big, round head and my tiny body. She did not marvel at the wondrously freaky mis-proportions of it all, the head a quarter the length of the entire body, the nearly adult-sized eyes and the comparative lack of a chin or nose. All these things, if carried into adulthood would result in an alien-looking being with a beach ball-sized head, baseball-sized eyes and severe neck problems. Instead, she saw something beautiful. She sported that glazed look of motherly admiration, that instinctual love that has been blindly bred into mothers for millions of years. That look of being exhausted from ten hours of labour, strung out on hormones and painkillers and, for my mother, about two minutes away from becoming her old self again.

"He's gorgeous," she said.

"He's small," my father said, watching his wife hold his son from across the room where he leaned against the wall. His idea of perfect was quite different from the nurse's. Father didn't have the same millions of years of inbred instinct that Mother had.

"No he's not," my mother replied. She looked to the nurse. "Is he small?"

The nurse's forehead wrinkled, a frown. "He is a little below the average length, a little thinner than average but he is perfectly healthy. Those are just averages, some babies are longer, some are fatter, others are shorter and skinnier. All babies are different but all of them are beautiful."

"See," my father grunted, pushing himself from the wall and walking to the bed to get a closer look. "He's small."

Mother gingerly touched some of the gick that covered me and recoiled. Her eyes cleared, her beautiful eyebrows dropped and her face seemed to fall.

"What is that?" she asked. My mother pointed, her finger wiggled an arc at the top of my vision.

The nurse inspected me. "That's called a haemangioma. It's a mass of constricted blood vessels. It's kind of like a birthmark. Nothing to worry about, really."

"It is rather hideous though," Mother said and poked the top of my head. "Will it go away?

"They mostly disappear over time," the nurse replied. "It may grow a bit more but it should go away in a few years."

My father sighed.

My mother's eyes were unconvinced. She scowled for a moment.

"Can it be ... taken off?"

"It can if it's posing some kind of health risk. Sometimes they form on or around organs and impair their function. It's usually not good to operate on newborns though. That one will go away in time. Even if it doesn't, it won't matter because the little fellow will have a full head of hair."

Mother scowled at the blemish for a while longer and then, resigned, examined the rest of my body.

"And what's that?" she asked. Her finger dropped below my vision.

"What?" The nurse's mask flexed and contracted when she spoke. "That's an anomalous patch of terminal hair." She muttered. "Again, nothing to worry about."

"Terminal hair?" My mother's eyes widened in horror and the corners of her mouth dropped, exposing her lower canines.

Mother had beautifully white teeth.

"Yes," the nurse replied. "The body is covered with hair, called vellus hair. Hair follicles respond to androgens, hormones like testosterone, and thicken into what is called terminal hair. Usually this happens at puberty but occasionally babies have a patch of fuzz like that. It's a cute fuzzy patch, I think." The nurse's eyes smiled at me over her mask.

"He's not going to turn into one of those Mexican wolf-men is he?" Mother grimaced.

"Testosterone," Father mumbled to himself and smiled.

Mother sighed.

Father coughed.

"I'm going out for a cigarette, dear," Father said and sauntered out the door, not waiting for a response.

"He's a very handsome boy." The nurse cast a stern gaze at Mother. "You have a beautiful baby boy, not a Mexican wolf-man."

With that, she stormed out of the delivery room and I was left to continue bonding with my mother. This consisted of her holding me awkwardly and making strained kissy faces in between glances at the door and out the window.

Four days later, bundled in an odourless blue blanket and cradled in my father's arms, we stepped out into the bright sun and crossed the parking lot to a shiny new green AMC Pacer. My father wore a green cardigan and sported a thick, but well-groomed, brown beard. The glass shimmered in the sun as Father handed me off to Mother and opened the door for her.

"Blitzkrieg Bop" by the Ramones screamed through the speakers as the engine roared to life. "What is this?" my father said and poked at the radio pre-sets. "Where did ABBA go? They used to be on all the time and now there's this nonsense." He fumbled around on the seat between us and found an 8-track cartridge. Without taking his eyes from the windshield, he scoured the dashboard with it before inserting it in the player.

"There we go," Father said with audible relief. So began my first experience with ABBA, something that everyone does, or at least should, remember. Unfortunately, the kids nowadays hear "Dancing Queen" on a drunken night at some retro-dance party. They fail to see the depth of ABBA, the depth that my father saw, their first ABBA experience ruined by some DJ-of-the-moment's "Dancing Queen" remix. Just out of the hospital, swaddled and warm, there was something in the air that forever tied me to those Swedes.

The engine roared and the Pacer turned out of the hospital parking lot onto the main street. Father lit a cigarette and the smell of it filled the car. That's the smell I remember of my father and, in the future, that's a smell I would always associate with the man. It would remind me of the first words I heard from his voice and of playing catch in the backyard. It would remind me of the feel of his green cardigan, scratchy and warm, and how his beard looked when I gazed up as he carried me out of the hospital.

Mother rolled down her window a bit. Smoke slid out of the crack like a waterfall.

We were going home. We were a family.

I don't remember much of my early days at home except the general things. There was a lot of sunshine coming through clean windows into large rooms with vaulted ceilings. There was the smell of freshly mown grass coming through open windows and the sound of kids shouting in the distance, over the rows of fences, in someone else's backyard. I remember the air being fresh and sweet. It was a morning feeling, one where there was the clink of dishes and cutlery from another, faraway room and the sound of the vacuum cleaner running downstairs.

Then there was the barbecue where I got to meet more of my

family. A warm breeze blew across my face where I lay in a bassinet, in the backyard in the shade under an orange tree. "He's gorgeous." My aunt's face beamed down.

I was wearing a blue cotton unitard with attached booties. There was a button-up hatch in the back. I also wore a fuzzy bonnet. I remember always wearing a hat when I was a kid.

"A little darling," Mother agreed. I could not see her but I knew she was close by the sound of her voice.

"Have you settled on a name?"

"Jack wanted to name him Jack Jr.," Mother said.

My aunt frowned and rolled her eyes.

"But I think I've convinced him of Richard," Mother continued.

I giggled and my aunt's face melted into a smile.

"Richard Trench." She contemplated before turning a wiggling finger to my chin. "Hello, little Richard," she said. "I am your Auntie Maggie."

"He likes you, Margaret," my mother said.

"Tony," Auntie Maggie called over her shoulder. "Come say hi to your nephew."

"What's that?" came a voice from somewhere.

"Come here, damn it," Maggie said. "Say hi to your nephew."

A man's face appeared in my vision, beside Auntie Maggie's face. He had a heavy brow and a square jawline that was covered in silvery stubble. The man smelled of grilled meat and barbecue sauce. He held a bottle of beer at belly level. His head was quite a bit bigger than Auntie Maggie's, his eyes were a little wide-set. The bridge of his nose was flat and the rest of it was rather bulbous, giving him the look of a syphilitic boxer. This man, my Uncle Tony, revealed two rows of crooked teeth as he smiled.

"Leonard, come here and meet your cousin Richard," Tony boomed over his shoulder. "Now, damn it." Pause. "Hold my beer, Mags," he said, handing Auntie Maggie the beer, raising a camera in front of his face, fiddling with the focus and then clicking a picture.

Uncle Tony slung the camera around his neck and bent out of my vision for a moment. When he reappeared, he held up a small child with a round face and a runny nose.

Leonard.

Uncle Tony presented him like a gift, holding him out so he could touch my arm. Leonard, who would become my best friend in childhood and through my adult years. Leonard, who would always have a scheme and would share so many moments and memories with me. Leonard, who, being two years older than me, would protect me from bullies, break ground and map areas for me such as girls, driving, alcohol and so many other wonders of the world.

Leonard pinched me hard.

I cried out in pain.

"Leonard," Auntie Maggie's voice was stern. "Use your nice hands now."

She patted the backs of Leonard's hands in a vague and noncommittal form of discipline.

Mother mistook my surprised yowl as an order from the bar and lifted me from my bassinet.

From this new vantage, I took in the backyard. It seemed to go on forever. My father stood at the end of the deck, poking at the barbeque with a confused look on his face and a cigarette hanging out of his mouth. The grey-blue smoke from the end of the cigarette blended with the grey-blue smoke drifting into the air from the grill. Uncle Tony put Leonard down and tapped him on the butt, sending him scooting across the dark green grass, away from the orange tree. The colours of the flower garden were vivid and alive. Roses stood thick and majestic near the deck. Clematis climbed the trellis near the fence where a bright yellow bird sat and sang. Leonard made his way to the clematis and hit the trellis, causing the bird to trill and flap away. He laughed and tumbled backwards onto the grass. Auntie Maggie wandered away from us, toward Father. Her gauzy dress, swirling blue and green, patterned like an ocean wave, rippled in the breeze.

And then my face was plunged into my mother's breast.

When I was pulled away again it was from under a blanket. I was in a grocery store. Fluorescent lights, far overhead, stung my eyes. The air smelled like a mix of vegetables and cardboard. The floors were polished to the point of being blinding, if a tan shade of brown could ever be blinding.

"Jack," Mother said, calling to Father.

"Wha'?"

"Go get me some of that udder balm Maggie was talking about." She was hissing now, her eyes darting to see if anyone was close enough to hear. When she deemed it safe, she continued. "My tits are chewed raw." Father wandered off, nodding and breathing through his mouth which, combined, came across as a look either of retarded wonder or cerebral palsy.

We were sitting on a stack of pallets full of Campbell's Soup across from a row of glossy magazines at the end of an aisle. Opposite us was a freezer full of Swanson's Hungry Man turkey dinners. "Mean" Joe Greene glared at us with the threatening claim that spending ninety-eight cents and half an hour with an oven would result in a succulent Thanksgiving dinner.

A heavy-set woman wandered up to the freezer and, with a finger attached to her chin, contemplated the meals. She took two and then spotted us. Her face softened to a smile and she pushed her cart with a wobbly wheel over to us.

"Oh my God, you are so cute in your little ball cap. What's your name?" she asked.

"This is Richard," Mother replied for me.

"How old are you, Richard?" the woman clucked, reached out and rubbed her finger up and down my cheek.

"He is just turning eight weeks," Mother replied.

"Aren't you adorable?" the woman cooed and made a clicking noise with her tongue against the roof of her mouth. She took a step back in admiration before waving bye and pushing her Hungry Man dinners over to the magazines.

Mother sighed and looked up the aisle for Father. My eyes followed the woman across the aisle to a rack of magazines. She selected a fashion magazine and started flipping through it. Several heavy bond paper inserts slid from the pages and skidded across the aisle. The woman huffed and scrabbled around collecting the inserts.

I would see those magazines later in life but then they would be faded and dog-eared, the covers creased and coffee-stained. On the covers there were skinny models with turquoise blue neck scarves and big, bug-eye sunglasses. In the background there were beefy, hairy chested brutes with facial hair, moustachioed or bearded, and with ill-defined but undeniable musculature.

"Is this the stuff?" It was my father jolting my thoughts and holding forth a yellow- and green-coloured tin with a smiling cartoon cow face framed by gaudy daises.

"I think so," Mother said and adjusted me so she could open the container. She poked two fingers in and scooped out a gob of white paste. She thrust the wad of goo under her shirt and rubbed.

I hiccupped and puked up a little bit. Mother took this as a request and my face was plunged under the blanket and into her breast. The balm had left the distinct, sanitized smell of the hospital.

When I was pulled away we were in a parking lot, sitting in the Pacer, which was parked beside the sickly yellow light of an overhead lamp. In the light, I could make out slivers reflected off of the glass and steel of the surrounding cars. I could also see the slivers reflected off the tears on my mother's cheeks. The images outside the car were blurred by condensation on the windshield. I couldn't tell whether it was on the inside or the outside. The window was open a crack; the glass was foggy.

I smelled Father before I saw him. I smelled his cigarette even before he opened the driver's-side door and before I felt the suspension sink under his weight as he plopped down. The car keys jingled in his hand.

"Well," he grunted, smoke puffing out of his nose like a pissed-off cartoon bull. "What the fuck was that?"

The car was silent for a moment.

"Today, at the grocery store, a woman talked to Richard." Mother gasped and whimpered. "I wasn't even there."

Father looked at her dumbly. The cigarette hung out of the corner of his mouth, dumbly as well.

Mother continued. "She didn't talk to me or even look at me. She talked to Richard. I wasn't even there. And now, I just wanted a fancy dinner with some friends and Richard starts acting up and they asked me to leave. I went. I couldn't do anything else."

"Oh, I missed that," Father mumbled. "All's I know is, I went off to take a piss and you were gone when I came back." The cigarette bobbed up and down in the corner of his mouth, the ember at the end drawing circles in the dark as he talked.

"You didn't think to come looking for me? I've been here almost an hour," Mother said.

"Well, I had to finish my dinner ... It was steak," Father said, "and lobster. I thought you were in the can changing him or something."

"Take him for a minute."

My world jostled and shifted. Then, I was looking up past the steering wheel to my father's face. Mother rummaged through the purse resting at her feet. She found an orange bottle and rattled the pills inside before taking one.

"Shit, honey. When did you start the Librium again?" Father's beard frowned.

A bit of ash fell off the end of his cigarette and landed in a soft, sooty pile on my cheek, right below my eye. Nobody noticed but me.

"It's not the Librium. This is Valium. It's better," she said. "I'll be fine. If I have to dine in the food court at the mall with all the other moms for the next eighteen years, I'll be fine."

Silence followed the sound of Mother putting the rattling bottle back into her purse. A pudding-brained instinct made me giggle, kick my feet and reach for the rattling noise. This bothersome reaction would persist for a while before evolving through several stages including the instinctive giggle-kick-reach that comics and ice cream would bring out, and later, tree forts, homemade bike jumps, and drum kits, and later still BMX bikes and covert porno-magazine glances in the alley on the way home from school, and finally the boobs and butts of the real thing.

It's all instinct.

It happens.

Can't fight it.

CHAPTER 3

Bagged—Champion Sports Rhino Skin® Style

Leonard laughed.

The veins in his neck sticking out told me it was a real hard laugh, one of those grab-your-knees-and-squat-a-bit-because-you-may-just-piss-yourself-you're-laughing-so-hard kind of laughs. Then he squeaked, a long high-pitched siren noise. It was one of those squeaks that came from laughing so hard he couldn't control the flow of oxygen because he was busy trying to breathe and not throw up at the same time.

I caught all of this after the metallic *ping* sound of the Champion Sports Rhino Skin® Dodgeball faded from my head and from between my legs and before I hit the pavement in the courtyard behind the school. The sound had faded but the red rubber sting remained.

Leonard squeaked again.

I hoped he pissed himself.

Only two things were endearing to me about Leonard at that point. The first was that he still wanted to hang out with me though he was two years older, which I thought was pretty cool even if I had to tolerate a certain amount of abuse and embarrassment. The second was that Auntie Maggie and Uncle Tony always had the best stuff. They had just sprung for a Commodore 64 and I had a horrible addiction to fighting grues and zorkmids in the great underground empire of *Zork*. *Zork III* would be out next month and I was dying to play.

These were subconscious thoughts, though. They ran behind my active thoughts and tempered my reaction to the current situation. I wasn't mad. I just felt like throwing up as I lay on the pavement clutching my nuts. There was that and there was also me wishing Leonard would piss himself laughing in front of the crowd of kids that started to gather. Mind you, Leonard would find some way to make pissing himself look cool. He could do that; he was that good. To remain friends with Leonard at that age required taking the occasional hit, such as a simultaneous strike to the head and the nuts by Champion Sports Rhino Skin® Dodgeballs thrown by him and a buddy.

I was crying, I guess, because all of a sudden I was able to let out a howl and I could no longer see through the tears. All my muscles clenched as if I was trying to squeeze out of the world and slip into some dark unknown place in the universe. I know it seems a bit over the top but it just hurt that much. Even so, I don't know what was worse, the sting on the side of my head, the throbbing, sickening pain radiating up from what I protectively clutched between my legs or the fact that I was bawling in front of a growing crowd of my peers.

There was no hiding it, no saying it was sand in my eye or anything like that. I was a tight spasm of twitching little boy on the ground, bawling with abandon, snot flowing out of my nose and down my cheek, strings of gob sliding from the side of my mouth, tears streaming and falling from my face making wet dots on the sand and pavement where I lay on my side, fetal and rocking slightly in the grit.

There was no way to make that look cool.

That was the kind of thing that stuck with you.

That was the kind of thing that earned you nicknames that followed you well into high school, nicknames like "Dodge Balls."

That was the kind of thing that shapes your life and either makes you strong or turns you into one of those black trench coat-wearing kids who is always reading mail-order catalogues for throwing stars and talking about buying a sword.

Another nickname for someone who is clutching his nuts in public. "Ricky Ricky Grabs His Dicky." This one was particularly clever given that it incorporated rhythm, rhyme and my name. Though, my dicky wasn't the problem.

"Man, that was radical." Leonard finally calmed down enough to wipe his eyes and cough out a few words. He straightened up and stumbled closer, oblivious to the gathered crowd of kids. Leonard didn't need an audience to be cool.

"Seriously," Leonard laughed. "Are you okay?"

Leonard got down on one knee beside me, put a hand on my shoulder and curved his body into a *C* shape in order to line up his face with mine.

I made a loud *whaaaaap* sound as I breathed in a gulp of air between sobs. A glob of snot dropped from my cheek, making a sugary puddle in the sand and pavement.

"Come on, people are watching." Leonard's smile faded and it seemed the seriousness of scrambling my eggs sunk in. "You want me to go get the nurse?"

"Whaaaaap," I said and shook my head. My cheek brushed the sandy snot glob and it strung up from the ground.

Someone in the crowd giggled.

Another muttered, "Big baby."

Leonard spun around to see who it was. Everyone respected Leonard and the main ingredient for that respect was fear. This is something every six-year-old understands. The law of the jungle applies nowhere more than in the schoolyard at recess.

Leonard demanded respect. He had been held back a year and was still a grade ahead of me. He was eight, we were six and at that stage, age was not so much a number but a size. He was two years bigger than us. He could be mean, he could be unpredictable and more kids had him to thank for a bruise or a black eye than any other.

Remember earlier when I said there were two endearing things about Leonard? I just thought of a third. He was on my side.

I managed to sit up, one side of my face looking like a sugar doughnut and the other red from the Rhino Skin bitch slap. Both sides were wet with embarrassment. I forced myself to stop crying. I took a deep breath. I wiped my face on my shirt sleeve and got sand in my eye, which caused it to well up again. The snot from my cheek left a glaze on the fabric.

Leonard was prowling around the crowd, looking kids in the eye as if he could intimidate them into the suicide of admitting they had slighted me. Kids were nervously trying to break from the group without being noticed but, like in the wild, there was safety in numbers. The larger the group, the less likely you were to get singled out. Common practice was to wait until Leonard had passed and then try to make your way to the back of the herd before slowly breaking for the school doors.

Don't make any fast moves, it attracts attention.

Nice and slow.

Leonard turned his attention back to me once the crowd had cleared sufficiently. He smiled and helped me up, draping one of my arms across his shoulders and snaking his arm around my waist. He walked me over to a nearby bench.

I felt like limping, so I did. Anything else still hurt too much.

"You coming over after school?" Leonard asked after he settled next to me on the bench.

"Rad," I wheezed. "I think my parents are coming over for supper anyway." I clutched my nuts once again, it seemed like the thing to do as a bit of pressure eased the pain slightly.

Auntie Maggie and Uncle Tony had a satellite dish. The previous night Leonard and I had watched MTV and wandered around dumbly for hours playing air guitars and making stupid guitar-player faces.

"We can play *Zork* or watch TV or something," Leonard clapped me on the shoulder and I winced.

The recess bell buzzed and Leonard popped off the bench.

"You still got snot on your face," he said and ran to line up to get back in the school.

Recess was over.

In 1982, I was not aware enough to think of the bigger world and the progression of time. I was a kid. As Leonard and I walked home after school, the year 2000 was the distant future and, if it were to have crossed our thoughts, it would only have been as an abstraction. In the back of our brains, the year 2000 was a static of teleportation, jet packs and flying cars. It was a fantasy of robot slaves and laser ray guns. As far as we could comprehend, the future happened sometime after summer vacation, which was still three weeks away. After that, the world did not even register.

As I grew older, I would start to learn that the more I knew the less I really knew. I would learn that there are things going on all over the world that conspire, in time, to contribute to a moment and that connectedness of things. If you could follow all the details, they would comprise the anatomy of that moment, and could be used to predict the future. Leonard would figure this out in fourteen years or so; I would figure it out too late.

As for now...

I had no idea that in Hamilton, at the same moment Leonard pushed me from the sidewalk and into traffic only to pull me back just before getting hit by a car, a big, maroon Monte Carlo was rolling off the assembly line.

"Saved your life." Leonard grinned and squeezed my arm hard.

The engine, a big, mean, *Mad-Max*ian, eight-cylinder engine under the hood was so clean that it shone on its own. The low-grade nylon carpet in the trunk had a plasticky new car smell. This car was being shipped to Toronto; a sixty-eight-year-old lady named Margaret Koshushner ordered it from Franco Popodini's Niagara Escarpment Pontiac Chev-Olds dealership with the inheritance money from when her husband died in a Pinto accident.

"Now I own you until you repay the debt." Leonard's grin spread at the thought of having an indentured servant.

Leonard was always saving my life. I guess I had to be thankful.

Margaret Koshushner had little knowledge of the Grimshaw vs. Ford Motor Co. product liability case that had gone on in California, in which Ford paid over $6 million in compensatory and punitive damages because a Pinto exploded and someone died and someone else burned.

And why did Leonard own me?

"It's a Ninja Code thing." Leonard lunged up the front stairs to his house two at a time. "I saved your life and now you have to be my servant until you save mine or one of us dies, whichever comes first." He was big into ninjas.

I wasn't sure the Ninja Code applied if you almost killed someone just so you could save them so I couldn't argue the point.

Margaret Koshushner's husband didn't die in a Pinto explosion, though. He had been warming up the car when he died. He had just forgotten to open the garage door.

Leonard burst through the front door of his house calling, "We're home."

Leonard lived in a new two-storey house on a cul-de-sac about five blocks from school. There was a garage attached on the side and a dusty gravel alley behind. My house was about another five blocks, past the 7-Eleven where we got Slurpees and across the soccer fields where we rode our bikes.

Mother and Father always drove over to visit Auntie Maggie and Uncle Tony. They never walked. They were already there, I could hear Father mumbling in another room and the tinkle of ice in a glass of something that would undoubtedly be amber-coloured. That would be Mother.

"Boys," Auntie Maggie called from the back room.

Leonard led the way.

"Jesus Christ," Father said. "Leonard, you get bigger every time I see you. Look at the size of that son of a…"

"Hi, Dad," I said.

Mother sat at the end of a brown and tan paisley couch with a glass in hand. She was glazed, her eyes fixed on the sunlight coming through the window to the backyard.

"Shush, guys," Uncle Tony said. He got up from his recliner and crossed the room to turn up the television.

The newscaster announced something about Pan-Am flight 759 crashing in Louisiana and killing everyone on board. There was a video of a panicked crowd and some wreckage and then a still shot of a hospital. Father and Uncle Tony sat on the edge of their seats, elbows on knees and beer bottles held in prayer between hands. They muttered at each other periodically.

"Sonofabitch."

"Bound to happen every once in a while."

""'Nother beer."

Grunt.

"What did you get up to at school today?" Auntie Maggie asked us.

My face flushed red with the memory.

"Nothing much," Leonard smiled at me. He was so obvious.

The newscaster reported that it had been over one year since the US Centers for Disease Control had begun officially monitoring a rare and persistent form of pneumonia seen only in patients with weakened immune systems, and an ever increasing number of cases in countries around the world had some calling this an epidemic.

"Here's your beer."

"Thanks."

"What I miss?"

"'Nothin'."

"When's supper?" I asked Auntie Maggie.

"Shush, guys," Father said, got up, crossed the room and turned up the news.

"Why don't you go play out back?" Auntie Maggie said and beamed at us. "Barbeque and a slideshow later."

The newscaster talked about the splash a new band was having. Metallica played in some sweaty club. Dave Mustaine whipped his hair around. The newscaster mentioned heavy metal, mentioned thrash.

"They look like girls."

"Yep."

"Whatever happened to ABBA? Now that was music."

"Dunno."

"Shame really."

"Have I got a treat for you later…" Uncle Tony smiled and nodded to my father. His eyes were kind of glassy, maybe a little drunk already.

"Supper in about an hour," Auntie Maggie called after us.

The sliding door shut, cutting off the television noise.

Leonard and I stood on the deck and surveyed the backyard, a little patch of earth squared in by weathered fences. A warm breeze, high up in the trees, rustled the leaves. The yellowing grass had brown trails worn into it, one led to the shed and the other led to a row of trees along the back fence. The trail to the shed was to get tools for tweaking the faucet in the kitchen or hammering in a nail to hang a new picture. The trail to the back alley was to take out the garbage in the cool evening air. It was not as well-kept as my back-yard, the yard where I'd first met Leonard. Regardless, something was more attractive about the ratty, untrimmed bushes lining the fence and the weedy patches of thirsty grass. It was a living space full of history, stories and adventure.

A splash sounded in the distance.

My skin tingled. Something mysterious was going to happen; I could feel it.

Leonard smiled when he saw that I was sensing something out of the ordinary.

"What?" I asked his grin, looking at him out of the corner of my eye.

Another splash from somewhere beyond the fence. It sounded closer than the last one. "Wanna see a naked girl?"

The breeze that had been blowing high above the ground seemed to suddenly drop into the backyard and give a passing, floating touch to any patch of exposed skin.

Before I could answer, Leonard rocketed off the deck and across the backyard. I followed, more out of habit than anything else. Leonard and I scrambled through the bramble until we came to the slats of the fence. For the most part they were too close together to spy through, but it seemed that Leonard had found a way—experience led him directly to a gap. A vertical band of light played on his face as he peered through. His iris dilated.

I eased down next to him, squatting on my heels and knowing all too well that the dry leaves and twigs shed by the bushes made for a difficult covert operation.

Leonard watched for a while and then sighed.

"Check it out," he whispered.

Leonard shifted out of the way and gestured at the space between slats.

I was torn. At that age, I didn't really want to see a naked girl so I wanted to say no. There was a passing curiosity, though, to see what all the fuss was about and, for some reason, the splashing coming from the other side of the fence was intriguing so I wanted to say yes. On the other hand, there was a squirming feeling about watching someone without their knowing it so I wanted to say no. But then there was the pressure of Leonard urging me with a hushed whisper and a head tilted toward the gap in the slats. That sealed the deal. I had to say yes.

I duck-walked a few small steps to the left, took a deep breath and leaned forward to look through the gap. Framed by the splintering wood, the neighbour's yard opened before me like a studio-lit still life. The sun shone directly into the backyard. The grass was a vibrant green and was weed-free. At the far side, I saw the house with its sliding glass doors to the living room. The glass doors reflected an image of the patio, which was made from concrete slabs. There was white patio furniture made from metal frames with a plastic mesh stretched and woven over them. A beach towel, striped with the colours of the rainbow, was draped across a lounge chair and the twinkling water of the swimming pool reflecting the sunlight.

"What do you see?" Leonard hissed close to my ear.

"Shut up a minute," I whispered back.

I focused on some movement, something under the water. A shape rippled and slid, causing a slight liquid ridge above it. Then the shape broke the surface. A woman erupted from the water and hoisted herself up onto the edge of the pool.

I gasped.

"What is it?" Leonard hissed again. "Let me see." He pushed gently but I resisted, hoping Leonard would know that the fence wasn't soundproof and would lay off so we wouldn't get caught.

The woman spun so her back was to me and sat on the edge of the pool. Water flowed down her skin leaving sinuous, dewy lines.

"She's not naked," I whispered, noticing with some degree of relief mixed with a dirty dash of disappointment, that she was wearing a flesh-coloured, two-piece bikini. Regardless, there was something powerful going on that I did not yet understand. It was there in front of me, the tantalizing look of long, glossy wet hair between her shoulder blades, the slight plumping of her buttocks where they met the concrete, and the smooth curves of her skin.

She was no girl, I thought. She could be as old as Mrs. Brennan, my math teacher, but she was still beautiful.

Leonard slapped the back of my head, causing my forehead to bounce off the fence slats with a thud. I peeked through the gap again to see the woman spin around, looking for the source of the noise.

"Go," I spat.

The two of us scrambled, Leonard stifling his giggling with a hand. We crab-walked out of the bramble into the backyard with less care for noise than we had shown going in.

"Run," Leonard said and merged onto the trail leading to the back lane. We stopped briefly to fling the gate open and then we sprinted up the alley, gravel rolling under our sneakers.

My panicked mind could do nothing but tell my legs to follow. I hoped the woman didn't hear us but I was sure she did. I hoped she wouldn't go to Auntie Maggie's and Uncle Tony's to tell but I was sure she would.

Ahead, near the end of the alley, Leonard stopped running. He laughed, seemingly unconcerned. I was terrified.

"She wasn't naked," I said, hoping my face wouldn't betray my calm words.

"One time she was. It was radical." Leonard puffed a little from the run.

"She wasn't this time, though," I said. She was pretty, I thought.

Leonard and I wasted time in the alley, kicking rocks and talking about the woman until Auntie Maggie called. Then we raced back to the yard. Leonard won.

"There you are," Auntie Maggie said from the patio door.

Uncle Tony was fiddling with the propane tank under the barbeque. Mother sat at the picnic table on the deck. She wore bug-eye sunglasses and a wide-brimmed hat that shaded all the way out to her shoulders. Her glass sat beside the fashion magazine she was flipping through. It was empty save for one waning ice cube and a fingernail depth of tawny coloured booze.

She looked over at me and smiled. "Come sit with your mom." She patted her knee and slurred, "You handsome fellow."

I joined her. Uncle Tony's mutterings of "fuckin' thing" and "bitch-whore of a thing" subsided and shortly there was the smell of cooking meat in the air. Mother and I looked at her magazine.

"Look at this," she pointed with a free finger, the rest wrapped around her glass. "This is how the year 2000 will look, and it's happening now. Isn't that amazing?"

I didn't say anything but looked as pages flipped by. Space-age materials hugged galactic heroes and space vixens as they strutted down glowing runways. It was amazing. The designer names passing by were as exotic as the models: Thierry Mugler, Azzedine Alaïa…

"Oh, here. Look at this," Mother said breathily. "Yohji Yamamoto."

Sharp shoulders, round hips, Lycra and Viscose, two-foot-long spikes of hair and dark racoon-eye makeup. Material that made me think of the woman in the pool. All of this was wrapped in the heady faint chemical smells coming from the ink on the glossy pages and from between Mother's lips.

I looked over my shoulder at her and smiled. She wrapped an arm around my belly and gave me a limp squeeze.

"Aren't they gorgeous?" she whispered.

I could only nod.

Then she scowled.

"How did you get a splinter in your forehead?" she asked. Without waiting for an answer she spun me into a more accessible position on her lap and pinched at my forehead. She tweezed the end of the splinter between two fingernails and slid it slowly out of the sheath of my skin.

"Come here, Rich." Father's voice boomed from near the barbeque.

I looked over and was blinded. The sun was setting and hovered just above the fence. I squinted and saw Father holding a football. He faked a throw and I flinched. I couldn't tell if he was laughing. I slid off Mother's lap and wandered down onto the grass.

"Catch the ball," Father said.

With the sun behind him and no further prompting, he threw the football. A flitting shadow blipped across the sun and then there was a quick pain in my shoulder before I spun around and landed face-first in the grass.

"Jesus, Jack. Be careful," Mother said.

"You gotta get behind it and cradle the catch," Father called to me and mimicked the move.

I heard a loud squeak from Leonard laughing on the patio. The noise was silenced by a slap to the back of his head from Auntie Maggie.

"Burgers are up," called Uncle Tony.

I pushed up and brushed off my knees and the front of my shirt. My shoulder throbbed deep under the skin. I couldn't cry anymore today. I wouldn't, especially in front of Father.

We all made our way to the picnic table. The sun dipped below the fence-line and my mind drifted from my hamburger to the deep pain in my shoulder to the woman in the skin-coloured bikini who had been just on the other side of that fence.

The evening cooled and we gathered around the firepit where Uncle Tony built a fire. The adults drank scotch and chatted against the crackle of burning wood. Uncle Tony got up and opened the patio door.

"Come look at this," he said to Father. "You too, boys."

We went into the living room. Uncle Tony took out a small silver disc and put it into a machine.

"Wow," Father said, "a CD player."

Uncle Tony, always with the latest gadgets, smiled.

"We just got these in. A Sony CDP-101," he said. "Two channels. Sixteen-bit PCM encoding at a 44.1 kilohertz sample ratio per channel."

Father let out a low whistle and ran a finger along the top of the machine. Leonard and I looked at each other. I wondered what Uncle Tony meant and looked to see if Father had understood.

Father let out another low whistle when Uncle Tony held up the case for ABBA's *The Visitors*. Uncle Tony turned up the volume and we listened for a minute before heading back outside. Uncle Tony was the last out and he left the door open so we could hear the music.

With every second the future was bearing down on each of us. As we watched the embers from the fire rise into the warm summer night air, all of us in our own stupor, we kids worn out from a long day, Mother floating on Valium, Father and the Auntie Maggie and Uncle Tony floating on scotch, none of us there thought about it. Time would prove *The Visitors* to be ABBA's last studio album. Time would push each day from one to the next and the seasons would slip from one to another, all leading toward some end that was yet unclear but already in motion.

In the #713 Fire Hall on the other side of the city, unknown to us, a fireman named Gary Fairway stirred a pot of chili and laughed with some of his co-workers. The shift was just starting and would end quietly. There would be no fires or accidents to attend, the alarm would not sound. In the morning hours, Gary would drive home through the long daybreak shadows. He would chat with his wife before she went to work and he went to bed.

Far away, Margaret Koshushner washed a thin, porcelain teacup with none of the sinister foreboding that she should have. She did not know the role she would play in the eventual death of the six year old who was drifting into a heavy-lidded sleep, lying in the grass surrounded by the smell of earth and wood smoke and the sounds of "One of Us" coming through the patio door and into the night.

Her new car arrived two weeks later.

CHAPTER 4

The Little Miss Beef Cattle Pageant

An organic smell hung in the air. It was a palpable mist, a sticky mixture of dusty hay, fresh mud, and large mammal feces. The air in the big tent was warm and the temperature climbed a little more every minute. It was humid. I felt it on my skin. The red and white canvas walls worked to keep any outside breeze from stirring the stagnant air inside. "Fresh as a cow's ass," Father grunted before heading across the hay-covered dirt floor toward the metal bleachers opposite the stage. He blended into the crowd as he climbed into the murmuring herd of spectators.

It was true: the smell and feeling must have been the experience sought by a fly hovering a millimetre over a fresh, steamy cow patty.

After seeing Father off to the bleachers, Mother ushered me toward the long curtains making up the backdrop for the plywood stage. We passed a sign displaying the day's schedule of events:

11 am   Wal-Mart Little Mister and Little Miss Beef Cattle Pageant

12 pm   Esther Keen Memorial Chili Cook-off and Pickled Goods Competition

2 pm	Wal-Mart Mister and Miss Pre-Teen Beef Cattle Pageant
3 pm	Wal-Mart Miss Teen Beef Cattle and Miss Beef Cattle Pageants
5 pm	The Kentucky Fried Chicken Fry-off and Baked Goods Competition
6 pm	Beef Cattle Judging
7 pm	Steer Judging
8 pm	Beer Garden (Feat. Giddy Up Tiger and the Come Quicklies)

We pushed through the loose weave fabric curtains. A matronly volunteer directed Little Misters to the left and Little Misses to the right.

There were a few screened-off areas in the open cathedral of the corrals behind the beef cattle show floor. The staging area bustled with yelling kids, running here and there along the wood-lined chutes and maze-like fences. The occasional lowing from the beef cattle could be heard from outside, on the other side of the canvas wall. Their show was later in the evening. Large, metal pot-lights hung pendulously from bare power lines that traversed the air ten feet above the chaos of the corrals.

Mother led me across the corrals, took me behind a screen, stripped me and then started to rewrap me in a tuxedo from the top down.

"Such a handsome little guy," she said, kneeling and tugging at my bow tie. "Stop it," she said to my scratching and pulling of undies away from my ass.

There was hay in my underwear. I was embarrassed, changing behind that curtain with all of those people bustling around on the other side. Every time someone walked too close to the screen it billowed out, offering me a brief glance at the kids and adults tromping back and forth through the hay, around the corral fences and sidestepping errant cow-pies.

If I could see them, they could see me.

We had driven for four hours to get there. We passed nothing but fields and farms for the last three and a half of them.

It had all been Mother's idea.

In two years, when I turned ten, we would still be making this trip except I would be competing in the Mister Pre-Teen Beef Cattle competition and two years after that it would all be over. After the age of twelve there were no more Misters, only Misses. Miss Teen and Miss Beef Cattle. I guess little boys are no longer cute by then. I guess, behind the veneer of a beauty pageant, little girls grow into something to be leered at by handsome young farmhands mulling over their chewing tobacco cuds, scratching their sun-reddened skins and stretching kinks out of their wiry muscles.

"You said a little competition was healthy," Mother had said to Father when we loaded into the Pacer.

"I meant sport. Real competition. Not parading around a barn in front of an audience. I meant football. I meant baseball." Father's voice strained, almost to the point of whining.

They often talked in front of me as if I wasn't there.

Father ran a yellow light and we were outside of the city.

"Beauty is nothing to scoff at," Mother said. "It is the workings of good genes and good morals. This is a real competition, a competition of morals. This is the most important kind of competition."

Father blinked.

Fields rolled by outside. Little wooden buildings drifted by. Tractors and broken down old cars in fields floated by.

"Ugly people, fat people, pimply people don't take care of themselves. They are slothful, they are unhealthy, they are dirty. They live poorly," Mother continued. "How you live your life is a choice. If you choose to take care of yourself, invest a little in your looks, be healthy … well, that's a moral choice. Those who drink, smoke, slut around, they choose to live immorally and wind up ugly because of it. All of these things leave a mark on your appearance. Inner beauty is mirrored by outer beauty."

Father sighed and lit a cigarette.

Mother rolled down her window a little bit.

"Football makes you healthy," Father said quietly through a mouthful of smoke.

"We should all aim for this," Mother continued, ignoring Father. "I mean healthy, beautiful people are happy. The mind and the body are so tightly linked that what happens on the inside shows up on the outside. It also works the other way around. Beautiful people are happier, they get more out of life, they have more friends, get better jobs, get paid more. Dr. Sloane says that unhappiness is a sickness, a disorder. Sickness can be cured."

Mother had read a lot lately.

"Most sickness can be cured," Father muttered.

"Dr. Sloane has studies that show ugly people are less happy than beautiful people. Dr. Sloane says a beautiful mind creates a beautiful body. Richard is a beautiful boy. We should be proud to share that. We made a happy, moral-minded boy."

We passed a ranch. Cattle slid by, dotting the land to the horizon, grazing on dry grass as we sped along. Fence posts ticked by, the barbed wire between them invisible.

Mother and I stood backstage at Clearwater County Fair in the beef cattle wing of the Livestock Complex. I sweltered in my tuxedo and surveyed the other hopeful little gentlemen in the Little Mister Beef Cattle Pageant. Mother, dressed delicately in anxiety, had an open and hopeful look on her face.

I hadn't seen her take a pill in a week.

I didn't remember having ever seen that look on her face.

In the past week, she had read three Dr. Sloane books. It seemed she was always reading his books.

The pageant started fifteen minutes ago with the first pairs of kids disappearing through the canvas onto stage. None of them came back. My stomach knotted each time two new contestants were called.

The Little Misses competing for the Little Miss Beef Cattle crown were on the other side of a splintery corral fence being subjected to last-minute preening and being fussed over by grown-ups. Sheets of fabric had been draped over the fence, seemingly at random, in order to offer a little privacy to both sides. The fencing led from the corrals to the split in the fabric that shielded us from the stage.

"Little Mister Forty-Seven and Little Miss Sixty-Two, please report to the stage," the call came over the PA.

"That's you," Mother squealed.

My stomach flipped.

Mother pushed her way through the crowd to the back side of the stage, dragging me behind.

I was next. I stood beside a little girl in a striped dress that made her look like a bee. Each Little Mister was paired with a Little Miss for their walk across the stage.

From our vantage, through an opening in the backdrop, we could see another nervous Little Mister and Little Miss stomp across the plywood stage. They barely interacted. The Little Mister rushed from one end of the stage to the other, missing the part where you are supposed to face the crowd, smile and wave while the announcer in the auctioneer's booth read bits about your life from a questionnaire that was submitted with the entry fee. The Little Miss stood alone, front and centre stage, her eyes wide open and her hands clenched into fists by her sides.

"Little Miss Paige Green's favourite classes include Art and Drama. She enjoys painting portraits of her dog, Princess, and wants to be an actress or dressmaker when she grows up," the tinny voice of the announcer squeaked though the speakers.

Paige glanced over her shoulder to see her Little Mister disappear stage right and she smiled like a terrified monkey. She grimaced to the audience and hurried off the stage.

"Our next stunning couple," the PA squealed for a moment, "is Little Miss Abigail Spencer and Little Mister Richard Trench."

Four judges were positioned in front of the stage at a folding table draped in a white plastic tablecloth. Three women in ball gowns and one gentleman in a suit sweated elegantly onto plastic folding chairs. They made quick notes after brief scrutiny of each contestant. Those chosen from this first round moved on to the talent portion. The winner was crowned after that.

I was not paying attention; I had been watching the judges. Mother shoved me onto the stage, already two steps behind the giant bee. A hollow mix of Kenny Loggins' "Footloose" and the announcer's commentary blared over the PA system, keeping a beat that confused the Bee. I caught up to her, my heart racing two beats for each step I took. I made it work; I walked naturally, recovered the distance between us gracefully. The Bee and I stopped at the front of the stage, smiled and waved. I put my arm around the Bee's waist and she put her arm around my shoulder.

The crowd, dimmed by the spotlights aimed at the stage, was a bumpy silhouette against the red and white canvas stripes. The heat under the spotlights was intense. I thought to look for Father but worried that I would lose my concentration. I was even more worried that I would find a disappointed look on his face were I to spot him.

The judges scribbled on their notepads.

The Bee and I looked at each other and nodded: a consensus was reached. We exited stage right.

Mother met me on the other side of the curtain. I knew I did well because she sported a big smile.

"That was wonderful," she exclaimed, almost knocking over Bee Girl to give me a hug.

"Thanks," I said. "It was fun."

"Next thing you know you will be wearing Ralph Lauren in London." She beamed with distant eyes. "I don't know if that girl will make it though." She cast a critical glance at the Bee.

"I couldn't see Father," I said. "The lights were too bright."

"That's okay, honey. I'm sure he was there. I'm so proud of you. You were fabulous."

"I think I messed up a bit at the beginning." I glanced at Bee Girl. The announcer had called her Abigail.

"Don't worry, baby. I think we just need to practise a little. I can see you in Azzedine in ten years, in Paris. Or maybe Thierry Mugler in Milan." Mother's eyes wandered toward the ceiling. "Oh, don't forget your mother when you reach the runway, dear."

"Okay, Mother," I said, a little confused, having never seen her like this before.

There was a moment before she said, "I am so happy."

That's what it was. I swelled with pride. I made her happy. I wanted that moment to last forever.

Eight more pairs of Little Misses and Little Misters crossed the stage before we were all brought out before the judges for their decision. When it was our turn, Bee Girl and I walked out onstage holding hands, more out of anticipation than nervous support. We stood under the spotlight. The temperature in the tent had risen past hot to stifling. Sweat rolled tickly trails down the small of my back. The Bee glanced at me out of the corner of her eye and smiled. I caught her eye and held it for a moment before smiling back.

"Little Mister Forty-Seven and Little Miss Sixty-Two…" a judge announced to us and started shuffling papers.

In that break, awaiting judgment, I gave the crowd a quick scan. I thought I saw Auntie Maggie waving at me. The judge flipped through papers. Beside Auntie Maggie was a smaller figure that must have been Leonard. The judge continued shuffling, a scowl crossed her face. I couldn't see Father or Uncle Tony in the crowd.

"Ah," the judge exclaimed, "you have both passed on to the talent round." She smiled at us.

With that, the Bee and I rushed offstage. There was still a crowd of kids to be judged but I couldn't see how they did because Mother whipped me back into the corral and behind one of the screens. My clothes were gone again and I was being wrapped in leather pants, a white T-shirt, and a black and red leather jacket with colours that made a *V* on my chest.

"You were so good. I knew you were going on to the talent part," Mother fussed. "I can't believe that girl made it though. You really pulled her through."

Someone walked by the screen and it billowed out. A boy milling about outside pointed at me and poked his mother to get her attention. I flushed. The curtain fell back.

"Do you remember the routine?"

"Yes." We had only practised it every spare moment for two weeks.

"Remember it's not just about going through the steps. You have to feel the moment, make it yours. Those judges have to see your character, you, shining through. Make them fall in love with you. Want them to fall in love with you and they will. You can perform perfectly and not make that connection. You need to connect with them. Let them know you. Let them in. That's the way to win." Mother fussed over the leather jacket.

My outfit cost $300, a fact Father wouldn't let us forget for an hour after we bought it.

"Coulda' got a full set of hockey gear for that much," he had puffed.

I nodded as Mother sat back on her heels for a final look. She finger-combed my hair a little, avoiding the divot the haemangioma had left in my skull once it had disappeared.

"This is important, you know." She wouldn't make eye contact with me; her gaze wandered every part of me but my eyes. She was tearing me down and rebuilding me.

"I know," I said.

She contemplated me for a moment. "I don't know if you really do."

There was a pause where I wondered if she would tell me or if I would remain ignorant.

"Good people win, they deserve to," Mother continued. "Good people do well in life and I want you to do well. This is so important, it's your first big test." Her eyes began to well up. "This is an early test as to how you are going to do, how your life will turn out. I think I have raised a good little boy who will turn into a good man. A man who will succeed, who will be happy. I want you to be good at life because I lo…" Her chin dimpled and her lip wiggled. She forced a smile through her emotion.

My chest felt like it was going to explode. In eight years, those first eight of my life, I had never experienced such love from her. I felt that I was responsible for her happiness and at that moment she was happy with me. I felt I had already succeeded. I felt what she was about to say before becoming so choked with emotion. I truly felt it. She loved me and I loved her in return.

She sighed an uneven breath. "…because I longed for this so much. I have put so much into this. I have sacrificed … make it worth my while. Win this contest." Her hand flew in front of her mouth and she darted out from behind the curtain. It flapped as she ran past and I stood there confused.

Mother did not accompany me to the stage for the talent portion of the show. I didn't see her as I made my way through the corrals alone to stand behind the Bee Girl, in line to get on the stage with ten other Little Misters and Little Misses. I didn't see her from where I peeked through the curtains from backstage, my stomach in a knot, wanting someone to tell me this would all be okay. I didn't see her as I moonwalked my way through Michael Jackson's "Thriller," doing the monster dance we had practised and pulling it off flawlessly.

I looked for her.

I looked to where I had seen Leonard and Auntie Maggie earlier in the show. I could only peek occasionally while I was onstage.

She didn't meet me when I exited through the curtain offstage.

"That was great."

Those words weren't from my mother. They were from the Bee Girl.

"Who're you looking for?" Bee Girl asked my swivelling head and darting eyes.

"Have you seen my mother?" I asked her.

Where was I supposed to go next?

What was I supposed to do?

Where were my normal clothes?

Was I abandoned there to be forever dressed like Mike?

Tears of panic welled up and there was the tingling in my sinuses that I always felt before I cried.

"I haven't seen her," Bee Girl said. She saw my distress and reached out to touch my arm.

"Neither have I," I huffed, "for quite a while."

My eyes searched the corral. It was empty of children and mothers and was filling up with folding tables covered by red and white checkered plastic table cloths. The show was reaching its end and the cook-off was setting up. Old ladies were plugging giant, floral-patterned Crock-Pots of chili into extension cords that snaked through the hay. Some already stirred bubbling vats and cackled to their neighbours, giving the occasional hungry glance to the children gathering behind the stage. Chunks of meat and beans glistened under the sweaty lids of those cauldrons. Gnarled fingers grasped wooden spoons, bringing spicy grease to withered lips, a vile taste test by pasty tongued hags.

I watched a tongue slip out of a woman's mouth and wet her lips, all the while she watched me. I could smell the sickly sweet barbecue smell coming from her chili.

"My mom can help us," Bee Girl redirected my attention away from the witches' Little Mister Beef Cattle Chili Cook-off.

Without further prompting, she grabbed my hand and led me to a tall, plump woman with such a kind face that I wished I could wrap myself in its safety.

"Who's your friend, Abigail?" the woman asked.

The question was really directed at me.

Here is where my training kicked in. I shouldn't talk to strangers. I looked away and caught sight of the corral full of chili cookers. I did a quick risk analysis before responding.

"I'm Richard," I said.

"Nice to meet you Richard. I'm Ms. Spencer, Abigail's mom," she replied.

Instantly, my panic subsided.

"Richard can't find his mom," Abigail said.

"Come here, honey," Ms. Spencer said. "They're about to crown the winner. We'll find your mom after."

All the finalists were called back onto the stage and the judges read off several names, the Little Misters and Little Misses who were eliminated. There were some tears, there was some loud wailing and a few angry parents until I stood there with one other boy and two girls. Abigail was gone.

"Ladies and gentlemen, the judges have narrowed down all the wonderful Little Misters and Little Misses that we have seen here this morning to these fine guys and gals." There was a shriek from the PA before the announcer continued. "I am pleased to present Little Mister Beef Cattle 1984, Little Mister Richard Trench."

I heard a scream and saw two up-thrown arms sprout from the stands. I spotted Mother's shadow backlit from the glowing red canvas wall, and smiled the biggest smile I could.

My world blurred into handshaking, flashbulbs, clapping and lots of teeth glistening behind smiles. Someone pinned a blue ribbon on my chest. My title was printed in gold letters on the button in the middle. Someone else handed me a hundred-dollar gift certificate for Wal-Mart.

The next thing I remember was Mother snatching my hand from Mrs. Spencer and storming off with me to where Father, Auntie Maggie, Uncle Tony and Leonard stood at the entrance to the swine wing. They stood at the junction of the dairy cattle, sheep, swine, goat and poultry pavilions, near benches under a sign that read *Sittin' Room*.

"This place smells like shit," Father was saying.

Uncle Tony nodded gravely.

Auntie Maggie spotted me and came barrelling forward, squat-walking with her arms outstretched.

"Gimme a hug, Little Mister Beef Cattle," she said through a smile.

When she hugged me, all I could think of was that Father was right. This place did smell like shit.

"It's noon." Father stated, looking pointedly at Uncle Tony. "Let's find us a beer garden and some lunch."

Uncle Tony grunted his agreement and we entered the swine wing. We walked past a series of livestock wash racks between two rows of swine stalls, which we needed to pass through to exit the livestock complex.

I paused briefly to look at one stall. There was a placard at the gate that read *Ian*. Ian had a blue ribbon beside his name with *swine racing* printed in gold letters on the button in the middle. Before being called along by my beaming mother, I watched Ian roll in some filth.

Outside the Livestock Complex, the sun beat down. The animal smells dissipated as we wove our way through the crowds and snaking spaces between big canvas tents. In the distance, I saw half of the Ferris wheel spinning over the tent tops.

Father piped up when he spotted a beer garden, a fenced-in open-air area with a straw floor and patio furniture shaded by umbrellas. A sign at the entrance read, *No Minors*. Leonard and I were ushered into an adjacent corral under a sign that read, *Milk Bar*. We sat at a table on the other side of the fence as our parents.

Three frosty pints of milk later, I looked across my filmy glass at Leonard.

"...so they are going to take her title away because of some nude photos she supposedly had taken of her before the competition. What kind of message does that send? Here she is, the first black woman in the sixty-three year history of the pageant and they scandalize her." Mother was talking.

"Who are we talking about?" Uncle Tony asked.

"Vanessa Williams," Mother responded and nodded to the waitress for another round.

"I would scandalize her," Father muttered to Uncle Tony.

"We have to pee," Leonard said.

"What?" Mother asked Father.

"Oh," Father feigned surprise, "I didn't say anything."

Uncle Tony smirked and gave Father a look.

"What are we to take from that?" Mother continued. "Are we supposed to be ashamed of a woman's body? Is it because she's black? What's offensive about a beautiful black woman's body?"

Next year, Sharlene Wells, a twenty-year-old Mormon from Utah would be crowned Miss America. Her life goals, when asked, would be to get married and raise a family at home.

"We have to pee," Leonard said again.

"I don't have to pee," I told Leonard.

"Yes, you do," he hissed back.

"Nothing wrong with naked beautiful women," Uncle Tony smirked to Father.

"Nude women," Mother corrected. "Nudes aren't some porno girlie pictures. They're a celebration of perfection through beauty of form."

"We have to pee," Leonard piped in louder.

More beers arrived at the parent's table.

"Boys," Auntie Maggie said sharply, reaching for her beer. "Just go, for Pete's sake."

Leonard grabbed my hand and dragged me from the table and out under the *Milk Bar* sign.

"I don't have to pee, Leonard. And the bathrooms are the other way."

"Shut up, I don't have to pee either but I'm so bored. We're going to the midway. I want to see the games and rides. Anyhow…" he jerked his chin over his shoulder in the direction of the beer garden, "they could be there all afternoon."

Once we were around a corner from the beer garden, Leonard let go of my hand. We wound our way between people, past cotton candy and mini-doughnut stands, toward the Ferris wheel. At one point, we were drawn to the sound of screaming engines coming from behind a fence. We went to the fence and tried to peek through but were thwarted by several big signs.

Motor Sports Arena!

Antique Tractor Pull Tomorrow … Agripowered by Annex Ethanol!

Come in and check out our Safety Wall! New This Year!

A fat man in an undershirt staggered up and shooed us along before taking a piss on the fence.

We followed the noise of a crowd and the Ferris wheel beacon and rounded a corner to the blaring music, bells and whistles of the midway. The air smelled like diesel and vomit. With mouths open and awe-filled eyes cast upwards, we wandered the length of the midway in wonder. Hair, legs, arms and screaming mouths blurred from the rides. At one point, I was narrowly missed getting hit by a set of keys that seemed to fall from the clear blue sky. Once we reached the other end, we stood between two tents, gape-mawed at the twirling metal and flesh stretching out along the midway.

Strong hands latched onto my shoulders from behind.

I screamed in surprise and Leonard spun to see where the little-girl noise came from. I glanced over my shoulder as I squirmed in panic. At the end of the arms attached to the strong hands was a pitted, sunburnt face of a man. He was wearing a carnie uniform, a stained, red T-shirt and jeans that were blotchy with grease and filth. He pulled me close enough to smell oil and sweat. He held a rusty nail between the yellow pegs of his teeth. In my glance, I saw the white paste in the corners of his mouth and the brown flecks of food stuck between his teeth.

I screamed and struggled harder.

"Hey," the carnie barked through his foul grin.

I pulled and twisted. I caught a glimpse of Leonard running forward and kicking his shin.

The grip released. Leonard and I retreated out of arm's reach and stopped, scared to keep our back to the man.

"You little bastard," the man spoke around the nail and rubbed his shin.

Leonard held my elbow and I felt his grip tense, ready to run or ready to fight, I wasn't sure.

"I was talkin' at ya," the carnie said. He seemed to think for a moment. "You guys wanna see something different, something really far out?"

His eyebrows rose. Ours followed suit.

"What?" Leonard asked though his grip didn't lessen on my elbow.

"I don't know if I wanna tell ya now you gone kicked me."

"What could you have to show us?" Leonard asked.

I made to leave but Leonard's grip on my elbow stopped me.

"It's something so far out, they tell us not to show anyone," the carnie continued. "Something that even makes the management nervous, something we ain't even supposed to talk about," the carnie paused and gave an exaggerated hurt look as he finished rubbing his shin. He pulled the nail from between his teeth, a string of spit dragged out with it. "Can you boys keep a secret?"

How could we not?

The carnie continued to talk, the white gobs at the corner of his mouth migrating as his lips moved, "You can't never tell no one. Not your parents, not the cops, not nobody. Promise?"

"Promise," Leonard said.

"I ain't sure I can trust the two of you. How can I know you'll keep a secret?"

Leonard took a step closer.

"Oh, you can trust us. We won't tell anyone. We already promised."

The carnie rolled his bloodshot eyes from Leonard to me and then back to Leonard. Then he seemingly made up his mind. "Y'all will love this." The carnie smiled. "Foller me."

How could we not?

We followed the carnie's baggy, stained jeans and skinny shoulders around the back of a tent. He checked over his shoulder to see if we followed and gave a crooked smile when he saw that we did. He stopped at a tent, hiked up his jeans while he glanced about and pulled a flap open on the tent.

I peeked in. It was mostly dark except for a dim glow coming from somewhere deep inside.

"This way gentlemen," the carnie said.

There are many moments in life that conspire toward making you the person you turn out to be on your deathbed. All of the events, the people, the places you go, the things you do and have done to you, everything foreshadows the person you are at the end. Final hindsight is like the cover of the puzzle box: it shows you the big picture but during life all you get are the pieces.

What was in that tent would change Leonard and me forever, in very different ways. The pieces are all coming together but they can only be seen in hindsight. Leonard and I were too young to realize this. We had the puzzle but not all the pieces were there yet.

I followed Leonard through the tent flap.

It dropped behind us with a wet sound.

CHAPTER 5

Tokyo Is in Flames

"**W**elcome to the big one-oh," Father yelled, then grimaced over the screaming kids at Bullwinkle's. "Happy Birthday, Kiddo."

The table we sat at was ringed by Leonard, Auntie Maggie and Uncle Tony. Our table was surrounded by other tables full of kids celebrating similar milestones. Those full tables reminded me that I invited ten kids from school and only Leonard showed up.

In an outer orbit around the tables were banks of coloured spotlights roaming the darkness and large speakers with poor sound quality. These pumped out a static and pop version of "Rock Me Amadeus," adding to the seizure-inducing quality of light and noise. Falco's lyrics were lost on us.

Occasionally, a comet of a waiter or waitress would fly through and drop off soda pop and food. Invariably, the server was a teenager with a face like the moon's—waxy, pale and cratered.

Father was putting on a brave show of enjoying himself so I followed along, pretending like none of this bothered me. If he could put in the effort, so could I.

All the tables faced an animatronics *Rocky and Bullwinkle* show that played every half hour. Boris and Natasha joined the bull moose and flying squirrel halfway through the ten-minute show. The few kids paying attention would boo at the villains. The lights were kept dark even between shows, save for the roaming spotlights. The only thing on the menu was pizza, but there were thirty different kinds of it.

Mother was notably missing. Father thought it best if he smiled a lot in her absence and pretended like she had never been there, anywhere, in the first place.

"She's gone off to fix her Tanqueray smile," Father had said the first day she was gone. "She'll be back in a month."

At the time, I figured it was something like a tan. It sounded exotic, like she was lying on a beach somewhere next to the ocean with a dentist or something. I just wished she would have said bye before she left.

Father had mumbled something about her never being able to stand the sight of a full glass.

Now, I realize, the grown-ups stopped drinking beer when they hung out, about a week before Mother disappeared. Nobody drank after she returned either, even though Mother often prompted them, following her encouragement with the disclaimer "I'm fine," in which she dragged out the *i* sound in the word "fine."

"Here's the pizza," squeaked our adolescent waiter in his violet-coloured hat and shirt. He plunked it onto the table before wiping his hands on the seat of his pants.

It had taken two shows to get here. Two rounds of jerky mouths opening and closing out of sync with the voices on the loud speakers, two recitations of the same jokes. The machines went through the same dialogues, same script, and the same awkward motions, as they would twenty-four times today, working away in the dark.

"Dig in boys." Father smiled at me and Leonard.

"Thanks, Father," I replied, smiling hollowly as well. I grabbed a piece of pizza. It was cold but good.

Leonard watched me for a minute before grabbing a slice. We sat there chewing, looking at each other. He was getting too old for this; he was too cool for this. Everything about him said that he didn't want to be there.

"Happy Birthday, Richard," Auntie Maggie glowed. She always seemed to glow.

"Yeah, here you go buddy." Uncle Tony leaned across the table holding a present he had pulled from the seat beside him. "This is from Auntie Maggie, me and Leonard."

I put the box on the table and tore apart the wrapping paper, saying thank-yous before even seeing what it was. I was so grateful they were there; otherwise, it would have been just me and Father and the overhanging accusations of being a loser because nobody showed up at my birthday party. I had one friend close to my age and I was related to him.

"Hey, Rocky." The spotlights flared up on the stage and the animatronics Bullwinkle ground into action. "Watch me pull a rabbit out of my hat."

I looked at the box. It was a picture of a kid standing on something that looked like a plastic Saturn but the rings were so tight it squeezed the planet enough to make it bulge on either side of its equator.

A girlie squawk came from the floppy flying squirrel. "But that trick never works."

"It's a Pogo Ball," Auntie Maggie said excitedly. "You inflate it, stand on the platform, pinch the top part of the ball between your ankles and off you go, hopping."

I smiled with equal enthusiasm.

Nobody could ever see me use this thing.

"Like a pogo stick but a rubber ball," Auntie Maggie said. "Leonard loves his."

Bullwinkle pulled a bear's head up from his top hat. A static roar played over the sound system. One kid laughed.

The Pogo Ball was neon pink with a fluorescent green ring.

Nobody could ever know I had this.

"I don't have one," Leonard said.

"And now for something we hope you'll really like," Rocky flopped precariously to one side of the stage.

"Let's go to the arcade," Leonard said to me.

"Can we go to the arcade?" I asked.

"Go to the arcade," Father sighed and started cleaning up around the table, stacking plates and cutlery, crumpling wrapping paper and boxing the remaining pizza from our plates.

As Leonard and I walked past the stage and into the next room, there was a scream and bells started ringing. The room was full of video games, mini basketball games and mini bowling games where you earned tickets for sinking a ball in the right hole. You could redeem your tickets at a booth manned by the adolescent server's clone. In exchange, there were things like a whistle or a toy car, a small plastic army man with a parachute or a plastic dinosaur in a top hat.

Leonard and I worked our way through the crowds and sidled up to the group of kids around the *Rampage* video game. Some kid was playing as the Godzilla-inspired character, Lizzie, and had made it to the Tokyo level. The pixellated lizard jerked her way up the side of a building, punched a window and ate a woman.

I glanced around the crowd of kids and wondered quickly if any of them would have come to my birthday party if they knew me. Were they here for someone else's party? I wondered what the other boy had said or done to get so many friends to show up at his party.

In the meantime, I decided, they were all at my party. That thought brought a smile to my face, a smile that was returned by a girl standing close to me. She looked familiar.

"Hello," she said.

"Hi," I replied, stealing a quick glance at Leonard. He was busy watching the screen.

"He's doing really good," she said, tossing a quick glance and a raised eyebrow at the boy playing.

"It's my birthday," I said.

"Happy birthday." She smiled. "What's wrong?"

"Only one person came." I pointed at Leonard. "And he's my cousin."

The girl gave me a sad look and reached out for my arm. We stood awkwardly, her hand on my arm, and watched the boy tear buildings down, swipe helicopters out of the sky and throw a city into chaos. She kept her hand on my forearm while the city collapsed; people were dying. The giant lizard hammered away at a tank, people ran screaming in every direction and her touch calmed me. Her arm resting on my forearm was all I could focus on. I stole the occasional sidelong glance at her calm face, flashing yellow and blue in the arcade-lit fires of Tokyo burning to the ground. I also stole the occasional glance at Leonard, not sure what I would have to endure having wilfully let a girl touch me but, at the same time, something kept me from moving away from her.

There was a collective groan from the group of kids. Lizzie had been shot off the side of a building. The electronic lizard's expression was a mix of pain and sorrow, as if it wasn't ready for death, it still had things it wanted to do and death had come too soon. There were still so many people to eat and buildings to smash up. Add to that the pain of falling ten storeys after being shot off of a building—it was unfair.

The crowd started to disperse. Leonard looked my way and gave an almost imperceptible frown, catching the girl's hand on my arm a second before she said goodbye and wandered off to a clutch of girls at a bowling game. Before Leonard could say anything, Auntie Maggie was on us.

"Let's get a picture of you guys," she said and dragged us toward a photo booth.

"I want to play *Rampage*, though." For all his newfound toughness, Leonard sounded very close to whining.

"Come on, you'll look back at this picture in twenty years and laugh," Auntie Maggie said. "Trust me on this."

I didn't have that much time. I would fall one year and four limbs short of Auntie Maggie's prediction. Not knowing this then, I trusted her.

I went along, my feelings torn between Auntie Maggie and Leonard, wanting to get a picture but wanting to be cool too. The cooler I could be, the more kids would come to my eleventh birthday.

Just as I finished that thought, Leonard and I were stuffed into the photo booth.

I could hear Auntie Maggie dropping coins in a slot. Two dollars for four photos. The booth was cramped. The backdrop was red and white vertically striped fabric.

"There, now you boys smile," Auntie Maggie told us, reaching up and dropping the booth's curtain behind us with a wet sound. The flashbulb fired.

It took a few moments for my eyes to adjust to the dim tent interior. I stood there dumbly next to Leonard. I could hear the carnie breathing close behind us, the rusty nail scraping quietly against his teeth as he shifted it slowly in his mouth. There were other people in the tent—some big, adult bodies moving around in the shadows. Their murmurings were hushed and seemed to pause for a moment when we entered, as if we were expected but had arrived an hour early. Outside, the noises of the midway were muted to the point of being distant screams in the darkness.

Somewhere in the dark came the tinny sound of an organ grinder churning out a variable speed version of "The Entertainer." The air was thick with a distinctly male smell, the musty smell emanating from the straw-covered ground, cigarette smoke, body odour and a sharp tinge from booze-soaked breath.

As my eyes adjusted, they were drawn to a series of dim cones of light, areas spotlit by weak overhead lamps. The milling shadows of people crowded the perimeter of each area. The crowd moved slowly, in a predatorial circle.

"Feel free to take a look around, boys," the carnie growled from close behind us. If a voice could leer, his did. "I'll be around if'n you want to be talkin' to me about anythin', but, in the span, take in these marvels of nature."

"Come on." Leonard grabbed my hand and led me to one of the spotlit areas.

We wove our way through the bodies to the crowd gathered around the base of one watery pool of yellow light. We worked our way through the cluster of towering people. There was a constant stream of mumbling and the occasional subdued laugh and snicker.

We stopped at a sign that read: *The Mighty Mite. The World's Smallest Man.*

Beneath the light, behind a low, handprint-smeared Plexiglas wall, was the Mighty Mite. He was about half as tall as me. He was shirtless. His tiny torso was top-lit by the spotlight, accentuating the frail fingers of ribs wrapped around his chest.

The Might Mite, a primordial dwarf, one of a hundred in the world, was two feet tall and weighed twenty-one pounds. He had a severe overbite, a cone-shaped face ending in the point of his nose and a presence that likely instigated every pixie legend in the world.

He sat at a tiny table playing solitaire, his bird bones manipulating a deck of cards which seemed as big as a book in his stunted fingers. A cigarette smouldered in an ashtray on the table, giving a blue haze to the air in the enclosure. A small black-and-white television set sat at one end of the table, playing a fuzzy soap opera.

Occasionally, the Mighty Mite glanced at the television set, then focused on his card game again.

"Ugly little thing," someone in the crowd said.

"Like a real person," came a reply, "only smaller."

There was some snickering.

The Mighty Mite must have been able to hear the comments but gave no indication. He glanced at the television, reached out with his stubby fingers and took the cigarette from the ashtray. He brought the cigarette to his lips and took a long drag. He coughed a high squeaky noise.

"Weird," Leonard said breathlessly, sounding amazed.

A creeping, uncomfortable feeling overcame me. It was the sense of voyeurism, the crowd of people gawking. It was the Mighty Mite, seemingly oblivious, doing his job just by being stared at. It was how hard I found it not to stare at him. It was the apparent dignity with which he did his job, the apparent strength with which he ignored all the eyes and the derogatory comments. It was almost as if we, the gathered crowd, didn't belong here, like we were invisible and watching him go about his life, alone in his home. It was a complex mixture of shame, empathy and wonder. We were the ones who were out of place here, not the little man. The Plexiglas acted to keep us out more than it did to keep him in. It was almost as if we, the crowd, were caged. We were the intruders, the freaks.

I glanced at the towering shadows around me. Eyes glistened in the weak light, intent upon the Mighty Mite. Even as whispers were exchanged, fascinated eyes did not stray from the Mite. This was a human zoo.

"That's the teeniest freak I have ever seen."

"Is all of him small?"

"Does he get ID'ed when he buys his smokes?"

The Mighty Mite looked at his wristwatch, stretched and put down his cards. He reached under the table and pulled out a sign to place on the top: *Back in 15 minutes.*

The Mighty Mite stood, grabbed his cigarettes and wandered out of the circle of light. As he left, someone took a picture. The flash fired, almost audibly, blinding me in the dark.

"Hey, I tell you clowns, no pictures." It was the carnie.

There was a scuffle in the crowd. The carnie snatched the camera from the shadow, opened the back hatch and pulled the film out.

"What the hell?" the shadow said and shoved the carnie.

"Let's move." Leonard pulled me out of the intensifying scuffle centred around the shadowed man and the carnie.

The voices grew loud and angry behind us. Once we were clear of the fray, we wandered, pausing once at a wax figure, the top half a naked woman and the bottom half a big fish.

Leonard read the sign aloud, "Mermaid: this specimen was caught in a fishing net off the coast of Montserrat." Leonard tilted his head. "She died three hours after being caught. She suffocated to death out of the water."

"She doesn't look real," I said.

"Oh, I'm sure she's real." Leonard gave me a strained look before taking off toward another group of people crowded around a spotlight.

We worked our way through a forest of legs ornamented with belt buckles topped by cowboy shirts with pearly snap buttons. When we arrived at the front of the crowd, we were confronted with the most confusing mound of flesh I had ever seen: over-stuffed, billowing pillows of skin, segmented by deep folds and creases, bruises on the flesh, crusted sores and sprouts of seemingly random, greasy hair. My eyes, wide in wonder, roamed the mound trying to make sense of the expanse of skin. The mound was on a slowly rotating pallet and in half a turn, it was obvious I had been staring at the ass end of the fattest man in the world. The pallet was set on an industrial weigh scale that displayed a red, illuminated, *1,021 lbs.*

The fat man had a boyish face, large as a pumpkin, set in one side of his body. He smiled as he spun by slowly. It may have been a grimace, I couldn't be sure.

As his side slid by, someone reached across the rope barricade and slipped a pen in between some folds. Someone giggled. The fat man squealed with surprise and began to jiggle. His arm emerged and flailed back to extract the pen, but it was too short to work its way around all of the flesh. A few people laughed. A few, with haunted looks in their eyes, broke from the group and wandered off to other corners of the tent.

I felt revulsion at the fat man but also pity for him. It was an instinctual clenching of my stomach at the smell of unwashed flesh, the sight of the sores and bruises, and the innocent smile that spun by.

How did a human come to this? I wondered. To care so little that he wound up a mountain of flesh, crippled and immobilized by his own weight, trapped on an industrial weigh scale by the size of his own body. The strength of the trauma to the psyche to get the fat man here, whatever caused it, would have been immense, and would have hurt worse than anything I had ever experienced. Then to be on display day after day, the jeers and pen pokings would have perpetuated that trauma. This fat man would die early and poorly. I couldn't escape the idea that I was watching a dead man flail on that pallet, in a freak show, covered in bruises and sores born from obesity, surrounded by prying eyes and poorly checked snickers, people looking in wonder at his death.

Not being able to extract a pen from your own fat folds is not a good place to be.

I glanced at Leonard. He was smiling, his eyes fixed on the quivering, squealing invalid on the pallet.

I pushed under the rope, put one hand on the fat man and leaned into his bulk to extract the pen.

The man stopped squealing.

I stood, instinctively wiping the hand I had touched him with on my pants, the pen in the other hand.

The spotlight blinded me to the audience so I couldn't see who said, "Stupid kid."

"Thank you," a muffled voice came from the fat man. His head was on the other side of the pallet. His voice was high-pitched, far-away and lonely.

The light flashed from bright to dark as I ducked back under the rope into the crowd.

"You touched him," Leonard winced.

"I had to," I replied, thinking Leonard was looking for an explanation. "I couldn't reach otherwise."

"What did he feel like?" He asked.

I wiped my hand on my pant-leg again. "Like a big turkey," I said, "before it's put in the oven."

Leonard pursed his lips.

We wandered past a display case that was not unlike Mother's china cabinet. Instead of shelves packed with trinkets and cups, these housed jars. There was a two-headed fetus. A snake with a scorpion in its mouth swirled in a cloudy yellow fluid.

"Look close," Leonard said, his nose pushed up against the glass. "The two-headed thing moved."

"It did not." I didn't want to put my face close to it.

"I guess not," Leonard said and then he stood on his toes and pointed. "Look. You can see where someone stitched the other head on."

"Really?"

I had questions like...

Where would someone find a spare fetus head?

Who would think to stitch it to the body of another?

"It's so fake," Leonard said.

Apparently he didn't think about the things I did.

"The fat guy was real," I said.

"Look, over there. Come on." Leonard was off.

I caught a glimpse of the carnie with the rusty nail in his mouth out of the corner of my eye. He seemed to be watching us. Then a few dark figures broke my view. For a moment, I feared I lost Leonard in the shadowy crowd. Then I saw him, waving me forward. The crowd around this spotlight was not as thick as the Mighty Mite or the fat man.

"Look," Leonard said, "Teen Wolf." He pointed.

I looked. My stomach seized.

Mother's voice: "He's not going to turn into one of those Mexican wolf-men, is he?"

Standing in the light was a boy my age. He was wearing only a pair of white boxer shorts and what looked like a fur suit. Head to toe, he was covered with shag-length hair. His eyes seemed particularly bright, framed by dark hair; they stood out in sharp contrast. The black dots of his irises scanned the boundary of the spotlight. His eyes did not betray feelings of shame or fear; they were very lonely. When he saw Leonard and me among the gawkers, his eyes lit up. He smiled and waved.

"He looks like an excited monkey," Leonard mumbled and shied away. The wave had drawn people's attention to us.

I waved back.

The wolf-boy let out a grunt.

"You're going to get us kicked out," Leonard hissed.

"Well, aren't that sweet," the carnie drifted out of the darkness, seemingly floating more than walking toward us. "You gone done made a friend of Esteban there. I ain't seen him that tickled in months. Regularly though, it's only the grown-up folks in here he sees. You wanna meet 'im? He speaks Mexican mostly, but he knows some English."

"It's all right," Leonard said. "I don't want to."

"Sure," I said.

I thought of the patch of hair on my stomach, the dent in my head where the haemangioma had once been. I thought of my mother's finger wagging. Her voice saying, "What's that?" It made me want to know the wolf-boy Esteban.

"You're all right, kid," the carnie said and tucked his bottom lip under his teeth to give a sharp whistle. He rolled his hand in a motion beckoning Esteban to come over.

Esteban glanced around before making his way over. The crowd dispersed to other corners of the tent, into the darkness, as the freak approached us.

"Qué?" Esteban asked the carnie.

"These here boys is wantin' to say hi," the carnie spoke, his lips moving lewdly around the nail in his mouth.

Esteban smiled and beamed, "Hola. I am Esteban."

"Hola," I said. "I'm Richard."

Leonard didn't say anything and shifted from one foot to the other, then back again.

Nurse's voice: "That is an anomalous patch of terminal hair."

"And this," I gestured, "is Leonard."

"I was so happy to see you," Esteban spoke with a thick accent. "There are no niños here."

"Where are you from?" I asked.

"I am from Divisaderos, in Sonora," Esteban replied. "In Mexico," he added. His voice happy, the bristles around his mouth shook with each word.

"We bought Esteban for two thousand bucks," the carnie laughed. "That's like a million dollars in that backwater. His folks're now the richest folks there, happy to be rid of 'im they was. Now back to work ya li'l bastard." The carnie was still laughing, making his insult seem like a pet name.

Esteban nodded and said, "It was nice to meet you." His shadow worked its way back to the spotlight.

I thought about what it must be like to travel far from home, to be in a place where everyone spoke a different language, and rarely see another kid your age. A lonely pit opened in my stomach. Esteban had seemed so thrilled to meet us.

There was a spark as the carnie fired a cigarette. For that moment, his pockmarked face glowed like a demon's, each line and scar and wrinkle was thrown into sharp contrast from below. Then his face fell into shadow, except for the orange glow from the cigarette tip.

"You boys oughta see one more thing before ya go," the carnie said. The orange dot bounced in the dark.

I stifled a cough brought on by inhaling a gout of cigarette smoke. "We should get back to our parents," I said to Leonard.

Leonard looked at me for a second, a slight frown on his face. "What else do we need to see?" he asked the carnie.

The carnie pointed at a gap in the curtains that made up the wall of the tent. "Why," he said, "y'all should see Razor's Blades of Doom." The carnie checked his watch, tilting his wrist to make the most of the poor light. "Show starts in five minutes," he said tapping his watch.

Leonard went.

I followed.

I wish I hadn't—that whole adventure had been a mistake.

The gap in the curtains was black, threatening and made the big tent we left feel warm and comfortable by comparison. My heart pounded in my ears as Leonard's figure slowly dimmed from my sight when he passed the threshold and walked deeper into the darkness.

I paused, paralysed. Leonard was gone. My eyes darted for an escape route. They jumped from the Wolf-boy to the crowd around the Mighty Mite. I caught a glimpse of the fat man though I couldn't tell which bloated body part I saw, a leg maybe, before the gap in the crowd filled in. I couldn't tell where we had entered the tent. The flap leading to the outside had fallen, caging the area in. My eyes jumped, looking for any difference in the tent wall, any slight change of colour or line of light that would betray the exit and lead to the safety of the crowds outside. The midway seemed so safe and so far away. I spied the cabinet full of jars. The snake with the scorpion in its mouth and the the two-headed fetus, drowned in yellow formaldehyde, trapped in jars, the outside sounds muted and aqueous.

The smell of cigarette smoke and a clasped hand on my shoulder prompted a squeak. I wriggled free and darted through the gap in the curtains, into the dark, into the unknown. The carnie cackled and coughed somewhere close by. I strained to see but couldn't. I heard noises, feral animal noises all around me: grunts, whispers, shuffles, the rustle of clothes and feet on the dirt and hay-covered floor. The air reeked of people.

Something big was going to happen.

There was a pop and a bright light came on, illuminating everything.

I closed my eyes, easing them open as they adjusted, not wanting to see but feeling the need to for self-preservation.

I looked over at Leonard. He sat next to me in the photo booth with the red-and-white-striped backdrop. He didn't return my gaze though his face was tight. I was happy to be safe in that curtained capsule with my best friend.

"That's it." Auntie Maggie pulled the curtains back and we both climbed out.

The three of us stood in the electronic beeps and flashing lights of the video games. Children ran, screaming from one machine to another, from one group of laughing friends to the next.

Auntie Maggie grinned at us, her head swivelling from Leonard to me and back again. We avoided her beaming face. Two minutes passed.

The photo machine whirred and ticked before spitting out four tiny photographs. Auntie Maggie took them out of the metal tray and looked at them. She frowned.

"You boys aren't too cool to smile occasionally you know," she said as she tore the photo strip across the middle. She handed two photos to Leonard and two to me.

I looked at my two pictures. It showed us, the both of us, looking lost and haunted. I was wide-eyed, on the verge of tears, terrified. I looked terrified. I was terrified. Scared of the freaks in the spotlights two years earlier, the leering eyes circled around them, the snide comments, my inability not to watch them, what happened with the Razor and his Blades of Doom. Scared of my need to be looked at, my need to have more than only my cousin turn up for my birthday, my need for my mother to be here, my father to be here.

Sitting next to me in the photo, Leonard's eyes were blank and his mouth taut. There was a slight crease in his forehead, as if he was concentrating on something or trying hard to forget something. His face was a mask, hollow and papier mâché.

Would he look back on this photo and laugh?

I wouldn't.

The sun set as we wandered into the parking lot. Father carried a box of leftover pizza. The sky was a palette from blue to black, blue on the horizon where the sun had just disappeared and black on the opposite end of the land. It was huge, so much bigger than the parking lot where Father and I said *goodbye* and *thank you* and *see you* to Auntie Maggie, Uncle Tony and Leonard. The evening sky, endless in depth, spotted with billions of stars, was so much bigger than the space inside the Pacer. Even opening the window to let the cool air in did nothing to quell the feeling of claustrophobia.

Now, looking back on that night, my tenth birthday, one decade old, I can't believe I felt that way. As we drove out of the parking lot, we passed Margaret Koshushner's 1982 Monte Carlo parked in front of a medical clinic opposite the restaurant. Margaret was the last patient of the day. She sat on a cold examination table, wearing a blue paper gown. Her doctor was telling her that she had pancreatic cancer and would be dead within five years.

Funny. What a small world it is.

CHAPTER 6

Do You Know Why You're Here?

"**D**o you know why you're here?"

"Mother made me come. She made all of us come."

"And why's that, Richard?"

"I don't know. Maybe it's because she thinks we're crazy."

"That's not a nice word. We won't use that word. It's a judgment word."

"Okay. Sorry."

"Only ignorant and uninformed people use words like that. People who don't understand that we're all different and equally unique."

"I won't use that word anymore."

"Thank you. Do you think you're crazy?"

"No."

"Then why would your mother? Can you think of another reason, the real reason your mother would want you to come here?"

"Maybe it's because we're always fighting. That's what she says. That we are fighting all the time and…"

"Why are you fighting?"

"…sometimes I set things on fire…"

"You're fighting because you set things on fire?"

"No. You didn't let me finish. We're fighting all the time and sometimes I set things on fire."

"Oh."

"I mean, I think we're here because we're always fighting and sometimes I set things on fire."

"Is there anything else, Richard?"

"No. That's all Mother told me to say."

"She told you to tell me that?"

"Yes. Well, that's what she told me to say if we saw anyone she knows here or when I was asked. But I wasn't supposed to tell you she told me."

"So why did you tell me?"

"I don't know, because you asked I guess."

"How old are you, Richard? Ten? Eleven?"

"I'm thirteen."

"I see. Let me run this by you. I think you told me because there's some other reason you're here, one that even your mother doesn't know about. You don't necessarily agree with your mother that that's the reason you're here. Richard, do you sometimes not do what your mother tells you to? Do you sometimes disobey her?"

"Sometimes, I guess."

"Can you give me an example?"

"She tells me not to light stuff on fire. Sometimes I do."

"Can you remember when you started lighting fires?"

"Yes."

"Will you share that with me, please?"

"What are you writing down?"

"I'm taking some notes to help me remember what we talked about."

"Are you going to show them to Mother and Father?"

"No. I won't. It's just to help us out in these talks. The notes are for nobody else. You won't get in trouble here. I won't tell your parents anything and I won't show them these notes. The notes are just for the two of us."

"Can I see them?"

"No. Now, tell me about when you started lighting fires."

"I don't know. It was a while ago."

"I see. Richard, do you ever feel lonely?"

"No."

"Do you ever lie to please people, possibly to avoid getting in trouble?"

"No."

"Are you lying to me now?"

"Yes."

"Did you lie when you answered my last two questions?"

"Maybe."

"Richard, if we're going to continue, you have to be honest with me. That's the only way I'm going to be able to help you. We have to trust one another and explore these things together. Can we trust each other?"

"Yes."

"Please don't roll your eyes."

"Sorry."

"It's okay. Now, let's start again. Clean slate. Do you ever feel lonely, lie to please people or lie to avoid getting in trouble?"

"Sometimes."

"Can you tell me more?"

"Sometimes, I feel lonely."

"When?"

"Since Mother started home-schooling me. I didn't like going to school but sometimes I feel lonely when I don't see anybody my age for weeks."

"When did your Mother start home-schooling you?"

"A few months ago. She saw an article in the paper about that guy who drove around in his car asking kids if they needed a ride or telling them their parents asked him to pick them up. Then one got in the car and the guy took the kid away. Mother read it twice and decided to home-school me."

"Do you like being home-schooled?"

"It's okay, I guess. Some stuff that I didn't understand in class, I get now."

"But you miss your friends."

"I didn't have a lot of friends but I feel lonely because there's nobody around who is my age."

"Okay. This is a good start. I'm encouraged by our sharing. Thank you for sharing that with me, Richard."

"What did you just write?"

"I'm here to listen. I hope you're learning that you can be open with me. Already, I feel you're getting more adept at sharing your feelings and articulating them into words. It's a tough thing. Many grown-ups can't do it. This kind of communication is the only way to trust and learn from one another. You're doing really well … Now, let's talk about telling lies."

"…"

"Can you tell me a bit about that?"

"Oh, that was the question?"

"Yes."

"I sometimes have to lie…"

"Sorry to interrupt but, you *have* to lie?"

"Sometimes I have to, especially when Mother or Father is mad."

"Why do you lie?"

"Sometimes it's easier, you know, to fib. Sometimes, if I tell a lie, things turn out better than if I had told the truth."

"Can you give me an example?"

"Father wants me to lift weights and run for an hour a day, during school days. He wants me to get bigger. Most of the time I don't feel like it, so I lie and say I do, when I don't. What are you writing?"

"You aren't scared you'll get caught?"

"Father is at work all day. Mother usually has a nap in the afternoon when I'm supposed to be running or lifting weights. She doesn't pay any attention anyway; she takes her sleeping pills and has a nap."

"I see."

"Sorry, was that a question?"

"No. No, I was just thinking."

"About what?"

"Oh, a hamster. Do you understand?"

"No. Not really."

"Okay. Richard, please don't roll your eyes at me. It's disrespectful."

"Sorry. What don't I understand about the hamster?"

"I would like you to think about that and explain it to me. You don't have to answer right now but I want you to realize that all of these answers are in you. You just don't know how to order the questions to make sense of it all. It's okay, you're eleven years old…"

"I'm thirteen."

"…the answers and questions to all of these problems will come in time. You just have to trust in that. This is a confusing time for you. You're at the point when things you took for granted as fact come into question, things you thought were solid and true become grey and murky. It's scary because you don't know where these cracks in your foundation will stop. You're just starting to realize that your parents are human and prone to fault…"

"Just starting?"

"…like everyone else. This is when you learn that Santa isn't real…"

"He's not?"

"What?"

"Santa's not real?"

"Um. It's a metaphor."

"What are you writing?"

"Do you know what a metaphor is, Richard?"

"I think so."

"It's something that stands for something else."

"Like what? I don't get it."

"Like when someone calls working life a rat race. Do you understand?"

"Like when people say they're so hungry they could eat a horse?"

"No, that's hyperbole."

"Oh. A metaphor is a kind of a lie though. You're calling one thing something else. The people in the race aren't rats, are they?"

"No, Richard, it's not a lie. It's a different way of describing the truth, a different way of looking at a thing. Sometimes you have to look at something in a different way to get deeper into it, to understand it on a deeper level. Some would say a metaphor is really a more truthful way of communicating."

"I get it. It's like the hamster. The hamster is a metaphor."

"Exactly, like the hamster. Have you ever had thoughts of attempting suicide, Richard?"

"No."

"Are you lying?"

"No."

"Perhaps you ought…"

"Perhaps I ought to lie?"

"No, Richard. Perhaps you ought to think about attempting suicide."

"Do you mean metaphorically?"

"No. For real. Literally."

"Why would I do that? I don't want to kill myself."

"No. No, good God, no. Richard, no. That is not what I'm saying.

I'm not saying you should commit suicide. What I am saying is attempting to commit suicide."

"Oh."

"Yes. It's a very different thing that you were thinking of. My goodness, Richard. Very different."

"Yes, very."

"Let me explain. From our brief meeting so far, it's apparent that, under the surface, you have a strong craving for the attention of your peers and your parents. You feel that attention is owed to you and it's overlooking you. Everyone has the need for attention. Some crave it more than others. It's perfectly normal, perfectly natural. You shouldn't think of it as a character flaw … ever. Lighting fires is a way for you to get the attention you need, but it garners feelings of fear and alienation, anger and confusion in those around you. It's the wrong kind of attention, not the kind you want or need. Attempting suicide, on the other hand, brings forward sympathy, caring and a host of positive, motherly, nurturing feelings."

"I don't mean to scare people."

"No, no. I know Richard. It's something too complex for you to deal with consciously. It's a desire you're simply too young to properly process right now so you deal with it in other, easier ways. Don't let it get to you, there's plenty of time."

"There is plenty of time to let it get to me?"

"Richard, do you think often of attempting suicide?"

"No, you are the one who told me to."

Mother called from the other side of the room, "Richard."

"That's Mother calling. I should go."

"Who are you talking to, Richard?" Mother asked.

"This lady in the waiting room, Mother."

"Leave her alone, Richard. Dr. Sloane is ready for us now. Let's go."

Two years ago, Mother came back sober and renewed. Her eyes were different. They were deeper. Her face wasn't tense anymore.

She said she was sick and would be for the rest of her life.

She said there was no cure for her sickness; she would be in "treatment" from then on.

I thought that sounded defeatist.

I thought she had given up.

Had Dr. Sloane been a real doctor, he would have diagnosed her, coding her disease as it appeared in the International Classification of Disease Manual. In the ICD, every disease that could afflict a human is provided a numerical code. Mother's code was F10.2: *Mental and behavioural disorders due to alcohol, dependence syndromes.*

Father was different for a while, too. He was helpful and attentive. He lost his caustic edge until he figured out that Mother was back to stay.

Treatment made Mother stronger than she was before. She was also more focused on herself, on her illness.

Father and I seemed to drift peripherally, to opposite corners of her eyes.

Within a year, her treatment became all-consuming. She bought scented candles, spoke of life centres, envisioned positive action to channel the energies around her, and swallowed several pills of valerian root extract before bed. Twice a week, she had other women over to the house, women who didn't wash their hair regularly. Mother wore her illness like a fashion statement. She talked of nothing else.

Father had trouble with this shift.

I found it hard to talk to either of them, what with Father brooding and distracted by Mother's distraction and Mother skimming along a positively altered reality, each of them inhabiting a different bit of the world's spectrum. The sun shone blue on Father and pink on Mother. These monochromatic worlds bumped along until one yelled and the other glossed over the wrong issue.

Two years of parallel talking, parallel seeing, parallel living, brought us here.

Mother enrolled us in family counselling with Dr. Sloane.

For the past few months, once a week, we gathered in the clinic's waiting room with the other people needing help. Every week we walked from the waiting room, where I had made a habit of meeting other patients, into one of the more well-decorated rooms I had ever seen. Every week, Dr. Sloane would greet us with the same wide, white smile. The same graceful wave of a hand would invite us to enter the "Discussion Circle": a circle of cushions big enough for all of us to sit, cross-legged, facing each other.

I grew to think of it as "the arena."

In hindsight, that may have been more accurate.

"It doesn't work like that," Dr. Sloane's deep, smooth voice filled the air when Father had asked where the couch was on the first visit.

"We don't lie on a couch? What about chairs, can we sit in chairs?" Father had asked.

"The circle is the shape of continuance, completeness and honesty. There are no gaps, no breaks in the line. It is never-ending and it is the true shape of an honest discussion," Dr. Sloane said.

"Circular?" Father asked.

Dr. Sloane continued, "We can't converge as we need to when we are in isolated pods with barriers, space, furniture and desks acting as walls to our joining. It's not circular, Jack, it is continual."

A circle as a metaphor is also innate. It is a path you can travel forever and not go anywhere. A hamster wheel is circular.

"Okay," Father had said.

"Please don't roll your eyes at me, Jack. It's disrespectful. You and your family have asked me to join you as a portal to your wellness, as the gateway for open communication."

At the time, I was beginning to think of these metaphors. The lady in the lobby had been right; metaphor was a more honest form of communication. Dr. Sloane acting as a gateway made sense to me.

In hindsight, it was actually a simile.

Every month since that first meeting, Father asked Mother why we couldn't spend money on a real shrink, one who had gone to school at least, one who got an education, one who had a couch.

"Dr. Sloane is a well-respected life coach and spiritualist. You can't learn that from school," was Mother's reply. She wore a blissful grin.

"Welcome to the Discussion Circle." White smile. Gesture to the ring of cushions.

Mother, Father, Dr. Sloane and I stepped into the arena.

"Welcome, everyone," Dr. Sloane said. He started every session in the same way. "Debbie, Jack, Richard, let's open our minds to the healing power of communication. The expression of love, from one to another, is found in this honesty. Allow the universe into your heart. Share your heart with those in this circle."

Dr. Sloane closed his eyes. Mother followed with hers. The tightness in her face muscles loosened and a slight smile breached her lips. I lidded my eyes, but didn't close them fully, peeking into an eyelash-hazed room to give the impression of compliance to the outside world but allowing me to keep a careful watch.

Father's gaze travelled the three of us. He sighed.

"Good, Jack," Dr. Sloane said in a hypnotist's tone. "Let yourself relax. Let your body spirit open. Your thoughts align with the others in the room. All of us are working toward harmony." Dr. Sloane's voice continued its lull. "If you try, if you really listen, you'll hear a hum deep in your mind…"

Father still hadn't closed his eyes, I saw.

"…and that's the thoughts of the universe, a river where everyone's energies converge."

Mother gasped and breathlessly proclaimed, "I hear it. It's beautiful."

"Good, Debbie. I want you to remember this mind corner. This is where you'll channel your desires, where you'll let your thoughts mingle with the universal energy. It will respond. Does anyone else hear it?"

"I do," I said. The blurry image of Father's head swivelled to my voice. I concentrated on not reacting.

"Good, Richard," Dr. Sloane droned.

"I don't," Father said.

"Jack, don't let it frustrate you. You'll hear it when you become aligned. For some it's harder than others. Some are just slow…"

"My universe stopped," I interjected in a panic. What an awful feeling to hear the universal energy just disappear. To feel every other thing envelope you in its soothing drone and then, suddenly, disappear. I shivered. The room grew cold with a very lonely feeling.

"That was the air conditioning you were listening to, son," Father said. I'm responsible for helping spawn a moron, his tone said. What's wrong with my sperm, his tone asked.

"No, it wasn't," I said.

"Yes, it was," Father countered. "It was running and it just stopped."

I was certain I had heard the universe and now I was alone. I shut my eyes tightly, concentrating, straining to hear it.

"Jack," Mother commanded, channelling her warning directly into the universal energy.

It worked. Father was silent.

"Try and find it again, Richard," Dr. Sloane said.

"It's gone," I lamented. My heart raced, uncomfortable with being the heart of a universal orphan recently kicked out of the collective consciousness.

"It's not gone, Richard. It's always there," Dr. Sloane assured me. "Your mother and I are here, waiting for you and your dad. Don't force it, Richard. Let your mind find us." He was using that soothing tone again. "Let your mind connect."

I was desperate. The universe had shut me out. One moment I

was wrapped in such a sense of connection to everything, to everyone, that I could hear the soft energy and feel it wash over me. The next minute, the door slammed, leaving me on the doorstep, all alone in the rain of a cold, black night.

I wasn't really alone, I reasoned. Father was on the doorstep next to me.

"No shit." Father's voice was full of disbelief.

"Jack?" Dr. Sloane made Father's name a question.

"Hold on a sec," a beat of silence. "I got it. It is kind of a soft feeling."

"Yes."

"Kind of a fizzy noise you can feel more than hear. Kind of how an amber-coloured ribbon would sound if you could hear colour."

"Yes. That's it." No, that was ICD R20.8: *Other and unspecified disturbances of skin sensation.* Synaesthesia: experiencing one sensation as if it was another.

"I've heard this before."

"Really?"

"It's a bit like the trumpet progression in ABBA's "The Name of the Game," except a bit more sustained and a bit fuzzier ... other than that, ABBA nailed it."

I was alone, the porch was empty, the rain drenched me to the bone and the cold enveloped me, completely alone. ABBA had taken my father from the porch beside me and guided him through the door of greater universal understanding.

"Okay," Dr. Sloane said. "Let's open our eyes like we have opened our minds and hearts. Let's connect with one another as we did with the universal energy."

All eyes opened.

"Richard, what's wrong?" Mother asked, a look of concern crossed her face.

My face was wet. In the panic of being suddenly and completely disconnected from the entire pulse of absolutely everything, apparently I was crying. At the least, my eyes had started to water.

"I had it," I stuttered. "Then it was gone."

"I heard it," Father said, drowning out my last words.

Gobsmacked with disbelief, his expression said.

"That's wonderful, Jack," Dr. Sloane swelled visibly. Since we started these sessions, the relationship between them had fluctuated between -273°C and absolute zero. Dr. Sloane was obviously bathing in the icy cold waters of vindication.

I got the hang of metaphor, I thought.

I lost the universe that day. For all I knew I would never get it back. I had lost the attention of the circle, too. The gateway of open communication was closed and locked and the portal to wellness had disappeared. I needed it back and I had no matches to light fires with.

ICD F63.1: *Pathological fire setting.*

"Sometimes I think of attempting suicide," I said.

The room fell silent. The kudos evaporated and the testicular camaraderie between Dr. Sloane and Father shrivelled.

"Well," Father said, "that's just great."

"Jack," Mother snapped.

Perhaps if Father had intoned a little more sarcasm she wouldn't have.

Dr. Sloane smiled at me. "Don't be quick to judge, Debbie. Without judgment, that's the only way we can have open communication, the only way we can heal. I agree with Jack, I think it's great."

"Dr. Sloane," Mother gaped.

"Debbie, Richard is able to share. He feels comfortable here. We encourage that as we must encourage his thoughts."

That was not what the lady in the lobby said would happen.

"Why would you say that, Richard?" Mother asked.

"That lady in the lobby told me to. She said lighting fires was freaking you out so she said that this would be better."

"But it's not really you, Richard," Dr. Sloane said.

"Yes, of the two options I would prefer you light fires, honey," Mother added.

"Oh, don't encourage him, Debbie," Father said. "Richard, you will not light fires anymore and you definitely won't attempt suicide." Father struck up his disciplinarian tone, the one that ended conversations before they began.

"We can come back to this," Dr. Sloane said. "When the heat of the moment dies and rational minds preside. We need one minute to realign. Everyone, connect and reflect."

We held hands. A "Connect and Reflect" was like a time out for bad children. It was a metaphorical being sent to the corner to "think about what you have done."

What did I think about for one whole minute, there, alone in my brain, with no distractions? Dr. Sloane's and Mother's hands in mine became sweatier by the second.

A minute can be a long time. Is it possible to stop thinking? Even for one minute? I don't think the brain relinquishes that much control. Mine never did. It was the one in charge.

What do you think about for an entire minute?

At thirteen, I was beginning to realize that my parents didn't have all the answers. In fact, they had very little clue about a lot of things. That's unfair though, unfair because they couldn't defend themselves there in my brain. Honestly, I couldn't blame my parents for whom I grew up to be. They couldn't blame Grandma and Grandpa, so why should I get the privilege? They were easy targets, they were right here and becoming painfully more human in my eyes every day.

Nothing was their fault. Blaming them was an easy out, actually, it was worse than that. It was selfish. It was irresponsible. People who say their parents are to blame don't take responsibility for their own situation. Parents, including those currently connecting and reflecting there in the arena, try their best. They want the best for their sons and daughters. They become boundless martyrs because, sooner or later, the subject of their affection rebels and bites back. It takes a hero's heart to carry on day after day. They were selfless in the pursuit of that at which they would ultimately fail. They were stoic. They work with monomaniacal fervour.

I couldn't blame my parents for anything. That would be low and cowardly on my part.

The air conditioner came on with a low-level hum that seemed louder than before.

"Hey, Richard," Father broke the silence. "You can relax now. The universe came back on."

ICD F91.0: *Conduct disorder confined to the family context.*

ICD Z61.3: *Events resulting in loss of self-esteem in childhood.*

I could go on.

"Jack. We haven't reached one minute yet," Dr. Sloane said.

"Please don't disrespect this time in the circle," Mother said.

"We will start again. Now," Dr. Sloane let out a deep sigh, "connect and reflect."

No, I can't blame my parents, but I can look to them for answers on how I turned out. Not blame, just an explanation of sorts. It is kind of like adopted kids wanting to meet their biological parents to learn about their medical history. Clinically, it is a good idea to examine the mother-father-offspring relationship. You can find out if there is a family history of, say, obesity or cancer. Perhaps diabetes, alcoholism or heart disease runs in the genes. Sometimes you can even catch a glimpse for the genetic predisposition to inappropriateness, chronic social retardation or even one of these comorbidly enhanced by monomaniacal ABBAness.

ICD F28.0: *Other non-organic psychotic disorder.*

The brilliant thing about all of these: they were all diseases. As Mother once said, "Sickness can be cured."

CHAPTER 7

Alien Sex Light from
Ten Thousand Years Ago

I swatted a mosquito on my neck and smiled. The sky was a deep, af-ter-sunset blue and a jagged line of black spruce trees marked where the land started. The lake we looked across was as smooth as glass and was slowly fading into the warm darkness.

Leonard poked at the fire with a long stick, sending hundreds of glowing embers weaving into the shimmering air above it. At a height, one by one, they winked into nothingness.

"Someone will see the fire if you make it too big," Paige Green said. Paige was fifteen, like me. She was slightly on the husky side, unlike me.

"It's okay," Leonard said, looking across the fire at Paige's com-panion, seventeen-year-old Mary Koshushner, one of the "Max girls." Back at camp, Paige and I were known as Saplings, which the Juvenile Growth and Climax Forest campers shortened to Saps. They were Juvies and Maxes respectively.

Leonard smiled and stared at Mary, his eyes half-lidded and his teeth showing.

The fire popped, sending a few more sparks upward.

Leonard continued, "The bush is too thick here and camp is at the other end of the lake. Anyway, I really need to see you," he said specifically to Mary.

Mary smiled and her gaze dropped to the flames.

Leonard told me they had sex last year at camp, when they had both been Juvies. He told me Mary squealed and wriggled a lot, which woke up the rest of the Juvies in the dorm. She had been so embarrassed, Leonard told me proudly.

"A year is too long not to see you," Leonard continued, poking rhythmically at the fire with the stick but with his eyes locked on Mary.

I glanced at Paige awkwardly. She grinned at me. I fidgeted with my hands in my lap, wondering if she got a report from Mary like I had from Leonard.

"Someone tell a scary story," Paige commanded in an effort to break the awkward privacy that Leonard and Mary felt they had in the presence of a couple of Saps.

I had had that uneasy feeling before. I was watching a nature documentary with Mother and Father in the living room, that one where a lion mounts a lioness and they show all the thrusting, growling and biting for a couple of minutes. I couldn't switch the channel because I wanted to feel adult enough not to seem like I cared. I wanted to switch the channel because watching another species have sex, no, secretly wanting to watch another species have sex was awkward while my parents were in the room. The kind of awkward that happened around that fire.

"I have a scary story," I said.

Leonard glanced at Mary and directed a slight jerk of his head into the darkness.

Mary smiled and said, "Okay Richard, let's have it." She turned a patient gaze toward me, like a babysitter entertaining a child.

Paige shifted the log she was sitting on closer to mine, sliding it jerkily across the ground, pushing up a small mound of pine needles and dirt in its path.

"The title of this tale is Razor and His Blades of Doom," I said slowly, trying to add a sense of foreboding to the words.

Leonard's gaze snapped from Mary to me. His face seemed to blanch in the flickering orange glow. His smile disappeared.

"I don't think that story needs to be told," he said.

The fire crackled.

I looked down at the ground.

There was a pause before Mary asked, "Why?"

"It's just not right," Leonard said. "Let's go."

He stood and held out a hand to Mary. She hesitated before standing and taking it. They faded from the firelight, bushes rustling and twigs snapping with their passing. Paige and I sat in silence as their noise faded from our ears. We watched the fire for a few minutes before we heard a splash and some giggling from the direction of the lake. A few more minutes and there was some distant squealing.

"What's wrong with Leonard?" Paige asked. She punctured a marshmallow with a stick and held it over the fire.

"It's a true story. I guess he doesn't want to hear it."

"I still want to hear it," Paige said, reaching over and touching my arm.

I felt as though she delivered an electric shock with her bare skin on mine. I shifted a little and looked at her. She was smiling, her chubby cheeks bunched up and her eyes were the same as Leonard's were when he looked at Mary. My body tingled and my pulse wavered like the firelight.

Wanting. That was a good word for Paige's look and my feeling.

Horny was another.

"Razor and His Blades of Doom," I said again, slowly.

Paige smiled, peeled a gooey marshmallow from a stick and popped it in her mouth.

The heat from the fire seemed to grow hotter against the side of my face as I watched Paige lick her plump fingers.

"It was not a day the boys thought would end in death. It was not the type of day that anything terrifying should have happened. It was sunny on the fairgrounds, hot. People screamed on the rides outside but, inside the tent, the boys stood in a crowd, bodies pressed together in the dark. The air was damp. People were crowded like cattle," I said.

Paige watched me speak.

The fire popped.

"The lights came up onstage, blinding because it was so dark before. For the first few minutes, the boys had purple spots in front of their eyes, like after you glance at the sun. When their vision finally cleared, the boys saw a beautiful woman wearing a skin-tight suit. She was tied to a wooden wheel that stood upright and spun around slowly at one end of the stage. Her hair flowed like water as she spun. The wheel was as big as she was, with thick spokes. Her arms and legs and waist were bound by leather straps; her body made an *X* on the wheel. A man was on the stage too, standing at the opposite end next to a table. He was big and tall and dressed in flowing red material. There was some shuffling and murmuring in the crowd. It was so crowded. The boys were shoved around.

"The man smiled and lifted big knives from the table, one by one. His smile was horrible, his teeth glinted like the ugly, serrated knives in the stage light. Horrible."

The fire snapped; a shower of sparks corkscrewed into the night. I felt its heat and the blackness closed in around me like it had in that tent. I remembered the adult bodies pressing against me, jostling me one way and then the next. I'd looked for Leonard but we had been separated.

"Ladies and gentlemen," Razor boomed from the stage. His voice drowned out all other noise, adding to the claustrophobia. "Each of these blades is solid steel." He tapped two blades together. The clang made me start. "Each of these blades has been sharpened to a razor's edge." Razor stabbed the table with one knife. The blade penetrated the wood effortlessly, poking through the underside of the table. With his free hand, he drew a handkerchief from his sleeve and threw it into the air. As it twisted back to the ground, he sliced it, mid-air, with two quick motions. The handkerchief landed in three pieces on the stage.

"Each of these blades is real. The danger here is real. My lovely assistant, immobilized on that spinning wheel, will face Razor's Blades of Doom."

With a flourish he gestured to the woman. A knife flew from his hand with the motion. The blade spun through the air and sank into a wooden spoke in the crook of space beneath the woman's armpit.

Someone in the audience gasped.

Someone in the audience screamed.

Razor responded with a wicked smile.

The crowd shifted and I pushed back at the bodies between me and the stage.

"My lovely assistant does not fear death," Razor said, picking up a second knife from the table. Addressing the crowd, he continued, "She has faced this fear before—she is prepared to face this." He held up the knife. "The blade is only as thick as a fingernail and the edge is thinner than a hair."

The woman spun slowly upside down. I noticed how her body responded to the altered gravity. Her hair spilled toward the floor. The flesh of her face shifted slightly. Her breasts and stomach shifted slightly.

"My lovely assistant knows that with every throw, her life could end. With every throw, she is prepared. This is my lovely assistant," Razor raised an arm toward the spinning woman, "my lovely assistant and my wife, Anastasia. A round of applause, please."

Clapping erupted from the crowd. A few cheers and whistles pierced the air.

Razor threw the blade. It spun end over end, glinting in the light with each rotation, a strobe light of doom.

The applause continued.

Hungry eyes watched the blade fly. Hands pounded together. A cheer went up at the sound of the knife driving into wood, near the woman's inner thigh.

Anastasia's face went taut. Her brow furrowed. Her eyes popped wide open. Her beautiful red lips puckered in surprise.

The applause continued.

The inside of Anastasia's thigh turned liquid red as she spun sideways, flowing across the wood, making it black, cascading onto the stage.

Razor ran, yelling across the stage. The noise he made was not a word. It wasn't fear. It wasn't human. It was the sound of grief from deep within his body.

The femoral artery runs on the inside of the thigh, at the crook where the hip ends and the leg begins. It is under two and a half pounds of pressure per square inch and can bleed a body of its blood in less than four minutes. Under the right circumstances it can spray blood several metres.

The applause became confused and stuttered to silence.

Anastasia died.

The wooden wheel looked like a bloody Spirograph drawing gone wrong.

Razor brushed hair back from her inverted face. Sobbing, he kissed her bloody lips.

Right there was the connection between entertainment and real life. Right then it became real to everyone, the inseparable nature of reality and the fantasy that had enthralled us. The fantasy truly took place, it happened in reality, and that only just became apparent. With the thickness of less than a hair, there was really nothing separating the two.

Razor, desperately clutching at his lovely assistant, his wife, looked frantically for some small part of her that was still alive. His hands and her face were covered in blood and tears.

Razor's real name was Chad Strauss.

His lovely assistant, his wife, was named Eileen Fletcher. She didn't take his name when they had married. They didn't love each other any less because of it.

Screams and commotion rippled through the crowd. I fought to stay on my feet in the press of shifting bodies. If I'd fallen, I would have been trampled. Somehow, Leonard and I found each other and we were swept along with the crowd. There was an explosion of light and we were back on the midway.

The fire popped and flared, sending fireflies spiralling high into the night. I blinked at it. Somewhere from the direction of the lake, there was a splash and a squeal.

I looked at Paige, her face smooth and pretty in the flickering light. She leaned over and kissed me. I kissed her back with eyes wide open, staring dumbly at her closed eyelids. She put her hand on my chest and pushed with just enough force to tilt me and the log I sat on to topple. Our lips broke contact for a moment when we hit the ground, Paige's body on mine. Our landing hurt and winded me. I let out a small grunt which was punctuated by Paige's tongue entering my mouth.

We fumbled there, in the dirt, lit only by the flickering firelight. Rough caresses followed, awkward hands exploring each other's bodies through clothes, lips never parting for fear of neither of us knowing what to say. I ran my fingers through her hair. She tousled mine with her hand on the back of my head.

Paige pulled me up to a sitting position and lifted my T-shirt over my head. I was dazed momentarily, head covered in a sleeve of fabric, until it popped out the other side. My skin was alive, naked in the night air, warmed on one side by the fire, cooled on the other by the night.

Paige latched onto my mouth again. She tasted like fire-roasted marshmallows and her lips were sticky with sugar.

She ran a hand, floated it really, one molecule above my skin, from my chest to my belly button so that I could feel the sensuous absence of her touch gliding across the fine hairs covering my skin. Even so, I didn't clue in that she had done this before.

"What's that?" she asked through a mouthful of tongues, her hand rested on the patch of hair left of my belly button.

I heard Mother's voice ask the question, which wasn't right. It was the last voice I needed to hear at that moment. I pulled Paige closer and sealed our lips together to silence Mother, which I wasn't sure was so right either. I needed a distraction so I clumsily pulled her sweater up over her head, as she had done to my T-shirt.

"Ow. Stop," she said, reaching to pull her sweater back down.

I recoiled, fearful I had done something horribly wrong.

"My earring is caught," she said, her voice muffled by a veil of alpaca.

I stole a look at the smooth skin of her belly which almost ended the whole session for me. I closed my eyes and tried to think of something else, something infinitely unsexy. A multiplication table, some mathematical impossibility, anything to distract me from the horrible pleasure I knew I was about to endure. I tried to remember all the lyrics to R.E.M.'s "Losing My Religion." I ran through scenes of *Terminator 2* in my head until a pyjama-wearing Sarah Connor's bare feet squeaked sexily on the floors of Pescadero Mental Institution.

Eileen Fletcher spinning on the wheel flashed into my mind.

"There," Paige said.

Paige pulled her sweater off. Her hair was a static-cling Medusa wig. She smiled triumphantly.

I smiled expectantly.

The fire crackled happily.

Paige smacked me in the side of the head.

It was much harder than a caress should be, I thought, though I wasn't sure, being new to this and all.

"What the hell?" I sputtered, a little aroused by the foreign sensations all over my body but confused by the pleasure/pain combination.

"Shit," Paige straddled me, her warm thighs bracketing my waist. She smacked me in the head again, then grabbed it in both hands, twisting to one side. She started pushing my cheek into the dirt and pine needles. She was surprisingly strong as she grasped firmer and pushed harder when I started to struggle, using both hands to washboard my face back and forth across the ground. "Your hair's on fire."

"There," she said, "lemme see." She twisted my face to the opposite side. "Yep, all out."

I ran light fingers over the area, trying to assess the damage. I could smell the burnt hair but I couldn't feel a bald spot. A few patches of my cheek and chin felt gritty where dirt had collected in newly acquired scratches.

Paige sat atop me watching. As soon as our eyes met, she leaned forward and smushed her lips to mine again.

"Let's roll," I gasped, "away from the fire."

She heaved and we steamrollered away from the fire, a distance of one roll. Paige wound up on top of me again, her skin on mine. I wanted complete contact. I reached around her with both hands and fiddled with her bra, having only a vague idea of how the clasp contraption worked. I tried to get a peek at the clasp without breaking our lip-lock but, unsurprisingly in hindsight, the geometry didn't work. Desperation and inexperience made it a good idea at the time though.

Paige let out, what seemed to me, a patient sigh. She sat up, reached behind her and effortlessly released the garment and its prisoners.

There they were ... boobies. That's what they were called. Breasts were the things that would cost Dow Corning $7.3 million after a lawsuit resolved with the finding that silicone implants caused immune system illness. But boobies, those were just wonderful.

I reached up with both hands and squeezed them as if they would honk, go *beep-beep*, or make an *Ah-woogah* sound like some old Model-T horn. Paige took me by the wrists and guided me through the foundations of erotic caressing.

All the while I worked through the hardest times table in my head, the twelve times table, anything to distract my mind. I thought about the images I had seen on television: burning Kuwait, soldiers in gas masks, rockets blasting off. Nothing helped against the presence of Paige's naked skin.

Of course, I had seen parts of a dirty movie and a few porno magazines before. Sex there was so glossy, juicy, large and long. It was also very tidy. There were no smells, no extraneous juices until they were called for. Vocalizations were all scripted or dubbed in after the deed. There were no farty noises, no weird grunts or air expulsions. Talking dirty seemed erotic when someone else was saying it or writing it.

I found the reality of it was different.

Sex education classes, with their vaguely erotic technical drawings, taught me where everything was: the sexy parts and the not-sexy ones. Mind you, I had mixed feelings about the words used to label the parts, attached by a thin black line leading from the name to the part. The words seemed wrong, seemed funny where they should have been sexy. They weren't the words anyone would use later, in real life. "Labia majora" read the fletching of the black line that pierced the part. Mons pubis, clitoral hood, perineum, Bartholin's gland.

The guys are no more blessed with technical terms than the gals. Scrotum, corpora cavernosa, tunica albuginea, testicles, or funnier yet, testes. The words were speleological gear and the weird rock formations you found on spelunking adventures.

So, put all this together and there was a heavy session of coitus.

When Paige and I had coitus, my penis penetrated past her labia majora and minora, less than gracefully entering her vaginal canal until her mons pubis rested on my mons pubis.

Then she jiggled a bit, her hands on my shoulders and her arms straight, locked at the elbows. Her shadow vibrated. Then I was done. There was nothing I could do; no amount of distraction with obscure trivia or mind games could prolong it.

Paige kept jiggling and I was left with a rather uncomfortable feeling of being done but wanting to be polite to someone who had given so generously of her body. From what I knew, this was much stinkier, more uncomfortable and notably shorter than most couplings.

A rustle came from the edge of the circle of flickering firelight. Mary and Leonard had returned, stumbling into the light and stopping cold when they spotted us. Paige looked over her shoulder with a gasp and was dressed before I even had time to stand up.

"Nice," Mary said, eyebrows raised at me.

I spun around looking for my shirt and pants without much luck.

Leonard smirked, the lines on his face exaggerated by the firelight. He circled the fire, pulled my pants from a shadow on the ground and handed them to me. He gestured at Paige, who was wearing my R.E.M. *Out of Time* T-shirt, with her arms crossed protectively across her chest.

"You can never say anything about this," Paige warned, not looking at anyone of us.

"Oh, Paige," Mary said. "Trust us, our lips are sealed."

"Yeah, Paige," I said, taking a step to comfort her.

"Put your pants on," she said, matching my step with one in the opposite direction.

I did. Then I put on Paige's sweater. It hung, loose and itchy against my skin.

Little else was said that night. We put out the fire and stirred the ashes. Leonard and I peed on the spot once the girls started back to camp. Billowing clouds of stinky, steaming soot rose up. We followed Mary and Paige who walked slowly, picking their way through the dark woods. The pale moon lit the forest in greys and blacks. It robbed the dimensions from sight, making it like a walk through a painting of a forest at night. I could hear the girls talking quietly up ahead. Leonard followed me in silence.

I wanted to talk to Paige. I wanted to talk about the experience we shared. At the time, it was the deepest connection I had ever felt with anyone. But we couldn't talk with Mary there. I wanted to know what they were talking about. Was it about me? Then I didn't really want to know. My loneliness deepened with a giggle from the girls and the quiet noises of Leonard moving through the bush behind me.

The sound of a breeze in the trees drew my attention upward. I slowed my pace and looked at the sky. The trees were grey stripes, all converging on a hole in the canopy, a beautiful black space where I could see stars. The lights shining from up there were old. Whatever happened to them was already long over, thousands of years past. I wondered if any one point of light had a planet spinning around it where a little alien guy was walking through an alien forest after just having had coital relations. I doubted it and from that doubt came an overwhelming sense of wonder coupled with deep isolation. Reality was here. Fantasy was out there, in some alien sex light from ten thousand years ago.

I shivered.

We broke through the forest and onto the camp's compound. A few naked bulbs cast deep shadows on the dorm cabins. A gravel cul-de-sac looped around the buildings and back out through the dark spaces of trees to the highway a short distance away. A logging truck roared by, its headlights and yellow running lights flickering through the trees. For a moment, it drowned out the distant buzzing of the power line that ran to the camp from the lines along the road. It drowned out the quiet gurgling of water that passed through a corrugated aluminum culvert that redirected a stream under the highway.

We whispered good nights.

Leonard and I watched the girls go, their bodies side by side slipping from white to black through light and shadow. Their feet reported a muted crackle as they walked along the gravel lane. They rounded the girl's dorm and were gone.

"Want to go for a walk?" Leonard asked in a hushed tone.

I nodded. I was glad he asked. I needed to be around someone. The place was too quiet and, that night, the universe was too big. I felt too small. I wouldn't have been able to sleep anyway.

We wandered up the short road that led to the highway. A single lamppost, crowned by a yellow spotlight, marked the turnoff to the camp.

Across the highway was the large black spot of a recent cutblock. The space left behind where trees once stood was large, flat and empty. It smelled of earth and was a feeling that settled into both of us. The spotlight did not stretch far from the tarmac where we stood. There was a slight creosote smell from the lamp pole. We stood in the safety circle of light, looking in opposite bearings along the highway. The unknown tarmac stretched out in either direction. For all we knew, in the dark beyond our vision, the road may have just looped above, rising overhead and leaving us looking at each other in opposite directions.

"You feel that?" Leonard asked.

"Yep, weird," I replied.

"You got any smokes left?"

I had stolen a pack from Father on our way here. It had been in the glovebox and was easy enough to take when he stepped out at a gas station to go to the can.

"Yep." I fumbled around with my pockets and pulled one out. "Do you have the matches?"

A sulphurous smell flamed bright. Leonard held a match out and I puffed, coughed and handed the cigarette to him.

We stood, power lines humming overhead. A garland of telephone line was pegged to the same poles. The creek trickled hollowly through the culvert. A cicada chirruped in the night air from the direction of the clearing.

We stood, quiet enough that I could imagine the power travelling through the lines to lights in far-off places, coming out over empty dinner tables, coming through companionless television sets flickering in some distant neighbourhood. In a quiet, lonely suburb, someone switched off a bedside lamp and pulled the covers up snug. Leonard and I stood, far away from all of that, in a spotlit hole in the forest, a point of light like a distant star.

I imagined I could hear late-night telephone conversations, thousands of them, sliding through the little phone lines, simple thin wires carrying voices.

One of those calls was to the camp counsellor's office. A weary *hello* was exchanged between the counsellor and Mary Koshushner's mother. Mary's grandmother, Margaret Koshushner, had passed away that night.

Margaret had undergone the surgery for her pancreatic cancer five years ago and it had taken that long for the disease to catch up to her again. Margaret had thought of each year as a gift. She saw Mary grow up a little bit more. She had been able to visit with her friends for five more years. It was all she had hoped for.

In the end, she didn't mind dying. She missed her husband since he died in the Pinto and she truly believed she would see him again. She had never referred to herself as a widow. She always said she was separated.

Tomorrow, Leonard would learn Mary had gone home in the early morning sunlight. Tomorrow, I would try to speak to Paige and she would avoid me. I already knew that would happen but I didn't want to think about it. The horrible loneliness would return but, at that moment standing on the highway, the feeling was held at bay by Leonard, the spotlight above us and the cigarette we shared.

"Check it out. There's an airplane," I said. What I had thought was a star slid slowly in front of the others, smoothly as if the night sky were an ocean.

"Where?" Leonard exhaled smoke and passed the last centimetre of the cigarette back to me. "Oh, I see it. That's way farther out than a plane. It's a satellite, I bet."

"Cool," I said, not smoking, just letting the coal wink out against the filter. The first few drags had tasted horrible.

"How was your night?" Leonard asked after a pause.

I thought for a moment, my head swimming—from the cigarette or the events of the evening I couldn't tell. "I'm not sure," I answered.

Confusing, I wanted to say.

Sad, I thought.

Unreal and wonderful but so grounded it made me feel lonely, I wanted to say.

It didn't really make sense.

"It was so real," I said, "except it doesn't feel like it really happened. You know?"

Leonard gave me a sidelong look before shifting his gaze back to the darkness up the road.

"I know," he said. "You can talk to me if you want."

"I know. I'm okay."

"Okay."

The creek in the culvert plopped as if a stone had been dropped into it. The sound echoed metallically.

"Look," Leonard said. He pointed at a pinprick of light. A firefly.

Looking around, there were hundreds of them blinking across the clear cut.

There were signals everywhere. There were signs everywhere, all the time. Even at that late hour, in that dark spot in the middle of nowhere, flashing butts in the deep black, the chirp of the cicada, pheromones of a million ants disrupted by the logging, the burbling creek, signals from airplanes and satellites, power lines and static from distant stars. Thinking of it as silence was false. Stillness never happened. The night was full of radio waves, television broadcasts and phone conversations.

My feeling of isolation lessened.

Everywhere there were layers of activity and constant interaction. Even when things seemed so still and quiet, the world was full and moving and connected. The air was alive everywhere, at every moment, even those seemingly still and quiet ones. Something was always in the air. Things were progressing. Life was progressing.

The signals were everywhere.

The signs are everywhere.

CHAPTER 8

The Anatomy of a Model

Early summer, 1993, found me putt-putting my way south along the coast in Uncle Tony's rusty Chrysler Magic Wagon. Of course, Uncle Tony had a new minivan by that time, a year ahead of the rest of us with his 1994 model. He kept the old Magic Wagon for sentimental value. It had been his first, new from the dealer, loaded to the brim, financed to the hilt, automobile purchase.

"The Magic Wagon was the first front-wheel-drive small van of its kind," he told me proudly, admiring it in the garage with his hands on his hips. Birds chirped in the cool, early morning air.

When Uncle Tony had asked me to go pick up Leonard and bring him home from college for the summer, I jumped at the opportunity—freedom to get out of the city for a few days and road trip back with my buddy.

I clambered behind the wheel.

"The thing's a piece of shit on the hills. Totally gutless," Uncle Tony said, closing the driver's door with a creak behind me. He handed me the keys through the open window. "But it won't die and it's magic on gas."

Uncle Tony passed me one hundred dollars gas money and stepped out of the garage. I turned the ignition. The Magic Wagon failed twice but started on the third go, billowing out greasy blue smoke that filled the garage.

Despite its creaks and rattles, in my mind, the Magic Wagon was perfect. When I pushed the breaks, it slowed down. When I pushed the gas, it sputtered faster. The tape deck worked. Most importantly, the Magic Wagon was the thing that would get me away from the city.

The sun rose as I waited at a set of lights where the ring road marked the city limits. The cool morning air poured into the cab, flushing out the exhaust smell. Music came out of three speakers and static hissed out of the fourth: Pearl Jam's "Even Flow." The light turned green. I smiled at the long stretch of road before me. I pushed the gas pedal and the engine stalled. The speakers went silent when I turned the ignition off. The car behind me gave a long, uninterrupted blast of its horn. I flipped the key forward. The engine lurched and the Magic Wagon stuttered through the intersection, threatening failure until the speedometer needle jerked past thirty.

I hadn't told Father I was leaving. He hadn't been very attentive since Mother left, so I didn't think it would matter. The morning I went, he was sitting greasy-haired, and glaze-eyed in front of the television, watching *X-Files* reruns and smelling like he hadn't bathed in days. The house had been pretty quiet for three months. Only the blathering television noise crept through, muffled to different degrees depending on which room I was in. The air was stale. Windows hadn't been opened in months. Most of the curtains were drawn. Dishes were piled in the sink, on the counter and beside the couch.

The Magic Wagon, burning a steady cloud of blue up the coastal hills and easing up on the emissions on the less strenuous glide down the other side of the Continental Divide, couldn't really—safely—handle the main highway speeds. So, I mostly stuck to the cracked asphalt and gravel-filled potholes of the secondary highways and side connectors. It would take twice as long but I didn't mind.

I had woven my way through the mountains and along valley sideroads for three hours. Still, a few hours out from my destination, I pulled into a gas station in a small town sitting in a wide, sunny river valley to pee, check the oil and get some beef jerky before moving on. Everything was green and the air smelled alive. It felt good to stretch in the parking lot, chew some dried beef and breathe the mountain air before driving on.

Leonard had gone to college the previous fall, three hours down the coast if you took the freeway. He had written his last exam, completing his first year of journalism.

I hadn't seen him in as long. I finished my final year of high school and envied his freedom. He had escaped the city, lived with a roommate in the campus residence. I couldn't wait to catch up with him. So much had happened lately that I had holed up, stuffed deep down and needed to tell someone.

After a while of being lulled by the sun flashing through the trees and the buzzing engine, droning a higher pitch up the hills and relaxing to a lower hum coasting down the hills, I broke from the mountain forests and drove out onto the wide, bright coastal plain. The sun twinkled off the ocean and a dark square of a tanker ship sat between the shore and the horizon. It was big, seemingly unmoving, but when I looked away and then glanced back a minute later, I could tell it was heading south. The ship was so big and the ocean was so much bigger that it seemed inanimate.

Then I hit a skunk.

At first, it was a sharp bump and a heart-lurching moment of confusion. Then the smell hit me, that burnt plastic and frying garlic smell, and I knew what I had hit.

My heart beat faster even though it was sinking. I killed it. I could have avoided it had I been paying closer attention. Some distance passed, asphalt rolling under the tires. I gagged on the smell for a while and, as it lessened in the cab, it was replaced by a murderous hollow in my heart.

I had murdered an innocent being.

The tanker had moved an inch along the horizon.

Maybe it wasn't dead, I thought.

I slowed, spun the Magic Wagon around 180 degrees in a jerking three-point turn on the deserted highway and then started back.

Maybe I could save it, send death back empty-handed.

The Magic Wagon shuddered as the speedometer needle bumped against eighty.

From behind the windshield, my hopes dwindled as I approached the long smear of organic matter, a juicy exclamation mark on the asphalt punctuated by the corpse. Checking the rear-view mirror and finding myself alone, I slowed to a stop near the largest chunk, slid the stick to park and stepped out.

The Magic Wagon coughed and stalled. The reclaimed silence was complete and profound.

The tanker had moved another inch to the south.

I looked up and down the length of carnage, determining there was no hope for resuscitation and realizing that even if the animal had remained in one piece, I wouldn't have known what to do. I so badly wanted to do what was right. I wanted to fix what I had killed, but there was nothing to put back together, no going back in time to pay attention to the road enough to swerve out of the way. No way to put the animal back together and make all the bits work again. Some things, once done, cannot be undone.

So, I cried. I cried at how useless I was to fix the wrong I had committed.

I resolved to do the next best thing, to dignify and remember the dead. I would bury him.

I found a cardboard box in the back of the Magic Wagon and tore off a flap from the lid. I used it to scrape the smears off the highway the best I could. I put the pieces in the cardboard box, dragging it around behind me. I spent twenty minutes wandering the tarmac, scraping up small pieces of fur, flesh, bone and jelly. The whole while, I choked and cried, on both the smell and the sorrow.

Sweating in the heat, I dug a hole in the dirt just off the side of the highway and buried the remains.

One car, a Monte Carlo, drove by as I was saying a few words. A shadow swivelled behind the steering wheel as it drove by, watching me choke out a eulogy and wipe away globs of snot with my arm.

By the time I climbed back behind the wheel of the Magic Wagon, I had no more tears. I got the Magic Wagon started in a cloud of blue smoke. The tanker was nowhere to be seen. It had fallen off the horizon. The ocean was empty.

I drove north.

After a while, houses became more frequent, slipping past along the side of the highway. Traffic grew denser and eventually, I pulled up to the first red light I had seen in hours. I arrived, burning oil, exhausted and emotionally drained. Two hands clutched the top of the steering wheel and two arms hung from them. One block later, I pulled up in front of the dorm building. Leonard was there, sitting on a pile of boxes and chatting to a woman.

"What the hell happened to you?" he asked as I get out of the minivan.

The woman grimaced at me and said goodbye to Leonard. He kissed her on the cheek before turning his attention back to me.

I was covered with dust. My shirt was splotchy with rusty blood patches and snot smears and I smelled like sweat and skunk anal scent glands. My eyes itched from crying and, when I told Leonard what had happened, tears welled up again. While I confessed to murder, Leonard pulled a shirt and a pair of jeans from a box. He nodded as I recounted the funeral. He handed me the clothes and I changed there on the sidewalk, stopping my story only for a moment when I pulled my shirt off and put the clean one on. I told Leonard how lonely the funeral was, how empty the highway, the forest and the ocean seemed. How a life had passed from the world, how I took it and how I only wanted to do right now that I had done something so permanent and unforgivable.

"You're an idiot," Leonard said, not condescendingly but more out of a loving kind of pity. He grasped my shoulder. "Thanks for coming to get me."

"No problem." I blew my nose into my dirty shirt, looked at it, wadded it up and then threw it into a nearby bush.

"I'm all moved out." Leonard gestured to the boxes. "They needed me out by two o'clock so here's all my stuff. Let's go home."

We loaded the Magic Wagon and, on the way back out of town, Leonard suggested we stop at a pub to get supper and a beer. I reminded him that I was only seventeen but he brushed off my concern by saying, "I know this dumpy place just off the highway. All the students go there. They never check ID."

Leonard directed me past a scrapyard to a deserted service road. Twilight settled over the parking lot where the Magic Wagon putter-putter-stalled. A building clad in corrugated metal hunkered down in one corner of the lot, rusty tear-shaped stains dripping from where nails tacked the siding on. The only thing hinting at a place of business was a pink neon *Open* sign. An old biker wearing a leather jacket and bandana stood beside the door, sucking on a cigarette. The dull thudding of loud music played from within.

The old biker grunted and tipped his head at us when we entered. Inside, cigarette smoke hung like a film in the air, probably left over from the previous night. The bar, a large warehouse with wooden picnic tables, pool tables and a dance floor, spread out before us. Everything was lit by feeble bulbs strung from the rafters. There was a strong smell of stale beer and an organic waft from the straw fermenting on the floor. The place was empty save for one scantily clothed buxom beauty leaning against the bar talking to a beefy bartender who watched us suspiciously when we entered. We ordered the Road Kill Sampler Platter and a pitcher of beer.

People trailed in and the cloud of cigarette smoke grew thicker. Every time the door opened, I could see the old biker outside, smoking a cigarette and nodding at everybody who passed by. The music grew louder to the point where Leonard and I were leaning across the table, up on our elbows and shouting. We ordered more beer. Every table filled up and the buxom blond became a blur of waitress. The beefy bartender looked suspiciously at everyone who came through the door.

"I'm going to write obits," Leonard yelled.

"A bit of what?" I sloshed my beer, tilted my ear so I could hear better. Our picnic table had filled up with round, sweaty, biker bodies.

"Obituaries," Leonard yelled.

"Oh," I called. "I thought you were taking journalism."

"I am. I never realized how little I knew until I looked at other people's lives," Leonard said. "And you only really get to see what anyone does with their life after they die, otherwise they're still a work-in-progress. A finished life is at its maximum. It can't be anything greater."

I nodded, glanced sideways and caught a pair of beady eyes staring at me. They shifted as the porcine face they were embedded in moved awkwardly to face the tabletop.

"You know," Leonard yelled over the din of the music and people, "there are more people dead on earth than live ones? Like fifteen times as many dead people."

Spittle landed on my face whenever Leonard used a word with the letter P in it.

"And each one of them had a life as full as yours or mine," he yelled.

I nodded and thought of the skunk I killed.

"I want to know those people, know what they did. I want to know their lives. You can know everything there is to be known about them. You can even know everything through them." Leonard was excited. His eyes sparkled.

I glanced sideways and caught the man staring again. Again, quickly, he looked away.

Leonard's gaze followed mine with no pretense of discreetness. "Maybe he's a cop," Leonard said.

"He's looking?" I asked. My pulse quickened.

Leonard lifted his beer. "He's getting up and coming this way."

"No," I said but Leonard nodded. I couldn't bear to look. I was seventeen, with a beer and we had five hundred kilometres to go until we broke the city limits and got home. All this and I was being approached by a cop to be arrested, tossed in the tank, have Uncle Tony's Magic Wagon impounded and my licence revoked.

A hand clamped down on my shoulder. I jumped, my muscles snapped taut. I looked to the source of the arm. White smile, tanned skin, blue eyes, earring, hair that looked like it was cut yesterday, fashionable wireless glasses. Probably not a cop. "I saw you," he said.

"Oh yeah," I said. I pushed my beer as discreetly as possible toward Leonard, on the off-chance he was an undercover cop.

"Yeah. My name is Chester Leroy, I'm with the Agency. I was wondering if you've ever considered a career in modelling?" Chester extended a card and gave my shoulder a squeeze.

There was a pause so I filled it with my name. "Richard," I said.

Leonard's smug look slid into one of shock. I must have looked similar because Chester moved to fill in the silence with a stream of uninterrupted chatter.

"Yes, we represent hundreds of fashion models and a gaggle of actors and actresses. You have a look we could really sell. Things are changing right now, they always are really, but there is a shift coming, a big one, and I think the times are ready for you and you are ready for the times. There is a harmony to your features that I think the Agency could really promote. I represent several of the firm's top models and, for you, I see paycheques ranging into the tens of thousands per show if we position you right. I don't want you to rush and there's no obligation. Even if we meet later, there's no obligation to sign up or anything though I think a contract could be a very real option for someone with your look."

I glanced at Leonard who shrugged, still with a confused expression on his face.

"Sure, I guess," I said. "But we're leaving town tonight."

"Not after those beers, surely," Chester said.

Leonard closed his eyes and nodded.

"Take my card," Chester said. "I'll see you tomorrow morning at my office before you go." Without another word, Chester spun on his heel and exited the bar. As the door closed, I saw the old biker outside nod and tip his head, a cigarette held between his fingers glowed in the dark.

"We'll sleep in the van." Leonard smiled. "We'll leave tomorrow after your interview." He waved his empty mug for more beer and pointed a finger at mine, too. We still had seventy dollars of gas money to drink.

Mother and Father grew up in the sixties with icons like Burt Reynolds, Sean Connery and Christopher Reeve. Likewise, the models they saw in fashion magazines had ill-defined but undeniable musculature. The women were thin but still had curves and breasts. In the eighties, I grew up with icons like Sylvester Stallone and Arnold Schwarzenegger. Likewise models became beefier. The women became gothic muscle action figures like Sigourney Weaver in *Aliens* and Grace Jones.

A face and body that was erotic in one generation may be repulsive in the next. Overall though, the basic tenants of beauty remain unchanged. A healthy body—one in which the combination of parts is balanced and in harmony—is beauty.

I never got bigger like Father had wanted. Luckily the perception of beauty changes. My slim stature, the bane of my and Father's relationship, became a boon to my career. The "contrast effect" in marketing accounts for these swings. Basically one phenomenon, Schwarzenegger, is a foundation for the rise in popularity of the opposite phenomenon, me. Popular perception is framed in the context of the milieu so if everyone is beefy, the slender stands out. There was no planning on my part, no attempt to sway my body into a smaller pair of jeans or a tighter shirt—I just happened to coincide with what would soon be deemed beautiful. I would become the new foundation. The by-product me happened to fit into what was going on at the time. Models started to swing from chiselled men and shapely women to androgynous and childlike. The contrast effect. Had I been born five years earlier or five years later, none of this would have mattered and I would have been nothing more than an attractive barista or handsome accountant.

None of this was going through my mind when I woke up in the Magic Wagon in the bar parking lot, head pounding, grimacing against the early morning sun powering through the windshield. I stepped out of the wagon to stretch and pee. Leonard woke and drove us to the address on Chester's business card.

The receptionist let me freshen up in the bathroom, seemingly unfazed by my stale alcohol and body odour smell, as if strangers regularly wandered in to wash themselves as best they could in the cramped two-piece bathroom.

There were three people in Chester's office, all sitting. Being that there were no extra chairs, I stood. The office was small, close and crowded. I became very conscious of the smell of my underarms.

"Richard, right on time," Chester smiled, stood and extended his hand. Someone closed the door, which made the air seem heavy.

"Welcome to the Agency. We represent hundreds of models, many of whom I am sure you will recognize. It all started with this woman, Stella Supernova," he waved a hand at a picture on the wall. It was of a forty-something looking woman who may have been a drag queen. "Stella pulled this agency out of the limelight and into the spotlight over twenty-five years ago and she is still actively modelling. Here's our information package," he handed me a folder, "here is a benefits sheet," he handed me a sheet, "and here's a recent client list," he handed me some more paper, picked up a camera, and clicked a few shots of my face. "Now take your shirt off, I need a picture."

I lifted my T-shirt over my head, trying to limit the escape of the strong smell of my underarms and the nutty smell of my hungover, unwashed skin. Nobody in the room seemed to notice. Chester looked from me to the two unintroduced people sitting close by. They looked me over.

There is a mathematics to beauty that I didn't understand at the time. Apparently, Pythagoras mathematically answered the question: *What is beautiful?* The answer was 1.618. That is the ratio between two quantities as well as between the sum of those two quantities which, when seen in human features and proportions, is consistently and particularly more appealing than any other. It is a complex addition of both the individual parts as well as the combined effort of these parts to create a harmonious whole. It is inherent that beauty is not in the eye of the beholder, it is in the eye of some subconscious calculation that recognizes variation around the symmetry and proportion of parts related to this, the golden ratio.

Chester and the two unintroduced were mathematicians examining my face and body with the cold calculation of any master physicist or actuarial scientist.

Chester clicked a picture.

Symmetry, in artworks, in bodies, in faces, is the basis of what is beautiful. It portrays an absence of defects. Symmetrical growth is portrayed in our subconscious, good genes, good for breeding and therefore attractive on an animalistic level. Greek and Roman men, considered the classics of beauty by many artists and other mathematicians, were tall and muscular.

"He's skinny," one of the unintroduced said.

"And small," the other said. "Malnourished with an intrinsic sadness. Like those kids you are supposed to adopt from those villages on TV. Except he's without the bloaty belly."

Greek and Roman men with full heads of hair and strong jawlines were considered virile. The handsomest of them had bodies that portrayed health.

"I love it. Positively anemic," the first unintroduced said. "It is unhealthy. I think we have a new look for the Agency to get behind. We will make a beauty the likes of which the world has never seen. This is an opposite to the beauty that's on the market today."

Greek and Roman statues portrayed intelligence through high, wide foreheads and wide-set eyes, strong mouth lines and sharp noses, not unlike predatory birds.

Chester moved and clicked a profile picture.

"He has nice, thick hair. A good brow line. Nice and strong. Broad but not Cro-Magnon." Chester started his inventory. "There is a mysterious seriousness in those green eyes, not so much an intimidating intelligence but a misplaced one. If I could remove them and put them on a plate at a party, no one could deny snacking on them," Chester said.

"His nose is classic though his face is anything but," the unintroduced said. "Its angles are sharp and perfect and very similar in slope to that of the jaw."

"The lips are a little thin but seem to work well with the rest of him," Chester rejoined. "There is a lot here to work with. I'm a little concerned about the body though, the weight."

"He's positively emaciated," said an unintroduced one.

"We need an extreme counterpoint if he's to stand out," Chester said. "Five foot eleven and one hundred and ten pounds if I had to guess. It's good now but we'll have to watch that he doesn't grow into his height. If he fills out, we could lose him. Right now, we should get him into suits and swim trunks. His broad shoulders angling to the narrow hips, that's perfect for formal ware and beach ware. He's like a walking coat hanger. He's the perfect simulacrum for the new masculinity. His ass will send the swim trunks flying off of the shelf. It's sculpted."

"His hands are too plain, too workman," the unintroduced piped in. "And that weird patch of hair on his stomach will have to be dealt with."

"His hands would exclude him from product shots," the second said.

"Come on," Chester said. "With looks like his, I wouldn't waste him on hand modelling even if he had spectacular glamour hands. And there are ways of dealing with that stomach hair."

This went on for half an hour. At first I was concerned by the compartmentalization of each of my body parts. After signing with the Agency, it became normal to me. It should have been all along. I was signing the health plan when I realized the treatment of a body as parts is institutionalized. The health plan was compartmentalized too. I could claim from a dentist, a dermatologist, an ophthalmologist, a psychologist for work done on my teeth, skin, eyes and brain. The accidental death and dismemberment forms showed me exactly what one foot is worth. I was insured for 50 percent of the principle amount if I lost a foot. One eye, 50 percent. Both hands and feet, 100 percent. A thumb or index finger, 25 percent given that severance happens on the closest joint to the wrist. A fingertip doesn't pay out. You can't cash in on a pinky either.

All the parts, well, Chester was ready to represent them 100 percent. Every piece of me would be marketed and cashed in on. Every last little bit.

CHAPTER 9

The Handsome Boys' Modelling Guide to Beauty, Poise and Personality

"Ladies and gentlemen, welcome aboard flight zero-four-seven to Moscow. We'd like to ask for a few minutes of your time while we outline some important safety features of this aircraft."

Lately, life could have used a few safety features. Since signing with the Agency a year ago, I had spent most of my time strapped in the bellies of various Boeings beside beautiful co-workers. I had heard the safety speech to the point. I could recite the American Airlines version, the Air Canada version, the Lufthansa version, the British Airways version. All the speeches were pretty much the same, being written by various federal transportation agencies. The words were best coming from between the lips of the most beautiful stewardesses ever to seduce the skies, those of Singapore Airlines.

Singapore Airlines … I had sex twice in their washroom over the Pacific Ocean. Air Canada, sex once somewhere over Saskatchewan. Lufthansa, once over the Atlantic and once over Central Europe. British Airways, just before descending into Amsterdam. It's a very short flight from Heathrow to Schiphol. American Airlines, seven times over the continental US and once over the non-contiguous states.

"This aircraft has five exits, two at the front, two over the wings and one at the rear. Please take a moment to note the exit nearest you."

I had been driven directly from a shoot to the airport to catch flight zero-four-seven. The shoot was for Jungo undergarments. It was fabulous and took place in an abandoned parking lot downtown. A generator-powered bank of lights was the sun and a generator-powered fan was the wind. It blew my hair as I stood on a boat that sat on a trailer hooked to a tow truck. The driver sat waiting in his greasy overalls, chewing on a toothpick and tugging on a hangnail. I hung from ropes and draped myself across various pieces of nautical hardware, not knowing how any of them functioned but knowing how to look amazing with them. My skin was sticky with glycerine ocean spray. The generator had chugged and roared, not seeming to bother a guy who slept in a puddle of his own piss in the corner of the parking lot.

A photographer clicked black and white freeze-frames, stopping time's progression for an instant. Each photo captured a singular moment. Each moment held the promise of another to come and, along with it, the eventuality of celluloid immortality.

From the camera angle, I was in clear ocean air with virgin white sails billowing all around me. The line between reality and fantasy was altered merely by the way the shot was framed. Reality was a matter of perspective, what the photographer allowed the viewer to see.

"In the event of an emergency or sudden power loss, this aircraft has been equipped with in-floor lighting that will guide you to the nearest exit. In the unlikely occurrence of a loss of cabin pressure, oxygen masks will drop from the panels located above your heads. Secure the mask over your mouth and nose and tighten the elastic straps. The bag may not inflate, which is normal. We assure you that oxygen is flowing. Please don your own mask before assisting those in need around you."

That homeless guy, the one sleeping in his own piss near the roaring generator, I thought, would I assist him? Well, it wasn't so much that I wouldn't, it was that I didn't. Which, in the long run, is the same thing because I could have assisted him. I got paid well. I could have bought him lunch or a bottle of Big Bear or something.

I fastened my seatbelt.

Not helping him was the same as not wanting to. Did that make me a bad person? Well, nobody else was helping him.

"Please take a moment to ensure your seat belts are fastened, your chair backs and tray tables are in the upright and locked position, and your carry-on baggage is stowed under the seat in front of you or in the overhead compartments."

There is a safety reason for storing all of your baggage. It can cause harm if not stowed properly. Stowing your baggage securely, out of sight and out from underfoot, is a healthy practice. I vowed not to think of the less fortunate anymore. I vowed to live in the now, for the moment, without consideration for the past or the future. I vowed to let it all slide. I would live my own life. I was independent, free and jetting all over the world. Cameras were pointed at me. People were beginning to notice the new look.

"Transport and safety regulations dictate that this is a non-smoking flight. The bathrooms are equipped with sensitive smoke detectors. It is a federal offence to tamper with or disable them. We're glad to have you aboard. If there's anything your attendants can do to make your time with us more pleasurable, please press the attendant button and one of us will be happy to help."

I had smelled smoke when Leonard lit a cigarette on our ride from the Jungo shoot to the airport for me to catch flight zero-four-seven. He had parked the Magic Wagon beside the generator and stood there smoking while we finished. Leonard had just graduated. He got a position with the *Times*, but often had afternoons off so he drove me places. Leonard was an obituary writer. His co-workers called him names.

"Hey, Dr. Death," I said as I approached.

"Nope, this week I am Harold, of *Harold and Maude* fame," Leonard threw the butt to the concrete.

"Here, I found this at a used bookstore." He handed me a copy of *The Handsome Boys' Modelling Guide to Beauty, Poise and Personality* with a shrug. "Figured you could use it."

Leonard edged the minivan into traffic. He scratched his goatee and seemed distracted.

"What's up?" I asked.

"Oh, Kurt Cobain died and I didn't have a pre-obit done so I had to scramble," he said.

I looked at him quizzically.

"Yeah, I write up famous people who're going to die so when they do, we can go to press quickly. It avoids rush mistakes," he said. "Problem is, there are so many famous people you can't get them all. Some are easy to predict, the ones that have pre-existing conditions or are really old, but others…" he chewed his fingernail, signalled and changed lanes.

"Well, don't be too hard on yourself," I chided.

"Yeah," Leonard said in all seriousness. "I guess, but there has to be a way."

"A way to what?"

"To guess," he replied. "You know, when someone's going to die. There has to be a pattern or something," he said and jammed on the brakes. Distraction caused him to miss important traffic indicators such as illuminated tail lights at stop signs.

"They're holding a vigil in Seattle," he said. "Thousands of people are there. Cobain shot himself in the face. I should've seen it coming. I could've written so much better, made it relevant, if I had only known."

Police investigators figured Cobain shot himself on the sixth of the month though he wasn't found until the eighth. On the sixth, a plane carrying Burundian president Cyprien Ntaryamira and Rwandan president Juvénal Habyarimana was shot down. Both died and the attack sparked the Rwandan genocide. Western headlines were too distracted by Kurt to notice. Ten years later, there would be a candlelit vigil for the half million who were murdered in the genocide.

"You should call your dad," Leonard said as we pulled onto the freeway. "He phoned the apartment again today."

Father had become needy since Mother left and I moved out. Every week he would want to meet for lunch or have beers in the evening. He was trying to be a cool dad but always just wound up lecturing me on the latest protein powder, creatine mixture, or how I should join him at the gym after work. He had beefed up, though. He was buff. He had nothing else to do, I guessed.

I hadn't heard much from Mother since she moved in with her boyfriend. I got an *It's not anything you've done* letter and an *It's not your fault* phone call. I thanked her and said that I knew all of that.

"Yeah," I said to Leonard. "I'll call him when I get back."

"And Rachel is moving in with us," Leonard said as an aside.

Rachel was Leonard's girlfriend. They met at school. I first saw her in front of the residence building that summer I went to pick him up in the Magic Wagon. She worked for the *Times* too, reporting for the style section. I ran into her periodically at events, fashion shows and fundraisers.

Having her move in wouldn't change anything. I didn't care, I was barely ever there anyway. She was tall and pretty and natural. She might use too much time in the bathroom but she was a good cook and neither of us were.

I hadn't felt like I'd had a home in about a year, unless you counted all the hotels I stayed in for shoots and shows. They were all pretty much the same and could blur into one, stable abode if I squinted and tilted my head to the side. They all had the same bad hotel art, same lobby furniture, same big-city views from the window. When I thought about it, I realized those rooms were my home. Same linens, same tiny soaps, same hygienically plastic-wrapped glasses. The familiarity of it was home—each room was just an airplane commute away. Same bellhops, same minibar, same pay-per-view pornography. The lobby had become my living room, the hotel bar my lounge and the restaurant my kitchen.

"So, where're you off to?" Leonard asked.

"Moscow Fashion Week. Showing for some new designer called PG."

And then they were serving the inflight meal. I glanced around at the other passengers, peeled the tinfoil off, and spanked my chicken with a fork. Nobody was looking yet. Maybe after supper.

The lights dimmed and the movie started, something with a bunch of rugby players crashing onto a mountain and having to survive in the wreckage of their plane. I saw it two weeks ago coming back from London. It ends with them eating their teammates and then hiking out of the Andes.

I pulled out the airline magazine and flipped through it. Someone had done the crossword and I read it last week coming back from a shoot in Florida. There was a fascinating article about the Duyser Virgin Mary Grilled Cheese Sandwich. Story goes that Diane Duyser made a grilled cheese sandwich and, when she took a bite, noticed the face of the Virgin Mary staring back at her from a charred portion of toast. She and her husband, Greg, decided to save the sandwich for luck.

I glanced at the movie and then inspected my chicken for a likeness of the Virgin Mary. I could make out the outline of Vermont in one of the grill lines but that was it. I turned my focus to the woman sitting beside me thinking, perhaps, she would like to have sex. I smiled. She would do. She was something we in the industry called frumpy-chic, a seemingly homemade, loose-fitting denim dress and some kind of Third World-ugly wrap for a blouse. She was a little overweight, but that would soften the edges of the small washroom. She was approximately my age or maybe a few years older and her face had a comfortable familiarity.

"What're you reading?"

She put her book down and peeled the tinfoil from her meal.

"It's called *Passages*, by Gail Sheehy." She looked at me as if I should know who Gail Sheehy was and stuffed a piece of chicken in her mouth without looking at it.

She may have just eaten the Virgin Mary, I thought. Perhaps she wasn't worth the effort. I nodded to myself, which she mistook as an expression of interest, a prompt to continue.

"Sheehy broke people's lives into decade-long phases and, based on seemingly universal Western sociocultural issues, plotted the average person's 'life cycle' from the Trying Twenties through to the Serene Sixties."

She used the side of her fork to slice the chicken.

"That's a little like fate isn't it?" I asked. "A little defeatist."

The plane shook a bit from turbulence and I couldn't help but notice the tantalizing way she jiggled. She'd be worth the effort, I decided.

"It's true enough," she said, flashing views of the grey chicken bolus in her mouth. "Man goes to school, man graduates and gets a job. He moves out of home, buys a car, dates and gets married. He moves with the wife to the suburbs, raises two children, has the neighbours over for a barbecue. Man works hard, gets promoted to manager, buys electronics and a La-Z-Boy. Then he retires, putters around the garage and dies."

Shit, I thought, Father and Uncle Tony.

Maybe this woman wasn't worth the effort.

"I see," I said and looked around the darkened aisles for a different play pal.

"And woman, she goes to school to become a secretary, a teacher, a nurse. She finds a man with a car and marries him. She moves to the suburbs, has kids, quits her job. She joins the PTA, becomes a pillar of the community. She bakes and becomes the PTA president. She retires with her husband, putters around the garden and then dies."

Something had changed for women, I thought. Something got better.

"When was that book written?" I asked.

"The seventies," she said.

"Things change," I said.

"Indeed. This roadmap doesn't work anymore. I guess, in answer to your earlier question, it's not like predetermination. It's a record of what fate was. It's also proof that, with a little effort, you can change fate." She paused. "You see, my theory is everything changed in the eighties when the idea of the makeover became so prevalent."

I thought of Mother and Father. She broke the cycle and ran away with another man. I thought of Father desperately trying to cope with the unexpected turn in his life. Not being able to adjust, he settled for watching *The X-Files* and drinking beer.

"Once that was altered, it wasn't hard to twist the rest." She smirked at me. "Men just couldn't keep up."

Was she flirting or was I being insulted? Could I get laid? I was intrigued.

"You see, women broke their life cycle, reinvented it. It was really as simple as shifting the perception of youth. With makeover culture, thirty became the new twenty. Women rediscovered their youth, no, reclaimed their youth and that was the foundation for altering their whole life cycle. With an extra ten years, they could do anything. Altering and extending that youthful power, a little shift in the social attitude, a tube of lipstick and the chains just snapped. The point in the life cycle about meeting a man with a car, and all the steps after became moot. That altered the second half of the men's life cycle too but men haven't seemed to be able to fill in that gap yet, haven't been able to adapt."

"Reinvented the life cycle?" I asked, giving her a skeptical glance.

"Yep," she said, mopping up congealed clots of gravy from her plastic feed tray with a bun she had just peeled the cellophane rind from. "Changed fate."

"New rules…" I commented. "I am going to the washroom," I unbuckled my seatbelt. "The one at the back of the plane," I said pointedly.

Sex in an airplane washroom is a fetish for some, a fantasy for others and an unfortunately pervasive urban legend. Common misconceptions are that it is exciting, romantic and daring. These are fallacies spread by the legions that claim to have had sex in an airplane washroom but never have. These people haven't even given it much thought beyond the actual deed. Those few people who have actually flown and fucked will tell you it is necessarily rushed, totally practical and potentially embarrassing or even criminal, if caught.

Sex in airplanes is no small feat. The sheer impossibility of the ratio of bathroom patrons to bathrooms, combined with the confined quarters of the bathroom itself, is cause for creativity. The copious sex I had in airplanes was not some pathological mental disorder, it was alleviating boredom. That and I was eighteen years old, which in hindsight, may have been a mental disorder.

The logic goes like this: the more you fly, the more likely it is you have read all the magazines in the seat pocket in front of you, the more likely it is you have heard some variation of the story the stranger beside you has to tell and the more likely it is you have seen the inflight movie.

So, you start looking around. Then, while most eyes are fixed on the movie about the woman who meets the man and falls in love and loses him and gets him back in the end, you notice that a few others are also looking around with meaningful glances. While most eyes are glazed and mouths are open, a pair of well-plucked eyebrows raise at you and the next thing you know, you are fucking, grunting and gasping in confined quarters with one ass cheek sunk in the ass cheek-shaped sink. Next time you are on a plane, watch for these others because they are watching for you.

The vast population of liars will tell you airplane sex is easy to pull off undetected and that it is quite a rush. The truth is you must be calculating to avoid detection by the cabin crew and your fellow passengers. Logically, anyone who has truly done it will tell you it is just sex, above the earth, in a cramped, smelly closet meant to barely fit one person but forced to accommodate two.

The choice of partner is important. It is best done with someone other than a close seatmate so you are not stuck sitting through a number of awkward hours trying to converse with someone you just fucked when all you want to do is inflate your horseshoe neck pillow and doze off until touchdown. This is, of course, unless you are either already acquainted with them or they are one of the few practised and professional mile-high veterans.

Timing airplane sex is important. It is best done early in the flight before the perennial line of bathroom goers forms, as is the case by the second half of any transoceanic flight. Also, avoid stewardesses blocking aisles with carts of steamed chicken and cellophane-wrapped buns. Therefore, the ideal time is right after dinner and drinks are served, early in the flight.

Once in the washroom, a new suite of logistical issues arises. First, the inward-hinging accordion door makes the meagre space even smaller. Clothing, at least those hindering access to naughty bits, is best removed before both participants are inside. This lessens the awkward fumbling and the potential for becoming inextricably wedged, which has happened in the long and sordid history of flying and fucking.

Assume at this point all has gone well and sex can actually commence. It is imperative that one does not become so rapt in the act that it overtakes conscious control of actions and noises. Excessive thumping, primal noises or loud proclamations should be avoided. A misplaced "Please, harder," or "Oh God, yes," will signal trouble. An errant "Drill me, pig," or "Make me dirty," will result in discovery due to the fact that, on the other side of the centimetre-thick wall, sit the people in the last row of seats. These people don't sleep for two reasons, the seats don't recline and they are invariably parents with small children. Parents think being at the back of the plane limits the nuisances that are their kids.

It is difficult to get lost in the act, though. There is always the jiggling of the door handle from people testing to see if the door is really locked or if the 'occupied' sign is lying. There is the constant awareness of the various buttons and levers, which cause premature spraying in the washbasin, flushing of the toilet or soap to be dispensed. There are the hard edges of counters, racks and towel dispensers that must be accommodated. There is the ever-present danger of potentially wedging oneself due to unexpected turbulence or partner movements. Being acutely aware is necessary.

As is becoming apparent, the logistics are against you.

In the washroom, speed is essential. Anything that carries on longer than the length of a good dump, say ten minutes, will arouse the suspicions of the crew. Those who require foreplay before and/or cuddling after coitus should not partake. The rule is, get in and get out.

Say all of this went off without a hitch and everything is over. With two people, it is impossible to wash down or wipe up, leaving the best option to beat a hasty retreat. If both participants manage to get their clothes on, exit at the same time. If not, one gets out quick, then the remaining participant can pack up and leave a few moments later. If there is a lineup at the door best to behave as if everything is normal.

Sex on a plane is never great, but it is an entertaining way to pass the time.

Or, if you haven't seen it yet, you could watch the movie.

I ducked into the washroom, closed the door behind me. I dropped my pants, slid my underwear to my ankles, sat down and waited. Within a minute, my seatmate accordioned the door in and quickly closed and latched it behind her. The overhead light flickered on. With surprising grace for a heftier woman in a confined space, she had me on my feet and inside her in seconds.

She's done this before, I thought.

We were standing face to face, she with her back against the door, one leg up on the counter, her skirt hiked up to her knee and me very comfortably pinned in the joint of her legs. There was even enough room for me to get a good jiggle going. I could enjoy our reflections in the mirror if I looked to the left, though the attached sign that read, *Please be courteous and wipe down the basin for the next guest* got in the way a bit.

She leaned forward and bit my earlobe.

I squawked in surprise.

She grabbed my throat with one hand and pushed my head against the wall. I kept pistoning though I could feel my face flush hot and, with a glance in the mirror, I could see veins standing out in my neck and my face turning red.

"I know you like that," she hissed, her lips brushing my ear. "But shut the fuck up. Don't stop." Her look was a warning against either the noise I made or the possibility of my stopping.

She clamped onto my earlobe again as if daring me to react. This time, my vocalizations were squeezed into silence by her tightening grip on my neck.

"You better come soon because I'm going to. Then, I'm done with you." She panted in my ear.

She whimpered and her body trembled a little. I doubled my efforts, speeding up the cadence and force. She stifled a squeal and took one long, continuous intake of breath. I swore that she was about to push my head through the wall but I shuttered and came too.

All in all, less than five minutes I would guess. Pretty good.

Within seconds, she was clothed. The light overhead snapped off when she unlocked the latch and flung the door open.

In the process of her leaving, I was inadvertently knocked off balance by her elbow. The door slid closed behind her. I tottered but, with pants and undies constricting my ankles, I couldn't recover my balance. I spun and fell toward the toilet. One outstretched arm bumped the toilet's flush button and the other hand wound up in the bowl to brace my fall.

A tepid flow of Peevercor Aircraft Toilet Chemical Solution coated the bowl from under the rim and doused my hand in a dark blue-green, slightly greasy and slightly viscous blend of formaldehyde, glutaraldehyde, colouring agents and perfume additives. I managed to get my hand out before the trap door at the bottom of the bowl opened with a loud hiss.

Pushing myself into a standing position, I moved quickly to lock the door. The light flickered on and I looked at myself in the mirror, naked from the waist down, genitals floppy and retreating by the second, a glowing red earlobe, and both hands held up like a surgeon, one a deep tint of turquoise. Instead of the sterile smell of a surgeon, I smelled sweet like a chemical toilet.

My feelings aligned with the image reflected back at me: sad, used and alone. I looked away.

I ruminated on what had happened and I felt lonely wonder as I tried to scrub the stain from my skin under the tap with wadded-up paper towels. I didn't even know her name. I didn't know anything about her. I had lots of experience with anonymous sex in the past year and I had never felt this empty before, this incomplete.

I needed a deeper meaning for what we had done.

I needed something stronger than soap and water to get the chemical stain out of my skin.

I dried my now-pale, turquoise-coloured hand, pulled up my underwear and pants and returned to my seat with a newfound determination to build a connection.

"What's your name?" I asked as I buckled up.

She was reading. "You really don't remember me do you?" She marked her page and closed her book. "Razor and his Blades of Doom? Camp? Mary Koshushner and your cousin? Doing it by the lake?"

It clicked. I was stunned.

I wanted to know her so badly that night, as I wanted to then on that plane. None of the other women I had sex with in airplane washrooms, or any washroom for that matter, evoked such a need for connection.

Was it coincidence?

Was it love?

Did I love her, the way she used me, the way she looked?

"And what are you reading?" She asked, breaking my reverie.

I dumbly held up the book Leonard had given me when he drove me to the airport.

"No shit," she said. "Perchance you are heading to Moscow to model in the PG show?"

It clicked. Paige Green.

"Well, aren't we just Little Mister Beef Cattle?" She snickered.

I looked at her, my shock mounting and my need deepening. We had shared so much without even knowing.

She misread my look to be one of questioning and explained, "It's this kids modelling show that I was in a long time ago. It was a county fair thing…"

"No. I know," I managed to choke out. "I was Little Mister Beef Cattle 1984."

It was Paige's turn to be speechless.

It is easy to predict the future when all the bits come together. It is all about perspective. If I had the time and maturity to think of it, I could have been able to predict the future from some point in the past. If I could only have recognized the hints as they were happening.

It would be easy to say, "That's life," or "Small world," or "Hindsight is always twenty-twenty," or something as equally dismissive. That there are so many clichés dealing with this very fact means I am not the first one to notice. There was something going on. There was no coincidence, anywhere. Ever.

The critics loved Paige's Moscow Fashion Week show. Then again, critics always liked to 'discover' the next up-and-comer, any unknown with a modicum of talent. I think Paige outdid both Viktor and Rolf in press coverage. She definitely outdid Carolina Herrera. There was even a full-colour, glossy picture printed in *F Magazine* of her at the end of her show. She was on the runway, smiling and waving, surrounded by beautiful models.

If you look in the background, you could see me in the back row, on the left.

CHAPTER 10

Baker Grade IV

The need to support and constrain breasts is the underpinning of a billion-dollar industry. We were in Las Vegas, arguably the centre of all things breast-related, to celebrate and promote them. From honorable to degrading, with its elegant and rhinestone-clad dancing girls and glamorous, low-cut evening gowns, to its burlesque history and neon titty peep shows, in Vegas breasts are the great equalizer. In the same night, they are both revered and objectified by visitors and inhabitants alike. In Vegas breasts are a tourist attraction, a civic monument.

As a man, it may be a wonder why I was involved in a shoot for Gowan Dewar, the overlord of couture brassieres. Bridges and skyscrapers didn't have the structural integrity or attention to detail that Dewar's bras did. They were second only to their contents as works of beauty. I was the only man in the shoot because the ladies needed something to drape over and cling to while flashbulbs strobed the hot desert night. I was an accessory.

The idea for the shoot was a post-apocalyptic, wrecking-yard lingerie party. It had me naked to the waist, smeared with dirt and oil, wearing leather cut-off short shorts and surrounded by six of the Agency's most beautiful models sporting nothing but amazing underwear. It was the middle of the night. The wrecking yard was ringed by the yellow blaze from the natural gas flares of a refinery on the city's outskirts.

Photographers shouted directions, their cameras clicking like a plague of desert locusts and their voices rising against the dusty diesel breeze that blew across the scrub and open flats. A lonely coyote slunk about at the edge of the light, its eyes two glowing pinpoints floating in the dark.

"Show me ennui," shouted a photographer. "Great. Now, show me subtle resignation."

We stood on a pile of crushed automobiles, a tangle of metal and tires. The rusting, twisted metal mountain we crawled over was a snarl of shadow and light from the spotlights and strobing camera flashes. We worked every inch of that mountain of wrecks. Dripping engine fluids, slippery break fluid, stinking gasoline and sticky fluorescent puddles of antifreeze all became sexy props. It was hell on earth and I was Max Rockatansky of Main Force Patrol. I was a desolate shell of a man in my leather short shorts, doing all I could to survive in an oil-starved future gone mad. I was sure lingerie would be at the top of everyone's thoughts when the world ended, when the Lord Humongous roamed the wasteland with his band of crazed anarchists in search of precious gasoline.

"I want crippling domination," shouted a photographer. "Great. Now, I want munificent tyranny."

I tried to look tough but it was difficult because all the women were taller than me and I was busy trying not to cut any of my exposed bits while crawling over rusty cars. Forget the broken cubes of windshield glass and the nauseating smell of oil and gasoline, I didn't want to shear off a nipple or anything.

"Give me contumacious servility," shouted a photographer. "Great. Now, give me libidinous masochism."

Give me a dictionary, I thought.

One of the models, a slender brunette beauty named Donna Wanna, swore when she snagged her shoulder on a jagged muffler. A bead of blood, black in the night, formed from the cut.

"Fuck this," Donna yelled through a snarl.

"Beautiful, that's perfect. Such emotion." A voice marvelled from below.

"I'm out of here. You bastards can suck it."

Donna scrambled down the pyramid of crushed cars as daintily as any lady wearing stilettos, cheekies and a bandeau could. The tirade continued. She waved her hands violently every chance she got, punching the air and giving lewd gestures. She became a force of nature, a fast and intense downpour flash-flooding dusty arroyos, eroding ancient cliffs and moving sediment for miles.

"You fuckers ain't paying me enough for this shit. I have better things to do than crawl around here contusing myself."

Donna did that, used pseudo-words. She told me she had heard in an audiobook that people instamatically respect people with a hunormous vocabulary.

Her voice rose from yelling to high-pitched screaming as she carried on.

"Look at this. I'm fucking bleeding everywhere and you pricks keep fucking blinding me with your fucking flashbulbs. Stop it now and help me get the fuck out of this shithole. I'm bleedin' all over the fucking place." Then there was a long, amorphous noise that could best be described as sheer animal fury.

"Don't get any on the strap." Gowan Dewar rushed to meet her when she reached the ground. "Christ, that's a seventy-five thousand dollar creation you're bleeding all over. Take it off before you ruin it."

Give me my paycheque and get me the hell off this crushed AMC

Pacer, I thought as I pulled slimy leather from between my sweaty butt cheeks. Give me strength to endure these chafing leather shorts.

"Give me a martini. Vodka, olives, straight up," I told the bartender at the breast cancer fundraiser after-shoot soirée.

We had taken a limo from the junkyard to the MGM Grand. On the way, Donna peeled off her lingerie and slid into a stunning Valentino dress.

We whirled from the limo, through a crowd of staggering tourists and into the lobby of the Grand. The creamy marble floor reflected the thousand lights overhead, making the whole room feel like a departure gate of some futuristic spaceport and the spinning night seem even more surreal. A golden lion statue sat in the centre of the room, caged by bars of light. People alternately bustled confusedly around and stood gaping at shiny lights, shiny things and their shiny reflections. Our caveman minds were still in there and capable of mystification.

Donna grabbed my hand and dragged me through the crowd. She pulled me to a sign on a gold easel listing events and locations. My eyes wandered as she bent at the waist to get a better look in the pale amber glow of the room. She used a finger to poke at different events. There was a gathering of realtors, a poker tournament and some firefighter's conference: Gary Jan Fairway presiding over a session titled "Nozzles, Hoses and Reels."

"Richard," came a call from my left.

It was Leonard, walking toward me with his arm outstretched. We clasped hands, bumped chests and thumped shoulders. Rachel followed a few steps behind. We hugged and kissed cheeks.

"Donna, this is Leonard and Rachel. They're both journalists with the *Times*," I said.

Donna looked at me, awaiting an explanation of why this was important. She held out a limp hand, palm down, to Leonard who dutifully brought it to his lips.

"It's a pleasure to meet you," Leonard said.

"Yes," Donna agreed.

She glanced at Rachel, as if she were a stain, and then looked expectantly at me again.

"Yes, well," I said. "Rachel writes for the style section and Leonard is an obituarist."

"Style and obituaries, how … eclectical," Donna said.

Leonard raised an eyebrow to Rachel who bit her lip but failed to stifle a snort.

"Richard," Donna tapped my chest with a playful finger. "We're in the Garden Arena. Let's go."

"I'll be there in a minute. I want to catch up with Leonard and Rachel first."

Donna looked at me like I made a bad smell, "Well, enjoy your conflagration." She stormed off.

Leonard watched her go. "She is quite a vocabularian."

"Yes, she is," I agreed.

"Do you think she meant confabulation?" Rachel asked.

"Likely," I said and shifted my attention back to my companions. "I didn't know the two of you were going to be here."

"Ever check your emails or voice messages?" Leonard asked.

I didn't.

"Well, Rachel is covering a bra guy…"

"Gowan Dewar," Rachel added.

"…and it was seen fit that I attend the Second International Obituary Writers' Conference."

"Get out, at the Grand?" I asked and then thought for a second. "Get out, Obituary Writers' Conference?"

"Yes, there is such a thing and no, not at the Grand. We're at Thomas and Mack. UNLV is hosting. I figured I would visit Rachel and see how the other half lives," Leonard said. "The paper sent me here because I wrote that Howard Goldfarb, a great pioneer of professional poker, had died. I wrote," Leonard held out a hand to frame invisible text, "this legend worked to make poker every part the legitimate sport curling is."

"So?" I asked.

"Goldfarb didn't die," Rachel said.

"Not so much. In fact, he's supposed to be here tonight." Leonard grimaced. "I had to do a retraction and it apparently caused Goldfarb quite a bit of grief, explaining that he wasn't dead to all of his friends and family and the folks at the World Series of Poker. So, the paper thought I needed a bit of education and here I am."

"We should go," Rachel said looking at her watch. "The show starts in twenty minutes. You coming?" She asked me.

"I'll meet you two later for beer?" Leonard called as we disbanded.

Rachel and I parted ways once we got to the Grand Garden Arena. I looked around and saw shadows mingling in the twinkling pinpoints of light on the concourse overhead. Some leaned on the railing, looking down at the sunken arena basin which had been converted into a catwalk for the show. The seats were already starting to fill.

I was trying to figure out what exactly was wrong about Gowan Dewar holding the launch of his new bra line under the pretense of a breast cancer fundraiser when Donna swooped out of the crowd, grabbed me by the arm and hauled me toward the bar through the glittering masses in the twinkling cavern that was the Garden Arena. Her strapless Valentino was made a little less glamorous by the thick bandage taped to her shoulder. The dress did serve to remind me that she made four times my pay on every shoot.

If I was going to survive the runway show and Donna's drunken fuming over the junkyard shoot, I was going to need liquor. At the best of times, Donna was socially maladroit. That didn't matter though; to most in the Garden Arena, her assets were solely of the visual variety.

"Can you believe that junkyard shit? It's ironical, us modelling his trash in a junkyard. And now I barely have time to get a drink before I have to get up onstage in Dewar's next piece-of-shit contraption." Donna pulled a tube of Rectolone hemorrhoid cream from her clutch and smeared some under her eyes. Steroids constrict vessels, lessening puffiness.

"Get this," she continued. "I'm going to be in a fucking prehysteric huntress get-up. Chester told me five minutes ago and now I have this fucking shoulder-gash I have to somehow make look sexy. And how exactly can I make a shoulder-gash sexy? Do I look like one of those cave women who hunt dinosaurs? The ones I've seen in pictures were all hideous, with bones in their hair and…"

"Give me a martini. Vodka, olives, straight up," I said when the bartender pointed a gun-finger at me.

Vermouth, Vodka, chilled martini glass, olives.

"Reverend Mordant Toehold," Donna barked.

Lemon vodka, rye, melon liqueur, Chambord, orange juice, pineapple juice, dash of sweet and sour, splash of grenadine, egg whites, ice, blend, fishbowl glass, pink umbrella, melon ball and a curly straw.

"Mint julep." Chester sidled up to the bar next to Donna.

Bruised mint sprigs, bourbon, sugar syrup, water, Collins glass.

"Karkadé," came a deeper and wholly intriguing voice from the woman beside Chester.

Sudanese hibiscus tea. Dried hibiscus sabdariffa flower, boiling water, ceramic cup.

Believed to normalize blood sugar, uric acid and cholesterol.

Believed to reduce food cravings, wrinkles and even out skin tone.

Believed to be a folk remedy for cancer.

This tall, regal and vaguely familiar woman gave us a sidelong glance.

"Donna," Chester said with a sly grin. "Dewar's looking for his Wilma Flintstone. They need you backstage for fitting."

Donna gave Chester a black stare until the bartender placed the fishbowl glass on the counter. Donna took a long pull from her Toehold, the fishbowl glass looking ridiculously large in her dainty hands, before storming off.

"Thanks, Chester," I said around a sip of martini. "She's a handful, a bundle of foul words and poison." I paused for a thought. "In fact, I have never met anyone so disagreeable. Truly, I can't stand her."

Chester had become a father to me. At the age of nineteen, I finally found a mature male relationship from which I could glean a much-needed passive guidance. Chester wasn't critical. He didn't judge. He didn't lecture or chide, he quietly guided. He wanted the best for me.

"She is a repugnant little vixen but one heck of a model. That fiery hellcat attitude comes through in every shoot and every show she's in. She exudes 'man-eating harpy' which is the edge a lot of designers want." Chester chuckled and looked into his julep to find what to say next. "How's that whole relationship thing going between you two? How long have you been together? A year now?"

"It's okay, I guess. I can't help but feel that something's missing though, some kind … any kind of depth or connection," I said.

The sex was amazing though. The kind that's in porno movies.

Chester nodded and smiled as if reading my thoughts. "Well, you'll know what to do. You have so much going for you. You're a good kid and you'll sort it out."

The tall, regal, slightly familiar woman with the Sudanese hibiscus tea had been watching us. She cleared her throat.

Chester raised an eyebrow and looked over his shoulder.

"Apologies, my dear," he said. "Richard, I have the distinct pleasure of introducing you to one of the most amazing women I have ever met. I'm sure, with time, you'll be liable to agree. This is Stella Supernova."

That was where I knew her from, the picture hanging on Chester's wall back at the Agency's offices. She was the legend he told me about. I had been modelling for two years and hadn't gone a week without hearing some mention of Ms. Supernova. In an industry with a standard for badmouthing and backstabbing, the references were always positive.

There she was, offering me a hand and a smile. She was amazing. Her face was not classically, or modernly, beautiful, but there was such character and otherworldly grace in her features. Physically, she was equally impressive, a relative giant compared to most of the models I had worked with, full in stature and voluptuous in form where the others were skin-draped skeletons. She stood a head taller than Chester and me, broad-shouldered with well-toned arms, one of which, I was reminded, was held out to me in greeting.

"Stop staring and say hello, Richard," Chester said.

I stuttered out a greeting that didn't contain words, only sounds.

"Charmed." Her voice was as rare as her look. "Chester has told me so much."

"Now, Richard," Chester said with a glance at the stage. "I have to go make sure this show doesn't have any hiccups. Can I trust you to keep Stella company, as a gentleman would?" He emphasized the last four words to impress upon me that Stella was higher up our cladogram. Although Stella boasted no pretense, it was obvious to me that she shared most of the genetic makeup as the rest of the people in the Grand Garden Arena in the same manner that humans and chimpanzees share most of their genes.

Chester was off. Moments later, the speakers blared. Stella took a sip of tea and watched the first models strut down the catwalk over the rim of the teacup. I popped an olive in my mouth as an excuse not to say anything, anything stupid at any rate. Stella watched the lingerie, the bodies. I chewed olive pulp very slowly, turning tapenade into paste and paste into consommé.

Finally, Stella spoke, shouted really, over the beat. "This doesn't hold much interest for me anymore. It makes me sad and a little disappointed."

I swallowed and nodded.

"Come." She smiled and linked her arm through mine with effortless grace. She guided me from the arena, very unlike the way Donna had dragged me through the lobby earlier.

"There's a display I want to see," she told me once we reached the relative silence of the Studio Walkway outside the arena. "It's part of the fundraiser and I'm sure it's lamentably under-attended in lieu of that spectacle." She gestured over her shoulder with a gentle roll of her head.

A short saunter found us at the Studio Ballroom. At the entrance, on a golden easel like the one in the lobby, was a dusty rose-coloured placard with gold letters spelling *Milestones in Making Women Whole: A Recent History of Breasts.*

We stepped past the sign, through the door and the last remaining vestige of noise disappeared. The room was coloured a deep tint of indigo. It was like suddenly being plunged into a vast, quiet ocean.

Stella and I stood, arm in arm, at the beginning of what would prove to be a winding corridor of displays. A spotlight flashed on, an amber tassel of light illuminating a series of grainy, sepia-toned photos. There was a static audio-pop, as if a needle hit a record. A series of ascending tones saturated the air before a soft voice played.

"Welcome to 'Milestones in Making Women Whole,' a celebration of one hundred years of breast enhancement…"

"I don't like that," Stella whispered.

"What?"

"*Enhancements.* It is the wrong word, has the wrong implications. They're implants."

"…performed the first recorded enhancement procedure in 1895, a procedure that became all the rage for actresses and prostitutes of the time." A series of happy tones sounded.

I looked at the archaic before-and-after photos and wondered if there would have been cosmetic surgery advertisements in supermarket checkout-line gossip magazines one hundred years ago. Would this new breast enhancement procedure be advertised in the lower right-hand corner of the article about Oscar Wilde's criminal libel suit against the Marquess of Queensberry backfiring with a countersuit and Wilde getting sentenced to two years in prison for homosexual misconduct?

I wondered if there were celebrity gossip magazines one hundred years ago and, if not, what did people read?

Audio-pop.

"Immediate results were promising. Paraffin was injected into the chest cavity, which settled into a passable breast shape, though realism was lacking to touch. Unfortunately, a common side effect of this treatment was granulomas produced by prolonged exposure to the paraffin. These paraffinomas, along with high rates of infection, scarring and paraffin migration within the chest cavity, made this a limited and fleeting technology."

There was another loud audio-pop and the light went off, leaving us in the deep violet silence. A moment later, another spotlight went on over a display table a short distance down the hallway.

Stella shook her head as we made our way to the second spotlight.

"Can you imagine?" she said. "Back then it was scandalous to get caught altering your body. Not only was it physically hazardous but socially as well. Can you imagine the psychological suffering to make a woman risk physical danger and social stigmatization, exposing one's self, though unknowingly at the time, to cancers and scarring…"

Audio-pop.

We stood at a table with breast-shaped glass objects, sponges, a vat of yellow-pink gelatinous material, and several other unidentifiable objects and substances.

"Breast enhancement technology had advanced by the 1920s with innovative procedures and new materials that improved the shape and feel of the breast. Early adipose tissue transplants, removing fatty material from the buttocks and injecting it into the breast, returned positive initial results. However, over time, the fat absorbed unevenly leaving unattractive scarring and malformations. Injections of silicone followed, leading to natural-looking enhancements though some believed the chronic inflammation, serious infections and organ damage caused by silicone migration to be an irritant. Later, implants of glass, ivory, wool and ox cartilage were used but all resulted in substandard breast shape and texture. Massive tissue infections also detracted from the look of the enhanced breasts."

The light went off.

"All for breasts," I said quietly as we moved in the dark. "All for bigger, rounder breasts."

Audio-pop.

"As the world entered the space age, so did the breast. With a wealth of materials manufactured by the newly founded chemical industry, the breast moved ever closer toward its potential."

Audio-pop.

1949. Ivalon sponges made from a polyvinylic alcohol-formaldehyde blend.

Tendency to be toxic to organs and blood.

Audio-pop.

1959. Polistan implants made from a polyethylene derivative.

Toxic to the body, massive scarring and infection.

Audio-pop.

1960. Polymethane breasts.

Audio-pop.

1961. Polyglycomethacrylate breasts.

"All of this research," I marvelled, "in the quest for the most natural-looking, natural-feeling, artificial breast. All of that experimentation, all of those oozing infections, all of those poisoned organs to bring into the world the perfect breast, and it's fake."

"I beg to differ, my dear," Stella said. "The very presence of an implant is real and the fantasy of what a breast should look like, being made into reality by a physical implant makes it as real as any unaltered breast."

"But people were mutilated," I pleaded, thinking of the spectacle going on in the Garden Arena. "People died for this." I pointed at a picture. "This, two half-grapefruits sitting high up on their chest."

"They were people, nonetheless," Stella countered. "People no more or less worthy than you or I to live the life they wanted to. People with desires every bit as real as yours and mine. Their needs, wants, insecurities, imperfections and potential were every bit as real. People don't get implants for a laugh, there's a reason for them. The tragic part is that many had to die in pursuit of their potential. These implants are real, on real people; these surgeries are real and make people real. Such body modification is not simple vanity-induced mutilation, it's a cure for a concrete, tangible unhappiness at the point where the body and mind meet."

"I'm unconvinced."

Audio-pop.

"The year 1961 was revolutionary for enhancements. The first encased silicone breast enhancement brought new, unparalleled realism to the look and feel of the breast."

The year Stella and I stood at that display, Dow Corning collapsed under the weight of a lawsuit backed by half a million women unhappy with their breast implants. They weren't just unhappy—their silicone tits were poisoning them.

Audio-pop.

"In the 1990s, Mother Nature was recruited to fix persistent problems in her own design. Natural sources were tapped to enhance the breast. New implants utilized soybean oil as a medium. Though these became toxic as they degraded, they paved the way for the pinnacle of a century of breasts, the saline implant. Saline implants require minimal maintenance and have no known health effects.

"Thank you for visiting and celebrating 'Milestones in Making Women Whole.'"

"Minimal maintenance?" I asked.

"They have to be reassessed every five to ten years," Stella said sadly as we made our way back into the Studio Walkway. "They have to be monitored because they tend to wander in the chest wall. Scar tissue also builds up around them, constricting them. On the scale they use to measure, the hardest are Baker's Grade IV breasts, with so much scar tissue they are immobile, hard lumps, which is a constant source of pain and is in danger of rupturing."

"I never knew any of this," I stammered. "You seem to agree with all of this."

"To me it's not a moral issue or some judgment of vanity. I'm part of that. My breasts were cancer," Stella said. "I had a double mastectomy. It was something that affected me so profoundly, it crippled me with depression. I felt so incomplete, I wanted to die. A part of me was missing. I had to stop modelling. I had my chest reconstructed and here I am. I don't doubt it saved my life. I don't doubt that there are other women that feel the same way as I do.

"One hundred years of suffering," she continued, "and the result is not simply two half-grapefruits sitting high on my chest. The result of one hundred years is also making women whole again. The result of those hundred years is both good and bad, both painful and amazing. It can't be categorized as any one of those things."

I couldn't argue with a word she said. I watched Stella talk confidently. Her beauty was real even if her breasts were fake.

Fantasy became reality. The line between the two disappeared.

CHAPTER 11

Sexy Beef in the Slaughterhouse of Desire

Modelling is the communication of want, desire, sex and fantasy. At a show, when I rounded the corner from the back of the house to the front, I recited my anthem, my mantra. Lights blazed, flashbulbs fired, television-camera eyes stared and I had twenty seconds to make it all happen, to be watched, to be the one thing that was branded onto the soft grey tissue of their minds. I wanted to be the sun they stared into, the deep purple spot burned into their retinas that they would see every time they blinked.

In those twenty seconds, I expressed myself in the most primal way. My walk, my hair, the expression that I pushed through my face like a fist through glass, like a bullet through a brain. I didn't have to speak to tell them a story, no matter what country I was in. I didn't need to speak Spanish, Russian, French or Whateverthefuck because what I did translated into all languages and kicked through all cultural barriers. My mind projected through me and drove my look to something deeper, psychic and subconsciously perceptible that heightened physical attraction from good to great, from great to irresistible. It's attitude more than look. It's intense and personal and animal and it was there as I went around the corner and into the light of the most important thirty-five metres in Whateverthefuck country I was in. My mantra growled in my head.

I am pure animal lust.

I am the most desired slip of skin that ever walked.

I am a firecracker exploding in your face. I'm taking an eye with me. It's mine, now. I own it.

I fucked your wife on the hood of your Porsche.

I am a screaming baboon shaking a tree.

I am a hurricane laying waste to your jungle village.

I fucked your sister on the dance floor and yes, that Primitive Radio Gods song was playing.

I am the sexiest side of beef in the slaughterhouse of desire.

I am a holiday-Monday, sleep-in slow fuck.

I am a memory.

I raged off the runway and into the tight crowds of bustling half-naked bodies backstage. I made my way through the dark chaos to where I had left my duffle bag and draped my street clothes over a rack. The crowd parted and Stella Supernova towered over the throng. She smiled, winked and strode by leaving a swirling scent of apricots in her wake. I stared at her, open-mouthed and awestruck, as the chaos enveloped her again.

I spied Donna through the fleeting gap. She sat at a mirror framed with light bulbs. A makeup artist flitted from one side of her to the other. I hadn't seen Donna in weeks. Our schedules had kept us on opposite ends of the world.

As I approached, I noticed something different. Her face sagged slightly on one side. Worried thoughts sprung to mind. I had known Donna to occasionally partake in cocaine. I had known cocaine users to have strokes. My heart skipped a beat.

Did my Donna have a coke stroke?

"Donna." I clasped her by the shoulders. "Are you okay?

"I am so happy," she squealed, though her face did not move. A stitch of a wrinkle puckered the bridge of her nose. Her forehead had all the expression of a steak. The left half of her face drooped. The makeup artist elbowed her way through my embrace, maniacally powdering and applying lipstick, trying her best to even up Donna's face.

"Your face…" I stuttered.

The makeup artist glared at me.

"Isn't it amazing?" Donna screeched. "I got Botoxed."

"What?"

"Botoxed. They use it on spastics and stuff."

The makeup artist sighed and took a step back.

Donna looked at me as if I was a dog that pooped on the rug. "You know, multiply sclerotics and people with muscle spasms and stuff. It paralyzes the muscles, you know, to stop their flailing around." She waved her arms for effect. "And it gets rid of wrinkles," she squealed again.

I had trouble aligning the excitement in her voice to the lack of expression on her face. The disconnect was disconcerting.

"Dr. Bella sent me to Canada to get it."

The makeup artist shrugged and wandered off.

That evening became a blur, the show ending, the cab ride to the airport, Donna at my side on the plane. The cabin lights dimmed and both of us got ready for our first sleep in what seemed like months. I declined the sleeping pills she offered and wound up shifting back and forth in my seat for eight hours.

"Ladies and gentlemen," the captain's voice oozed through the speakers and into the dimly lit cabin. "Good morning from the flight deck. Myself and co-pilot Jeff hope you are having a pleasant flight. We're about halfway through our journey and are a bit ahead of schedule due to a friendly tailwind. Our lovely flight attendants are going to be coming through the cabin in a few moments to offer our inflight breakfast service. We do expect to encounter a bit of turbulence once we're over land again but the disturbance should be weak, so please, sit back and continue to enjoy your flight. On behalf of co-pilot Jeff, myself and your cabin crew, thank you again for choosing American Airlines."

Donna snorted in her drug-induced sleep, her head lolling to one side. A strand of drool hung glamorously from the corner of her wrinkle-free mouth.

I didn't do drugs though I tried them once. I can't really be more specific about what I took. They were the generic kind of drugs that one takes and then can't remember a thing about the previous night.

I took drugs on the evening I proposed to Donna. Donna was getting ready for her flight to Miami for her labiaplasty appointment. She had booked with a pre-eminent labiaplastist and had been on a waiting list for more than a year. I remember her telling me in detail how she wanted smaller labia majora and plumper labia minora. She told me labia medius was all the rage these days.

I remember Donna, smiling, looking down at me on one knee and nodding at the ring.

Me, welling up with pride, interpreting that as acceptance.

Donna, checking her plane ticket and saying, "I gotta run."

Me, saying something romantic like, "Baby, can I call you a cab?"

Donna, leaving in a taxi, her silhouette talking on the cellphone.

Me, waking up on the floor of a cavernous hotel room with an overwhelming pressure in my bowels and the sorest nipples I have ever experienced. I lay on my side, the arm draped across my chest wasn't mine. It was woven under my arm and belonged to whoever was spooning me. It was hard to focus at first but, after some rapid blinking, a sea of naked arms and legs spread out before me.

I glanced over my shoulder.

The arm belonged to Paige Green.

As I wiggled away from her, the pressure in my bowels eased. It was then I realized I had been impaled by the strap-on Paige was wearing. As it slid from between my greasy cheeks, she smiled and sighed but did not wake up. I was startled and slightly intimidated by the size of it, a deep blue latex phallus draped to the floor as casually as her arm had draped over me. I was also a little confused by how natural it looked on her, as if she had found the perfect Chloe clutch for a stunning Mouret gown.

There was a small, white tag with black print on it stitched to the leather between the studs, beside the snaps that bound the strap-on to Paige.

Johnson DeLong. Made in China.

What would the little peasants working in the Johnson DeLong Strap-On factory think of making giant penises en masse for export? Shelves upon shelves of droopy, multi-coloured phalli in storage, waiting to be boxed and shipped to North America. I was embarrassed for our continent. Surely the little peasant workers' sensibilities would have tended toward the more practical, such as food and clothing and the like.

I stood, wearing only socks, the sole vertical body in the room. I glanced out the wall of windows. Midday traffic bustled by in silence twenty storeys below. Those people down on the street, out there in the sunshine, were wholly unaware of the sleeping Twister game happening here; they were oblivious of my numb anus and aching nipples.

What city was this? I rubbed my nipples thoughtfully only to meet cold metal. My heart jumped and I looked down. I was thankful to find that it was only a pair of nipple clamps and not some weird piercing.

That was the moment I decided I didn't need drugs in my life.

I realized that if this is what drugs can do for me, waking up wearing only socks and nipple clamps after getting ass-raped in an orgy by a small-d designer and having no clue what city I'm in or where my Prada suit and Gucci sneaks are, I don't need them.

Surely if that sentiment could be squeezed into an anti-drug campaign to play during Saturday morning cartoons, there would be fewer kids on drugs.

I picked my way through the strewn bodies and into the bathroom. There were bodies there as well, two stacked in the tub, one caged in the shower stall, and one in front of the toilet who inchwormed away when I lifted the lid and peed. My head ached with the release of pressure.

Done. Shake. Shake.

I needed Aspirin. There was a small medicine chest on the other side of the room, beside the sink.

On the short walk to the sink to wash my hands, the slippery sensation of my butt crack led me to wonder. I flipped open the medicine cabinet and absent-mindedly fingered around for a bottle of painkillers before curiosity got the better of me. I glanced at the bodies reflected in the bathroom mirror to make sure no one was watching before spinning around and bending over. I craned my body to one side, like a swimming fish, to see my butt hole. I gazed at its reflection and felt a distinct disconnect from the puckered orifice.

How could it be that I had never seen it before, this unintroduced little stranger on my own body?

Without an intimate knowledge of my anus, I couldn't tell if it was any different after Paige's intrusion.

Was it supposed to look like that?

How could I not know every inch of my body after living in it for twenty years?

If I didn't know this about myself, what else didn't I know?

My butt hole was something on the outside, something that I could have seen if I had only looked. Yet there it was, a total surprise. Its presence led me to think, if I was such a stranger on the outside, did I truly know anything about myself? If I didn't know every inch of my own skin, where did I stand on bigger issues like how did I feel about the recent IRA action in Manchester? Was I a conspiracy theorist because I believed the crash of TWA Flight 800 was the result of an American missile attack? Where did I stand on fur in fashion?

Someone cleared their throat.

I bolted upright, immediately flushed with embarrassment, thrusting my hands in front of my creeping jimber in a hopeless bid for modesty.

"What are you doing?"

It was Paige, in a housecoat with the hotel monogram embroidered on it.

"Um, I'm looking for Aspirin."

"Probably won't find any in there." Paige laughed, crossed the room and kissed me on the cheek.

"Richard, you're amazing. We are so lucky we found each other, in this life I mean." Then she said in an even, unwavering tone. "I knew one day we'd be together. I used to watch you with the others backstage. The world seemed to just move as static around a crystal clear you. Once, I even hid behind a rack of evening gowns so I could watch you uninterrupted. I'd watch you onstage, my eyes getting dry because I didn't even want to blink. I couldn't take my mind off you, even in my sleep. I knew you'd find your way to me and we'd be together again. Forever."

What was she talking about?

"You should move in to my place," she said. "I have space in my closet for your clothes."

What happened last night?

"It only makes sense," she said. "You have a roommate and I don't. I'll call movers when we get back to the city. I don't see any reason to wait."

I glanced at my finger. No wedding band.

"You can go get a key cut and … what's wrong?" Paige asked.

"Aspirin, I don't see any."

I brushed a hand clumsily through the medicine cabinet, knocking some bottles over. One clattered into the sink. Another fell to the floor, popped open and sent a hail of candy-red pills bouncing across the tile.

"I'm going to step out to the store to get some," I said.

"Okay, sexy. When you come back, we can go for breakfast and talk some more and…" she beamed, "…I love you, too."

I wasn't aware I said anything to elicit such a declaration.

"I didn't want to say it back last night because if you didn't mean it I would have, I mean, I don't deal well with hurt, not at all. I didn't want to scare you because when I feel this way, when I say those words, it's intense." She shuddered. "Now, get out. I have to pee."

"Right," I said. She puckered, I dodged her lips and aimed a kiss at her cheek. It missed when she quickly realigned her lips and wound up being a clumsy peck on the side of her nose.

I tore through the room. In less time than it took Paige to roust the others out of the bathroom, I was standing in the elevator wearing the only pair of pants I found, ones that were too short and legs ending in constricting rings at my calves, a billowy orange blouse, and one shoe that was a size too small. I pretended to be absorbed in the numbers counting down above the door in an attempt to ignore the stares of my elevator-mates. I hobbled through the lobby and stopped dead when the concierge addressed me.

"Good morning Mr. Trench. I trust you're enjoying your stay. Is the room to your liking?"

I smiled politely and thought about how to get those people out of my hotel room.

When Donna came back from Miami, I didn't mention a thing. It wouldn't have mattered if I had told her about the whole drug-induced orgy adventure because she wouldn't have heard. She complained for a week about feeling like she was walking around with a pillow between her legs.

All that was several months before taking Donna to dinner to meet Mother and Father. Donna had become used to her new labia and her face had regained some expression. Her forehead was still lifeless and one side of her mouth drew higher than the other when she smiled, leaving the expression more of a sinister sneer.

The driver cursed and swerved.

I prayed for a horrible accident in which Donna would be shredded through a windshield cheese grater and I would be pulped in a car-wreck juicer. That was how I felt as we were driven from the airport to Father's house for dinner. For the first time since she walked out, Mother would be there. And she was bringing her boyfriend. Father told me her boyfriend was bringing his daughter who was in town visiting.

I had invited Leonard and Rachel to meet us at Father's because I wanted to see them too—that and I needed people in my corner of the ring. I could think of less stressful ways to introduce my fiancée to the family.

"Fuckin' drive much?" Donna shrieked as she was jolted about in her seat and grabbed at her seat belt, which hung pendulous and unbuckled.

I thought she was venting at the '89 Monte Carlo that cut us off but she was shouting at our driver.

"Sorry, ma'am."

The driver of the Monte Carlo actually didn't drive much. He was sixteen, fresh licence in his wallet and he had just bought the car for two thousand dollars from Mary Koshushner. He loved the car. It was his first.

"Easy, baby," I said to Donna. My heart was near exploding and I didn't know if it could take a Donna rant.

"Excuse me?" she asked, though I know she heard me.

I said nothing. I stared out the window. We turned onto the street I grew up on. It seemed older in subtle ways. The trees were taller, their trunks thicker. The pastel-coloured vinyl siding, flashing by the window, seemed out of date now. The pavement had a few more cracks and the lights in the evening dusk seemed a dimmer, more tired variety of orange than I remembered.

"Did you just tell me *easy?*"

She knew I did, she needed to repeat it to make sure I knew why she was about to emasculate me.

"This pecker damn near kills me," she jabbed a finger at the driver. I could tell she wished it was a knife. "I hit my head and you tell me *easy?* That fucker probably gave me a third-degree concrushion and you *easy, baby* me?"

The driver glanced at us in the rear-view mirror.

"It's concussion," I said. "And can we just get along tonight? I haven't seen my parents in years and I'm a little scared."

"Excuse me?" Donna looked at me as if I slapped her. Her mouth hung open, slightly crooked from the lingering Botox. "Did you just tell me to *just get along?*"

She knew I did. She needed to repeat it to make sure I knew why she was going to do the opposite. Before she could, I tapped the driver gently on the shoulder and pointed at a house.

"That one, please," I said.

He nodded and I felt the ounce of camaraderie I so desired. He pulled to the curb and we all got out. We stood there awkwardly, Donna fuming, me fishing in my wallet for a tip and the driver wondering why I was giving him two hundred dollars when there was no luggage to carry.

The Town Car pulled away and I watched the brake lights glow at the end of the block before disappearing around the corner. The smell of the evening air, mown grass and barbecue took me back to nights in the yard as a kid. I hadn't heard a night so quiet in years. A breeze rustled through the trees. I shivered, though the air wasn't cold. Donna didn't speak or unclasp her arms, but she let me place a hand on the small of her back and walk beside her to the front porch. The muscles underneath her gown were tight and I could almost feel a chill air cascade from her skin.

I rang the doorbell and said, "Can we just..."

"What?" She snapped.

Pretend to like each other, I thought, but before I could dig a deeper hole the door opened and we were awash in the chunky guitar and Moog synth of ABBA's "Hey, Hey Helen" mixed with the inviting sound of cutlery and dishes and conversation from within the house.

Without a word, Father lunged from the warm orange light of the house into the cool blue of the porch. He enveloped me in a hug. He smelled like a cigarette and his body was solid. He had been working out in the three years since I had seen him.

He held me out at arm's length and smiled. "You're small," he said. "Good to see you, Son."

His hair had become salty and the corners of his eyes had wrinkles that I didn't remember. For some reason, I felt like crying.

"Father," I stuttered, my voice weak with emotion, "this is my fiancée, Donna."

Sometimes I really hate her. What do I do?

"Welcome." Father gave Donna a smothering hug and then stepped back, holding her out to admire her.

Donna smiled, her hands resting like feathers on his biceps. The chill that had been there a moment ago had thawed.

With exaggerated gestures and many admiring looks and pauses, Father led us to the dining room. We were the last to arrive. Leonard and Rachel sat beside each other at the table and smiled as we entered. Mother stood and rushed over to us.

"Honey," she said, tears welling up, chin trembling, arms

outstretched. "Oh my Spirit Warrior, it has been so long. And Donna," she paused, "welcome to our family. We are so lucky to have such beauty in our souls. Richard, honey, your remember Mike Sloane?" She gestured to the man sitting across from Leonard and Rachel.

I swallowed, my mind reeling to the Sharing Circle and my abandonment by the universal flow. The deep feeling of loneliness I had felt at that time came back and I wanted to leap across the table and stick my fist through Dr. Sloane's teeth.

Instead I said, "Yes, I do." I nodded. "Dr. Sloane."

"Please," he smiled, "call me Mike. I'm you're stepdad after all."

I looked to Father, who was grinning stupidly and emptying a wine bottle into Dr. Sloane's wineglass, seemingly unfazed by the cascading madness. It seemed each word took my life one more step into lunacy. Father twisted the drop and left for the kitchen.

"Stepfather?" I had been gone for too long. "You're married. Married and moved to New York?"

"Yes, honey." Mother rubbed my arm. "I know you meant to join us at the ceremony but…"

I tried to remember if I knew about this. There was that voicemail a year or so ago from Father. I was in a bar in Tokyo. It had been loud, the reception was poor and I think Father was drunk. As I remembered, it went something like, "Your Mother's gone. It's all over. Come to New York on Friday. Call me."

I just figured she had died and the funeral was Friday, not that Mother and Father had divorced and Mother was getting remarried. I didn't call back because the next day I proposed, Donna left for her labiaplasty, I took drugs and … then there was the message the next morning from Mother. I checked it as I stood at the hotel door, being stared at by the doorman, wearing that orange blouse and someone else's shoe.

"Honey … it's Mother. Richard, dear, I know we haven't talked in a while…"

I had dropped the phone and it broke on the sidewalk. I had not heard from her in years and then, to my drug-addled mind, I was receiving a voicemail from my dead mother.

Here she now stood, a hand on my shoulder, introducing my stepsister Abigail.

"Abigail Spencer, not Sloane," Abigail said. "Dad's a chronic monogamist. My mom was two wives ago. You join a large clan, Richard."

Rachel looked uncomfortable and Leonard grinned, as if revelling in my family's madness, as if he'd missed being a spectator to it.

Mother clapped her hands and beamed from Abigail to Donna to me. "I wonder what your father has made us for supper," she said and we took our seats.

From the smells and curses coming from the kitchen, I guessed he was going to serve us a three-course meal of failure. The ruckus reached a crescendo and ended with a punctuated crash. Father came in wiping his hands on a tea towel, his biceps rolling massifs under his skin. Donna's functional eyebrow raised and she sneered.

"How's Chinese takeout for everyone?" he called on his way to the phone.

There was a mumbled agreement and the order was placed. Donna excused herself and went into the backyard for a cigarette. I followed. Leonard followed. Rachel and Abigail huddled conspiratorially.

By the time the patio door slid closed behind Leonard, Donna was halfway through a cigarette. She surveyed the backyard, her arm cocked at the elbow, her elbow locked to her hip and the cigarette held elegantly above her shoulder. Her eyes travelled from the dying orange tree, across the scorched grass, to the tendrils of weeds reaching up from the flower bed along the fence. She grunted.

"Donna," Leonard said. "So good to see you again. Congratulations on the engagement."

"Thank you," Donna sneered at Leonard. "Richard, why don't you introduce me to your friend."

"Donna," I said. "You've met Leonard. At Dewar's show last year in Vegas."

"Really. I see," she said. She waved her cigarette at the yard. "I am going for a walk around the gardens." She stepped off the deck and, within seconds, was at the back fence. She stopped, looked over her shoulder at us and, in five more seconds, was at the flower bed near the house. She continued this way while Leonard and I talked.

"Congrats, Richard," Leonard said. "How are things with you?"

"Great. Designers can't seem to get enough of me. I've been in ten countries in so many weeks. Tomorrow, I'm going to Milan. According to Chester, I'm top twenty in the industry, moving into the top ten by the end of the year."

"That's great," Leonard said, his eyes following Donna ricocheting around the yard, contemplating dead undergrowth. "I meant, how are things with you and Donna?"

"Oh, it's amazing. I hardly see her she's so busy. She'll be Kate Moss kind of legendary in a few years."

"That's great," Leonard said. "I meant between the two of you, outside of work."

"Oh, good. How are you and Rachel?"

"Really good. We're off for a break soon. I can't wait to just chill on the beach with her. Chat. You know?"

My look must have said that I didn't know. Leonard's face fell. We watched Donna for a moment.

"I'm going to run something by you, Richard. Don't get freaked out," Leonard lowered his voice. "I've stumbled onto something huge at work, something people would kill for, something almost as amazing as a fountain of youth but kind of the opposite. I'm still working out the details and it's not 100 percent perfect yet, but if I can iron out the wrinkles, this could change the world."

"You discovered something that could change the world ... writing obituaries?"

"Don't freak out, okay? But I've come across deaths, two people, three people, more, everyone all linked together."

I failed to see the source of wonder.

"I'm talking more than just two married people dying in a car wreck," Leonard continued. "More than a bus full of geeks plunging off a cliff on the way to a computer convention. I'm talking about far-reaching, seemingly abstract, seemingly coincidental deaths. I think I can prove that there are no coincidences in death."

"Great," I exclaimed, not sure what was being demanded of me other than not to "freak out," which I thought I was managing quite admirably.

Donna's orbit around the yard took her in a precariously close swing by us. Leonard waited until she passed.

He sighed. "Don't you see?" his voice hushed. "Death is predictable. There are connections between us all and our deaths are laid out before us, if we can only figure out how it works. There's a pattern, a huge web that connects us all."

"I don't get it."

"Oscar Wilde became legally entangled in a lawsuit over relations with the Marquess of Queensberry's son. Wilde went to prison, two years hard labour. Both Wilde and the Marquess died in 1900. Ten months apart. They were ten years apart in age."

"Wow," I said to the silence Leonard had let linger. I hadn't meant it to sound sarcastic.

"I was doing some research and … you know about the day that music died, right? So that morning, the band wants to get on a plane but it only seats three. Buddy Holly is on board, of course, the band can't go on without him. The Big Bopper has the flu, so his buddy Waylon Jennings gives up his seat. Ritchie Valens flips a coin for the last seat with his bandmate Tommy Allsup, who loses. They take off and later the plane crashes and Buddy, the Big Bopper and Ritchie all die."

"You said there was more to this than geeks plunging off a cliff. It's not some mystical connection they all died at the same time. Musicians dying in plane crashes, happens all the time."

"Hear me out. Know who else died that same day? Far away, in New York, a fellow by the name of Vincent Astor has a heart attack and dies. He was the son of John Jacob Astor the fourth, the fellow who, before dying on the *Titanic*, helped design the turbine engine on the plane that the Big Bopper went down in."

I glanced at Leonard. "It's not an exact science you're onto is it?"

"No," Leonard agreed. "Not yet. I've just started to figure it out. The part you don't seem to get, the world-changing part is, from this I may well be able to predict when people die."

There was a moment of silence when Donna swung by again as she roamed the gardens. What Leonard was talking about started to sink in. If you knew when you would die, you could live for that day. Retirement savings would be an exact goal. People could say goodbye to loved ones, write up their will the day before they expired, live life to the fullest, assuming they knew when they would check out.

Donna threw her cigarette butt into the garden and then lit a fresh smoke.

"These aren't the only ones," Leonard said quietly. "I have come across thousands of such deaths. Some are obvious, others aren't. Aldous Huxley and C.S. Lewis. John Adams and Thomas Jefferson, both on July 4th, on the fiftieth anniversary of the Declaration of Independence. I've barely scratched the surface."

A muffled doorbell rang from inside the house.

"So, have you got any predictions?"

"Prince Rainier of Monaco and Pope John Paul II could happen. Sometime soon after the year two thousand."

"What's the connection?"

"Both longest ruling monarchs of this century in the two smallest kingdoms in the world. I'm also banking on Paul Winchell and John

Fiedler dying on the same day as each other. All four of them are going to buy it in the same year. The connections run deep."

"Who are Paul Winchell and John Fiedler?"

"The voice actors for Tigger and Piglet."

"Shit," I gasped.

"I know," Leonard agreed.

Father slid the patio door open. "Food's on," he said.

Donna waved her cigarette and said, "I'll be a minute."

"You boys go in," Father said. "I'll keep my future daughter-in-law company. Tell everyone to start without us so the food doesn't get cold."

"When am I going to die?" I asked Leonard.

"I'll work on it," Leonard said as I followed him inside.

We ate. Donna and Father were not seen again until we were almost done reading our fortune cookies. Abigail introduced us to the fortune "in bed" game where you read your fortune aloud and said "in bed" afterwards. It works with every fortune.

"You'll find fortune and glory this year ... in bed," Abigail read.

"You'll be filled with friendship and love ... in bed."

"You are strong, wilful and fun. People like to spend time with you ... in bed."

"Oh my God, Richard, your Dad is amazing..."

That was what Donna said when the two of them returned, exploding through the patio door in a storm of giggles and breathlessness. Donna was flushed. Father glistened. They didn't even try to hide it and the funny thing was, I felt instantly lighter, happier and relieved.

Donna and I started our engagement on such shaky ground, what with the orgy and all, that I was not surprised it ended the night she met my family. She wasn't out of my life. I would see her at shows. I would see more of Father, too, as he would be in the audience, supporting Donna.

I cracked my fortune cookie in half, pulled out the dry piece of paper and read one of the more disturbing fortunes I've ever seen. "Past troubles will pale in comparison to what is to come..."

CHAPTER 12

There Are No Fat Angels

Light flashed so bright it was almost a sound. It burned every image seen before that moment right out of the mind, leaving the brain a soft, grey template ready for its first impression. A clean slate with no memory of past loves or previous traumas, happy moments or sad ones.

The pure white light faded to a pale blue as flawless and familiar as a lover's eyes. It was a colour that had its own soul. When I think about its beauty now, stumbling along with inadequate words and a broken recollection, I realize how insufficient language is to capture such perfection. I have to rely on the clunking tools of metaphor and simile to get close to an accurate description. Even still, it hits wide of the mark.

The blue was broken by occasional drifting wisps of clouds. They started as baby hair skiffs and grew more substantial as the seconds passed. They were white, so very white. Once the clouds were dense enough to stand on, the first few tones of music filled the sky: slow, sustained, electronic notes.

I stretched my feathered wings, light reflecting pearlescent from a fine film of lavender scented oils covering them. I stepped down onto clouds as firm as any ground I had ever touched. I took a tentative step and looked around, ready for the plunge back to Earth.

There is a Heaven, I thought. *I'm in Heaven.*

I looked around, uncertain.

To become an angel, to be blessed to walk among the clouds, I had successfully shed fifteen pounds of flesh that had barely been clinging to my skeleton in the first place. I had donned pants made from zippers and vinyl, pants that clung as tightly to my skin as my skin clung to my bones. A pair of aviator sunglasses crowned my newly etched cheekbones and my chiselled jaw. I wore a white shirt with black block-letters spelling out *Ozone Kills*. There were holes cut in the back of the shirt so my wings would sprout through and I could stretch my full five-foot wingspan. There were slits cut in the fabric of my shirt, the gaps stitched with a golden fleecy mesh through which my ribs could be seen, my collarbones, my breastbone making ripples under my skin.

This year, 1998, the same year I wound up in Heaven, was the year most developed countries finished their phase-out of ozone-depleting halocarbons in aerosol sprays and industrial chemicals. In Australia, under the magnifying glass of the biggest ozone hole ever recorded, people's tans had never been so deep and bronze. Only my skin, sparkling golden in the brilliant light, was more beautiful than theirs.

It took my mind a few seconds to overcome the vertigo and it took my feet a few more to trust standing on the clouds like they had once trusted the ground. When I was sure I wasn't going to tumble to the Earth below, I walked with a little more surety. A few more steps and it struck me that, if I were to fall, my wings could save me. The thought gave me confidence. A few more steps and I was getting up to speed. This was easy. A few more steps. A nod to old St. Peter. I rounded a corner, my feet pumping and my mind growling through clenched teeth.

I am the most desired slip of angel flesh that ever walked.

I am a firecracker exploding in your face. I'm taking an eye with me. It's mine, now. I own it.

I fucked your wife on the hood of your Porsche.

I am a screaming baboon shaking a tree.

When Chester had called a week ago to tell me he could get me into Ozone's Heavenly Show, he phrased it something like this. "Okay, don't shit yourself but I can get you into the Heavenly Show."

"No shit? Paris Fashion Week? Ozone?"

"I'm not shitting you, Richard. There's a catch though. Before I call them back to confirm, I need to know you're in, that you're committed."

"Shit, yeah. What do I have to do?"

"Lose fifteen pounds. I need you in fifty/eighty-six pants and an eighty-seven shirt."

Twenty-inch waist. Thirty-four-inch inseam. Maximum thirty-four-inch chest. Minimum thirty-two.

"Holy shit," I gasped.

"Yeah," Chester agreed. "But they don't make $80,000 pants for just anyone, Richard."

Were those proportions even possible?

Yes.

I could do it. I was twenty-two years old, my body was still malleable. I was close. Chester was right, fifteen pounds or so should do it. So I said, "Book it."

Chester hung up. A rush washed over me. I was in. This was the biggest thing that could happen to me. Ozone. Paris. This was the peak. Most people had to look back at their career to find the high point. I was fortunate to see mine coming, to be able to take full advantage of it. My career could not get higher. My head swam with the lack of oxygen at that altitude.

I was skinny and I had no idea how to shed fifteen pounds of flesh that I didn't have, let alone in a week, not without dying. But this was Paris. This was Ozone. This was worth dying for. I needed help. Luckily, I knew an expert. I grabbed my cellphone and speed-dialled 6.

Father answered.

Small talk. I was too distracted to remember what was said. I needed to get to Donna. Each moment that passed was an ounce of unlost weight.

"Put Donna on."

My thoughts raced. How had my weight become an issue? There is no more consistent a stigmatization than that of being overweight. The results of being obese are clear. Judgments about people, their morals, their worth are made first by physical appearance. It only takes seconds. In magazines, movies, advertisements, it is implanted in us. There are no fat superstars. There are no fat models. There are no fat angels. The world is rougher on obese people than anyone else...

"...and the fatties do it to themselves. They're lazy and dirty and smelly and self-decapitating, in the purest sense of the word, because they just don't care," Donna said.

I couldn't remember when my thoughts ended and she began talking.

Also, I think she meant "self-deprecating."

"They don't care about their appearances so they don't care about their lives or what they accomplish. They don't care about others. They're totally unmotivated and don't contribute and that's it. It's a sickness, in a nutsack, a sickness in the brain," Donna said. "Though I hear the fatties are jolly. If I ever get to know one, I'll have to see."

"I see." I needed to stay positive.

My psychologist, the one I started weekly sessions with after Donna ran off with Father, said positive feelings are a coping mechanism to help us live through the bad times. She said they make us look to a more viable, happy future that helps us endure the ever-difficult present. Negative feelings are also important because they validate the authenticity of positive feelings. One has less meaning without the other. She said that the perfect ratio for happiness is 2:9, positive to negative feelings that is. She had read it somewhere in a textbook.

"What did you want, Richard?"

"I need to lose fifteen pounds in under a week."

"Easy," she said. "Stop eating."

I knew I had come to the right person. Donna had stopped eating once. She watched a documentary about obesity in children and thought she needed a cause. She wanted to be a role model, so she boycotted obesity as if it were some seal hunt. She got down to sixty-five pounds. She stopped menstruating and her skin became translucent, so she stopped buying tampons and started putting on more foundation. She had chronic indigestion and got a persistent urinary tract infection, so she chewed antacids like candy and popped three antibiotics a day. Her doctor told her she had to eat or she would die. She laughed. Her fee had gone up by $20,000 a shoot. And then she collapsed.

"I have to eat," I said. "I can't stop."

"It sounds like you have a problem, Richard. How long have you been a chronic overeater?" Donna asked and then said, "Go see Dr. Bella. She'll make you better."

"I don't know," I said.

"It worked for my friend, Mila."

Mila's story was a legend told to scare new models as they snuggled down under 600-thread count Lauren bedsheets at night. Mila wasn't fat but she had her stomach stapled anyway, had it turned into the size of a thumb. She lost thirty pounds and her career took off. Top-ten model. She complained she was always starving. She had to eat every thirty minutes. She developed gallstones, osteoporosis and anaemia within a year.

She died during revisional surgery. Plastic surgeons never called it corrective surgery because it implied a mistake had been made.

The Cause: She starved slowly and painfully. She ate every half-hour but her body couldn't absorb anything.

The Moral: I wasn't really sure. I thought long and hard about what was worse, to be beautiful and dead or to be dead with friends and family knowing it was due to vanity. I still didn't know. The moral didn't matter. Mila was dead.

"It didn't really work for Mila though," I said.

"Well," Donna countered, "it did for a while."

"I don't want a doctor," I said. The feeling that calling Donna was the right thing to do was waning.

"Really? Because you're sick, Richard. Being fat makes you sad, you being sad made you reach out to me. A doctor can fix your body and then you'll be happy again. A beautiful body causes a happy mind."

I hadn't realized I was fat and sad until I called Donna.

Maybe I should go back to my psychologist.

Maybe I needed to get my 2:9 happy ratio realigned.

Maybe I should just hang up.

Donna was onto something though. I recalled my psychologist blathering on about physiognomy, something about how there is a close relationship between the body and the soul, how the two can't be separated, how one was a manifestation of the other. I just couldn't remember which manifested which.

"A good plastic surgeon is better than a good psychologist any day," Donna continued, seemingly reading my mind. "The reason shrinks never work is because they go at the problem from the wrong end. The problem is not inside your brains or wherever, it's on the outside. Once you fix the extremities, the intremities follow. Trust me, it works. You're talking to living proof."

I heard Father's voice in the background.

"In a minute, Jack," Donna said through muffling fingers. "I'm helping Richard. He's fat. Okay, I'll hurry." There was a staticky sound and Donna's voice became louder. "So, no liposuction then?" Donna asked.

Lipo, Donna's fountain of youth. Twenty-five years ago, doctors were just excising wedges of fat and stitching the body back together. The flesh left behind became a minefield of infection, gangrene and puckered scars. It wasn't until the seventies that a clever doctor figured out how to remove fat deposits without massive scarring and prolonged bleeding. The machine in that surgeon's hands had since evolved into the modern liposuction vacuum from its humble beginnings in abortionists' hands as the gynaecological cannula. From suction abortions to liposuction, progress is directional.

"No doctors," I said. "No surgery."

"Fine." I could almost hear her pout.

"You have just one option really. I wouldn't wish it on anyone but I want to help you get better and you leave us no choice."

"What is it?"

"Dulcolax diet." Without a pause, Donna described it to me and all I thought was how Heaven better be worth it. Looking back at my life though, I had never really wanted anything until that moment. I was dizzy with the idea of having a goal. I would do anything.

I hung up, put on my shoes and coat and headed for the nearest pharmacy.

The Dulcolax diet is basically an extended version of what patients do for three days before their lower gastrointestinal series, better known as a barium enema.

I was lucky on two counts. I had six days, not three, and I didn't have colorectal cancer.

The diet is clear fluids only, no solid food, not even a hearty soup. Additionally, take two Dulcolax every four hours and stay close to the bathroom. The day before the flight to Paris, I completed the final stage, inserting a bullet-shaped Dulcolax suppository.

Voila, seventeen pounds in six days. I felt so light I could have flown to Paris under my own power; that, and I was also half-delirious due to starvation and dehydration. I couldn't drink though, not that day, not any more than was necessary to keep my kidneys from shutting down. My urine may have been like a desert rat's syrupy dribbles but there were $80,000 pants waiting for me in Heaven.

On the flight, I watched a nature documentary. A narrator with a haughty British accent talked about avifauna. "In the bird world, the onset of sexual maturity is marked by the development of gaudy plumage and huge bulbous body ornamentation which is disadvantageous for survival, as it draws the attention of predators, but is evolutionarily necessary as it attracts the attention of a mate." Several images of birds humping flashed on the tiny, in-seat screen. I must have zoned out because when I looked again, the narrator was talking about plants reproducing. "This variety of orchid produces scents and grows dangly, bright baubles, which mimic the form of a female wasp." Flash to a wasp humping a flower. "This confuses the male into mating with the flower which leads to pollination."

The flight touched down at Charles de Gaulle in the early evening, the day before the Heavenly Show. I spied Donna and Father ahead of me in the Customs line and wondered why I hadn't seen them on the flight. Donna was wearing sunglasses and a scarf. Father was wearing sunglasses and a scarf. Donna carried a Fendi Baguette. Father carried four suitcases.

"Oh, first class sucked hard."

My gut clenched, either from the familiar pang of Donna's voice or remnants of the laxative suppository. She was talking to another model whose photo hung near Stella Supernova's on the Agency wall. I had seen her at a few shows but couldn't remember her name. Sienna or Savannah or something.

"The champagne was barely chilled and they didn't start service until we were in the air … Oh my God, are those new?"

"What, these?" Sierra glowed. "Yes. Do my nipples look off-centre though?"

Donna took a step back for better perspective.

Sahara thrust her chest out, "I feel like one is looking at the wall and the other at the ceiling."

"No, they're great," Donna said. "Okay, check this out." Donna hung her coat over Father and lifted her shirt to expose her midriff. "Jack got me an outie."

"I love it," Samhain squealed. "I gotta get me one. Innies are so 1986."

"My surgeon just started doing umbilicoplasty. She's amazing, an artist. I swear, every time I go to her my paycheque grows." Donna pulled her coat off Father, slung it over her shoulders and planted her hands on her hips.

The Customs officer said something to her.

Father prompted Donna to step up to the desk. She scolded him and then shrugged to Salmonella. "I can never understand what these Customs fuckers are saying, you know?"

Charles de Gaulle aerodrome is what Paul Andreu thought the future would look like from the year 1966. At that time, the future was a world of smooth, Plexiglas tubes covering moving sidewalks, all intertwined over a central courtyard cylinder. At that time, people still thought the future would only get better. There were so few angles in the building, I too couldn't help but feel fooled by the hope for a smooth, clean, soft future with no edges to bump into. It was a future of jetpacks and flying cars, a fantasy of robot slaves and laser ray guns that I dreamed about as a kid.

It was a lonely building though. The rest of the world still hadn't caught up.

I stood in the bustle of the spaceport and looked up the four-storey cylinder above me. I stood in the middle of a vision of a better world that hadn't quite made it. The longer I looked, the more I saw how the vision was breaking down. The Plexiglas tube enclosing the moving sidewalk spanning the second and third floors was hazy with scratches. There was a fuzzy white square on the railing to the central courtyard where someone had removed a sticker but left behind some adhesive. A dark smear of bubble gum blemished the otherwise-gleaming floor. There were subtle signs of decay everywhere I looked. It was as though the building tried to outrun the present but got caught in a dark alley.

I didn't see Donna or Father or Saliva on the other side of Customs. They must have found their driver and headed into the city. I couldn't find my driver, so I hailed a cab.

The ride to the hotel was a solitary affair. The driver smoked the whole way and mumbled at the traffic in French. At the hotel, the gentleman at the front desk would not speak English. He just shrugged at me until I put my passport on the counter, then he checked me in without a word. My room was a small, street-side affair with a Romeo and Juliet balcony overlooking the Opera House. I didn't turn on the lights. I stood looking out at the golden angel statues and listening to the foreign sounds drifting up from the street. There was the constant whoosh of traffic punctuated by the occasional sonar blast of a horn that echoed off the surrounding buildings. The voices coming from the sidewalk were smoky and exotic. It seemed everyone had someone to talk to, to stroll hand in hand with through the streets of Paris. They all seemed to have something they could say to bring smiles to their companions' faces.

In the dark, I picked up the phone and demanded room service deliver a bottle of San Pellegrino Chinotto, three lemons, a Cohiba Robusto and Taku Wild smoked salmon, raw buttermilk cream cheese and salted capers on a bagel. At that time in my life, obscure room service orders became a proxy of my loneliness.

Half an hour later there was a knock at the door. I opened it to find a tray on the floor with a small bottle of Perrier, two lime wedges, a packet of Marlboros and some stinking cheese and a baguette. I brought the tray in and sat on the bed with it beside me. I drank straight from the bottle, threw the limes across the room into the bathroom sink, lit a cigarette and cried while contemplating the cheese.

I gagged on the smoke. My mind sparked with the cigarette's crackle to the last time I smoked, fifteen years old and the taste of marshmallows on Paige Green's lips when we kissed by the campfire. I remembered the solitary light over the empty, black highway. The only thing between the stars and me was a buzzing power line. Standing with Leonard in the vast darkness, I never felt smaller until that night in Paris. I was small again but this time in a darkened hotel room in the middle of the City of Lights, surrounded by millions of people, on the eve of my greatest show ever, crying over blue cheese—or perhaps it was the baguette that made me weep.

The cigarette butt hissed when I pushed it into the stinking chunk of cheese.

My cellphone rang.

"Richard." It was Leonard. "I'm so glad I caught you. Where are you?"

"Paris. Alone."

"Is everything all right? You sound…"

"It's good to hear your voice, Leonard."

"What's wrong?"

"All of a sudden, I feel everything." I snorked back a gloob of snot that had somehow made its way onto my lip.

"What do you mean? Are you drunk?"

"No." I couldn't keep back a sob. "I can't … I can't eat the blue cheese."

"That's okay, buddy, few people can."

"No, listen. I can't eat the baguette either." There was silence on the other end, which I took as a prompt to continue. Maybe I haven't explained it all that well, I thought. "I probably shouldn't even be drinking this water. I'll bloat an inch and the $80,000 pants won't fit. I asked for San Pellegrino but they brought Perrier." I needed to get it across. I needed Leonard's help, not Donna's, I always had. "I have been shitting myself for a week. I needed to, no, I wanted to, so I made it happen."

"Richard, slow down. You aren't making sense. Start at the beginning."

"It started after the orgy, the one in Tokyo, I think. A few years ago, anyway, I had just seen my butt hole and my life didn't make sense. I didn't know my own butt hole and I got thinking that I didn't know anything. My God, Leonard. I realize I have never felt anything. I never felt love for anyone. I never felt the friendship from you. I always knew we were friends but now I can feel it. I never felt anything for my family but detachment. I never felt pleasure in my success. I've never wanted anything. It all happened and over the past few years, I've figured out that I can change things. I've always lived on the outside, outside my skin. Then, all of a sudden, tonight, I feel everything. The whole past twenty-two years is here tonight. All that stuff that has built up on the outside, now I can feel it. The past twenty-two years, all at once, and it's wonderful and terrifying and sad."

Native Americans would retreat into the wilds and, for weeks, they would starve themselves into visions. Fatigue and physical stress limits the brain's metacognitive abilities resulting in a breakdown of the ability to discriminate between internal and external stimuli. People rescued from the desert report lucid hallucinations, waking dreams so vivid that they swear they were guided through the dunes by Jesus or Obi-Wan Kenobi. Dehydration causes fluids and electrolytes to be depleted in cells and, in the brain, this is detrimental to intercellular communication. That's when the mind goes sideways.

I know this now.

My psychologist said I had Malignant Narcissistic Personality Disorder.

I had no clue what that meant, but that night in Paris, I understood.

"Richard, that's great," Leonard said.

I failed to see how.

"You have to come see me," Leonard said. "We have to talk."

"I can't," I said. "I have to go to Heaven."

"Shit, no," Leonard said. "Richard, don't do anything. Don't hang up. Talk to me. You aren't supposed to die until the year 2000."

There was a moment in which I thought I heard Leonard reprimand himself.

"What?" I asked, sobered.

"Nothing," Leonard said, unconvincingly. "Remember what we talked about? When you asked me to figure out when you were going to die? Well, that's why I'm calling. I didn't want to talk about it on the phone but I figure you'll die early morning, New Year's Day, in the year 2000. It's not a science though, remember? You said that."

When we were kids, Leonard would push me into the street and then pull me out of traffic. Each time, he claimed he saved my life and that, by our Ninja Code, I had to be his slave until either I died or saved his life.

It felt like the old days again.

"Thanks, I owe you," I said and hung up.

The phone began to ring again.

I wiped my eyes.

It was September 28, 1998. I would die on January 1, 2000.

I could feel now.

I felt like I had just awoken from a twenty-two year sleep.

I could feel.

It was like suddenly being able to see after living blind since birth. There was a glorious confusion of colour. The things I had pictured in my mind, through touch alone, I could now see.

The phone stopped ringing.

I had wants. I had desires.

I had just over a year to live a lifetime.

I was a baby in an adult body.

I felt the instant crush of time. I had just over a year to live.

I felt panic race through me. I embraced it bravely.

I felt the overwhelming immediacy of each second. I had just over a year.

The phone beeped; there was a voicemail.

I felt an invigorating rush of fear mixed sweetly with anticipation. In just over a year I would die.

Nothing adds value to time like the lack of it.

Everything I did until then would matter.

CHAPTER 13

Minutes to Midnight

Slender fingers with cinnamon-heart nails frantically undressed me. My fingers joined in the disrobing. My heart pounded and my hands trembled, flailing from one button to the next. A bead of sweat trickled a path from my hairline, tickled through the film of sweat coating the back of my neck and slid down the canyon of my spine. My arrector pili contracted, causing fine blond hairs to stand at attention. I panted with animal focus.

That other set of fingers, the ones with nails lacquered in glossy red, those belonged to a woman named Mitsi. Mitsi's lips parted and her pink button tongue slid from the centre of her mouth to the corner, leaving a salival sheen on the plump flesh in its wake. She worked the buttons of my pants. My shirt piled to the floor.

"Come on," I urged Mitsi under my breath.

The pants dropped, underwear too. Mitsi had her hands at my ankles, pinning the material to the concrete as I stumbled out of them.

A midget walked past.

Scratch that. I think that should be little person, not midget.

He looked familiar, though I couldn't guess from where.

The little person didn't seem to notice fumbling Mitsi or naked me. Not that he should, not with so many bodies crammed into this space, so many bodies in so many states of undress.

"Step in," Mitsi's tone conveyed she had no patience for midget-ogling.

Scratch that. Little person.

Mitsi was on a mission. She pulled up my new pair of pants. As they slid into place, the space my body filled displaced a puff of air. An acrid, musty smell wafted up, the scent of every man who wore them previously. The pants had travelled the world so regularly, so thoroughly, that it was unlikely they had ever been cleaned.

Mitsi sighed and slid a hand between the fabric and my skin. She made adjustments to everything before zipping up.

"No underwear," she said. "Doug says it makes his clothes look like shit."

"The underwear's not to blame," I said.

Mitsi smiled and I buttoned up a fresh Deacon Grande shirt. Since no designers are named Doug Melynachuk, Doug wanted everyone to call him Deacon Grande. If any reporter asked, he was from some obscure European place. I didn't remember which one but it caused Doug to spit when he pronounced it. Whatever we did, we were not to mention Estevan, Saskatchewan and under no circumstance was the word *Canada* allowed to broach our lips.

Doug was a douche.

Mitsi, on the other hand, was marvellous. Mitsi was a dresser. That was her job. Between catwalk appearances, there were as few as twenty seconds before we had to be changed and back in front of the cameras, which included first-looks from the director and final touches from Doug.

Doug was a monster.

Mitsi was a queen. She was great at her job. She didn't go to school for it; in fact, nobody knew where she came from. Given her name and comfort in the arena, I would have said she was in porn or was a stripper.

Scratch that. Adult film industry or exotic dancer.

Either way, I was glad she had our backs.

"You're good to go," she patted my bum and turned to disrobe Stella Supernova who had pulled up in front of a mirror with the elegance of a Mercedes at a racetrack pit stop.

"Richard, you look gorgeous," Stella said with a glance. "I saw you in the Heavenly Show last year and you looked…" She paused for a moment to construct an expression. When she looked sufficiently like she had smelled something long dead in a tropical climate, she continued, "…sickly. This is much more civilized."

"Trench, now," Doug barked from nearby.

"Oh, that man is so much more charming when he doesn't speak," Stella said. "Go now. Find me after the show. We'll talk then." Stella held her arms out to either side, slightly bent at the elbows. Mitsi draped a shimmering shawl across the crook created by each arm.

It was obvious that Doug was new. He fidgeted with his nose like he was on blow. He tugged and adjusted himself, seemingly trying to tailor his body to accommodate his bloated sense of self-importance. This was his baby, a fifteen-minute spot in the New York Millennium Fashion Show. Respectable designers like Pucci, Alaïa, they'd gone with Fashion Week. They were elsewhere tonight, observing the millennium at some fine party where the music was agreeable and the company better attired.

Doug's show was a mini event, in a tent half the size of Fashion Week's that sat on the squishy grass of Bryant Park like a flaccid reminder of better times. They hadn't even bothered to block off the streets around the park for this one. Everyone was over at Times Square. That's where the main event was.

Even still, the space we did have was packed. The flashbulbs were furious and the crowd was famous. As much as Doug was a poseur, the show wasn't half bad. Doug's show was called "Strippers, Gimps and Midgets."

Doug adjusted my clothes, and then my body parts under them, with much less finesse than Mitsi, before shoving me toward the stage. I pushed through the curtains and started the walk through a sexualized potpourri of bodies.

The atmosphere was a turn-of-the-century burlesque show. The runway was dim and what little light was available had the flickering quality of torches and the sick glow of sodium vapour lamps. It was meant to mimic the clandestine underground feel of illicit spaces and naughty places that early socialites and railway barons would have visited to partake in gallons of hooch and to get their kit off amidst the shadowed folds of the silken tapestries. It felt like a fitting send-off for the year 1999, for, in the last sweep of the second hand, it was believed that we would lose a hundred years to some computer glitch. The television news shows were in a frenzy that we would all be thrown back to this: the only electric lights in the house were flashbulbs and the strippers, gimps and midgets Doug put together to showcase his clothes thrived in the writhing shadows.

I had to hand it to him, he had tapped into something carnal with his freak show of body oddities, a smattering of sex-industry vixens, and a healthy portion of the sickest body idols available from Chester and the Agency. On top of it, cast the incorrigible Stella Supernova in the role of the Mistress of the House and there was magic in that small, second tier showing perched precariously on the cusp of the most dangerous New Year's Eve of all time.

There was a flashbulb lightning strike.

I scoped Donna in front of me on the catwalk. She was such a trooper, she didn't even limp. I couldn't even tell that, only two weeks ago, she had the second toe on each foot shortened so she could sign a contract with Oxygen shoes. Donna had suffered from a condition called Morton's toe, where the second toe was, tragically, a bit longer than the first. It's not actually a condition, it's just simple human variation. Regardless, Oxygen did not accommodate that type of person, so Donna changed to accommodate that type of shoe.

I scoped the midget I had seen backstage. He was wearing a tiny gown, the hem short at the back and long at the front. The back showed supports, garter and just a hint of panties. The front was long so that when he broke into his contractual cancan dance and lifted the garment above his knees, the hem seemed to even out.

I worked my way past the apogee of my orbit. As I rounded the end of the runway, I spied Father, little more than a glimmer of light reflecting from his teeth, glistening from the wing. His eyes were watery pinpoints, fixated on the billowing folds of the curtains where Donna had just left the stage.

The midget followed.

I followed.

The noise backstage was as cacophonous as the front though less coherent. My chest clenched and grabbed my breath, as it always did, from the cigarette smoke, the chemical sweetness of hairspray, the mingling of one hundred kinds of wet, musky, salty body odours. The assault was not limited to sound and smell. My eyes took in a clamorous mix of body parts, naked and clothed, all sliding past each other; arms passed through crowds of breasts that brushed past legs that slipped by shoulders. All of us created a super-organic creature that spat a steady stream of models out of its orifice.

"Gotta light?" Someone croaked.

It was the cancan midget. A cigarette hung from the corner of his mouth.

I opened my mouth to tell him I didn't smoke but Mitsi erupted from the crowd, grabbed my arm with both her hands and, the next thing I knew, I was standing next to Doug, his arm over my shoulder.

Smile. Camera flash.

Doug's arm around my hip. Smile.

A topless model passed between the cameraman and us.

Still smile. Camera flash.

Doug talked to a reporter. I stood there looking pretty. It was my job.

Another flash.

I hadn't smiled. There was a scream. It hadn't been a camera flash.

"Fuck," Doug yelled, excused himself to the reporter and stormed off. "Didn't you listen? No smoking around the hair designer. Hairspray is flammable. Let me see your hands. Shit, they're blistering already…" His voice was overtaken by the noise of the crowd and the steady rhythm from the front of the house.

The reporter's face fell momentarily before she turned her microphone to me. I couldn't help but notice how well manicured her hands were.

"Richard Trench," she said.

"Yes," I agreed.

She was right, after all.

"In 1998, your face was everywhere. Then you all but disappeared after Ozone's Heavenly Show. It's great to see you in action again but, I wonder, where did you disappear to?"

After the Heavenly Show or, more accurately, after that phone call from Leonard, I had vowed to make a difference and I believe I did. In the past year, all of my free time and considerable funds had been put to good use. I found meaning by living for others and had done so to the fullest. I had been so devoted that, on this night, the night of my death, with mere hours left to live, I could honestly say that I had reached peace with the fact that my life would soon be over. I had selflessly devoted myself to my cause.

"I've been working hard," I said, "to set up the NIC and I'm pleased to announce we've been successful in establishing the foundation of an independent homeland."

The microphone wavered.

"The Nunavut Independence Coalition," I said.

"The struggle for an independent Inuit country," I said.

"Northern Canada, Arctic Circle," I said.

Shit, I said it: Canada. Doug would kill me if this made it to print.

The microphone moved slowly away from my face.

Fucking Kosovo, I thought. I sink my fortune and my last year of life and everyone would know it if it wasn't for fucking Kosovo on the news all the time.

As the reporter backed away, Stella came through the curtain from the runway. She looked radiant in her neo-turn-of-the-last-century gown. She was plump and pushed up in all the right places and cinched and squeezed tight in all the other right places. Stella made her way to a mirror ringed with lights. I wove my way through the crowd and took a chair by her side.

"Stella, I'm done here tonight," I said. "I just wanted to pop over, say Happy New Year and thank you."

"Give me a kiss. Good tidings on the last night of the millennium aren't enough," she said and leaned toward me. "It's the end of time after all."

I kissed her proffered cheek.

Stella smiled. "I feel so honoured to have known you. But here we are," she checked a clock, "just under an hour until planes fall from the sky and every computer thinks it's a hundred years ago and decides to plunge us into a barbarian's darkness. It was only a matter of time, I guess. We had a good run though, didn't we? While it lasted?"

"You don't believe that," I said.

"No, not really." She gazed into the mirror.

"You sound disappointed."

Stella's reflection glanced at me, its smile tired. "When you have endured as many crises as I have ... My career has been up and down.

My bank account has been full and empty. My cancer has bloomed and wilted. My lovers have come and gone and, after everything, the only constant is that I'm still here." She brushed an eyelash from her cheek. "The next fifty-seven minutes won't make a difference. We'll still be here. We survive. We always seem to and no computer error is going to change that. Nothing will," she said. "But, sometimes, I wish it would. Just for a change."

I nodded. "Well, I just wanted to say it was wonderful to have known you. You are a truly singular woman."

"It's not quite the feat you make it out to be in such a mediocre world," she said. "Now give me one more kiss before you go into the darkness."

I stood and placed my lips to Stella's cheek. She put a hand on the back of my head and held me there. With her skin, soft and warm and alive against my lips, I hoped she didn't feel the tear that escaped the dam of my eyelids. That tear, drying on Stella's cheek, would get to touch her for minutes longer than I would. It's residue, dried to an imperceptible salt on her skin, would likely outlast me, I thought.

I glanced at the clock. With fifty-five minutes to midnight, I left Stella; her scent lingered on my lips.

I waited for Father and Donna on the street in front of the Public Library. Before the show, we had agreed to meet there and make the walk to Mother and Dr. Sloane's apartment together, in time to watch the ball drop in Times Square on the television. And from there, according to Leonard's prediction, I would die.

I flinched when an old car I was standing near backfired to life. The midget from the show passed by and clambered into the rear seat. The rusty door squeaked and slammed shut. It wasn't until the driver's window rolled down that my memory clicked. A gangly arm with knob-knuckled fingers tapped on the door as the Monte Carlo drove away. Between those knuckles, gnarled with pink-ringed, cloudy scabs, was held a rusty nail.

I had seen the midget before. He was the Mighty Mite.

"Richard," Father called from up the street. "Let's go." His arm was around Donna's waist. He sparked his lighter and lit a cigarette, his face glowing momentarily in the flickering orange flame. "Probably can't get a cab tonight. Traffic's all snarled anyway. We should walk. If we go now, we can still make it before midnight."

I stood for a moment, mouth agape.

"You creeping on the midget?" Donna called. "You should have seen the wolf-man. That show was transendational."

"Esteban," I said as I approached them.

"What?" Donna asked.

"The wolf-man. His name is Esteban. He's from Sonora."

"Oh." Donna blinked. "That's south of Canal Street, right?"

We embarked.

About ten blocks up Sixth, Donna piped up that she needed cigarettes. She popped into a convenience store with a red-on-white backlit sign above the door. Father and I waited on the sidewalk. Father shuffled his feet. I watched him from where I stood near the store window. His face was etched by shadows.

"You looked good tonight, Richard," Father said, his eyes following his feet. "You did good."

Traffic jolted up Sixth in fits and starts, engines roared and then idled. Exhaust billowed, flashing in the dichromatic strobe of passing headlights and tail lights.

Then I thought I heard Father say, "I don't know if I've mentioned it before, but I'm proud of you."

He may not have said that. It's what I thought he said, anyway. His voice was lost in the traffic noise and he may have actually said, "I don't like the ice all over the floor. It's loud here, too."

I blinked against the night, trying to process what I heard. Either phrase would have been just as unlikely as the other. As the awkwardness grew between us with each second, I began leaning toward the former. I felt warmth spread from deep within my chest. It was the first time Father might have said that he was proud of me.

"I have to ask you something," I said.

Father looked relieved that I spoke.

"Why Donna?" I asked.

Father chewed on his lower lip and watched the spastic traffic go by.

"It's because she tries. She always tries," he said. "She tries at life even though her enthusiasm is sometimes misdirected. She may not always be right, and she sometimes makes mistakes, but she has something. She never gives up. She doesn't let the bad get to her and she's always there for me." Father paused. "I still love your mother, too, but for so many years she gave up. She disappeared. I'm glad she found Mike and got her spark back. I know you and Mike don't get along but he's not that bad you know…"

That bastard Mike, Dr. Sloane, stripped me of the universe at an early age, I thought. He stole my family, stole Mother, and derailed my youth.

"…but even those last years, when she was still in the house, she was already gone. You were young. I was alone. Donna will never give up like that."

I didn't say anything so Father continued.

"I've seen a lot of that energy in you in the past year, Richard. You've built a good career. You've got a good group of friends and for all our fuck-ups, you've kept your family near…"

Donna erupted from the door, two packs of smokes in her hand.

"…and you're doing wonderful things with those Eskimos."

"Yep," Donna said, "Richard and his Eskimos. And I'm doing wonders selling those little African kids to people."

Father laughed and gave her a squeeze. "Donna, honey, the work you do with Orphan Care International is great as well. If this is how my life turned out," Father said, "then I'm a very lucky man. Now let's go, there's only forty minutes to midnight."

Father and Donna walked in lockstep, arm in arm. I followed a short distance behind with my hands buried deep in my coat pockets and my shoulders shrugged to my ears to ward off the cold.

A light, low cloud settled over Manhattan. It reflected the city lights back to the ground in a muted glow. We hit Central Park Street, trudging through slush. The glow of the streetlamps created a vision of sepia tones that softened the edges of the towering patchwork of buildings on our left.

It had snowed recently. The city had worked extended shifts to clear Times Square, getting it ready for revellers who wanted to be in the brightest spot in the world for the turn of the millennium. Everywhere, people wandered the streets. Everyone, waiting for it all to end. It was the cusp of the new millennium, thirty-five minutes to midnight and the city teemed with residents, each expecting that it would come to an abrupt halt once the clock ground past twelve. Thirty-five minutes until a computerized time warp threw us back one hundred years. Crashing computers, sick with a binary hangover, would cause planes to fall from the sky. The world would be forced to revert to horse and buggy, back to a time when buildings were built using simple carpentry, no power tools, no skyscraping towers.

We passed a 24-hour market packed with people. Through the windows, we saw line-ups that stretched back from the tills into the aisles.

"Look at them," Father said. "Topping up their stockpiles."

People with tired expressions held baskets full of batteries. Others pushed trollies of bottled water and toilet paper, first aid kits and multivitamins, coffee and blankets, tampons and canned beets, all in preparation for imminent doom. The expectation that it would all be over hung on their faces. Spectators of doom, they had a common, tired resignation and a complacent want for it to be over.

Thirty-three minutes to midnight.

We passed a crowd huddled near a bank machine, waiting for it to spew out its contents. People roamed the streets, some drunk, others terrified, all waiting for the sweeping tidal wave of blackouts as generators failed. The city would be plunged into the soft, flickering glow of candlelight. The high-rise towers would emit a wavering light, like giant candles themselves. From a space shuttle, the wave of blackness that swept over this dark half of the planet would leave the blackest night in a hundred years in its wake. It was as if the night had been waiting patiently for this.

Would the light from so many candles flicker strongly enough to be seen from space? I wondered.

My cellphone rang. Savage Garden's "Truly, Madly, Deeply" chiming a muffled ringtone from my coat pocket. I fished it out, listened to a line of the song and then hunched against the cold.

"Richard?"

"Hey, Leonard," I said. "Happy new year."

"Rachel's pregnant," Leonard blurted. "We're going to have a baby. We just found out a few hours ago. Three pregnancy tests say that we're going to have a baby."

"That's great Leonard, congratulations."

"I just wanted to call," Leonard said after a moment. "You know, to see if you're all right?"

"So far, so good."

I slowed my pace and dropped farther behind Father and Donna.

There was a pause before Leonard said, "I'm not really sure what to say here. I'm not calling to see if you had died or anything. Well, I guess that's partly it. Not that I want you to..."

"Leonard, it's okay," I said. "I'm glad you called. I wanted to say thanks. I don't know if I took the chance before but this past year was the best of my life, thanks to you. I did something I'm proud of. I've had a chance to get to know my family and friends better and..." I paused. "It's weird, but knowing I'm going to die tonight has brought me such peace that I can hardly put it into words."

"I've been wrong before…"

I thought I heard him choke on a sob.

"I know. Even if you're wrong and I see the sunrise, imagine what a beautiful morning it will be."

"But if you don't make it, Richard…"

"If I don't, well, this evening's sunset was the most beautiful I've ever seen. Either way, without you, I wouldn't have even noticed. The funny thing is, I should have always lived the way I have over the past year."

The phone line was quiet. I glanced ahead, squinting through a cloud of my breath. Father smiled, waved at me and pointed at his watch. I glanced at mine.

Breitling didn't matter anymore. The hands told that it was twenty-nine minutes to midnight.

"Leonard, I can feel it coming," I said to the silence on the other end of the line. "It took me years to acknowledge it, and now there's only minutes to come to grips with my role in the world. Leonard, thanks for being my best friend."

"You're welcome," Leonard's voice cracked. "Please call me tomorrow."

I smiled and watched my feet leave craters in the slush on the sidewalk like footprints in moon dust.

"I'll try," I said.

We hung up.

At the end of time, the air would be free from the clutter of phone signals and radio waves. Music would revert to intimate acoustic sessions. People would leave their cellphones, pagers and email and would talk to each other in person. The $600 billion spent on retrofits to keep the world we built turning wasn't enough. Technicians, not convinced it would work, now sat in the soft glow of computer screens. Alone in windowless rooms, away from their families, they monitored telecommunications, power generation and distribution, water and waste plants, subway and air travel—all of it in an attempt to keep the world's circuits firing and gears turning.

Police were stationed on the corners, waiting. Waiting.

"Let's go, Richard," Father called. "Donna just had a great idea."

"What's that?" I said with disbelief. I ran to catch up and almost fell on the slippery sidewalk. I was distracted by my misstep. For the first time, I wondered exactly how death would come. Would I slip in the slush, fall, and have my head bounce a fatal blow off the concrete?

"What's wrong?" Father asked once I caught up.

"Nothing." I smiled. "What's the idea?"

"We should stock up on supplies for the end of the world." Donna pointed at a liquor store across the street.

"That is a great idea," I said. I watched traffic up and down Broadway and thought, would I die crossing the street?

"Let's go." I leapt from the sidewalk and was assaulted by a barrage of car horns and the sound of rushing engines and squealing tires. There was a blur of blinding headlights and the hell-fire anger of brake lights. Then I was standing in a pile of slush on the opposite side of the street, the liquor store at my back and my heart pounding in my ears. I watched Father and Donna carefully time the gaps between cars.

"You're crazy," Donna laughed.

Donna and I stood in a trench of light coming from the liquor store window. Father went in, past the flashing neon *Open* sign. His presence was announced to the store by the jangling of bells tied to the door. The sound was cut short by the door closing on the night. .

Donna stomped her feet.

"Your dad says I should talk to you," she said.

"Yeah? About what?"

"He said he's noticed a change in you. He thinks I can help you like I did when you were fat, remember?" Donna's breath steamed out from between her perfect lips. "Are you happy, Richard?"

"Yes."

"Really?" Donna paused.

"I think so," I said and then thought for a moment. "No, actually I'm not. But I'm okay though."

Donna turned and looked through the store window. Out of the corner of my eye, I saw her wave and give a thumbs-up, presumably to Father. I caught her enthusiastic nod before she turned her attention back to me.

"You need someone. You're sad because you're alone," she said. "It's okay to tell me, I'm really good with feelings. Jack and I talk about them all the time."

Donna had feelings?

Father had feelings?

"Like sometimes," Donna continued, "Jack tells me he feels hungry. Then I usually feel annoyed because it's like, 'What the fuck do you want me to do about it? Go make a sandwich.'"

"I think alone is okay," I said. "Really."

"Sometimes," Donna continued, "it's hard for me to share my feelings, but I do have them, I just don't have words for them. I am not so elequaint when it comes to talking about feelings."

"What does that mean? 'Elequaint?'"

"God, Richard," Donna sighed a long stream of steam. It glowed fuzzy orange neon as it dissipated under the streetlamp. "Ever read a book? Elequaint means using words that are above, 'ele' as in elevate, quaint, as in simple words. But Jack and I have been exploring each other's feelings and he's teaching me. He's really great."

I could see what Father had been talking about earlier. Donna was amazing. She was so secure in the world she created, she never had to question the one she actually lived in. For a moment, I was jealous of the security she had. Maybe she did have the key to happiness.

"Your dad told me he was proud of you," Donna said.

"He hasn't said it much," I told her.

"He can't. Boys are so stupid around each other."

I contemplated. He *had* told me that earlier, quietly and muffled by the traffic noise. Maybe he had been telling me all along and I just wasn't translating the words properly.

"We done here?" Donna asked.

I nodded, not really sure what we had done here.

Donna spun and gave a come hither finger to Father who, presumably, was waiting for a signal before coming out to join us. He smiled sheepishly at me when he did.

Seventeen minutes to midnight and we were back on Broadway, each with a brown-bagged bottle in hand, laughing at how clever we were to have stopped. We had enough whiskey to survive into the new year.

We almost made it to Mother and Dr. Sloane's apartment.

It was three minutes after midnight. I was completely aware of each minute that passed. The suspense was killing me. I needed to know how I would die. To me, each minute was a lease, a bittersweet triumph and one more anxious minute closer to the unknown.

We were one block from the apartment.

We were walking past Verdi Square, a small triangular park between 72nd and 73rd. Donna was telling me how it was named after a great Italian opera composter, when we noticed our trio had become a duo. Donna and I turned in unison and saw Father lying on the sidewalk. The nearby streetlight reflected in the slushy puddle where he lay.

Donna and I ran to his side, us both falling to our knees, me searching for a pulse and Donna calling 911 on her cellphone.

Five minutes after midnight and the true impacts of the new millennium were becoming known to the world. There had been no sweeping darkness and no planes had dropped out of the sky.

In Delaware, 150 lotto machines went out of service.

In New York, one ticket dispenser on subway platform 56 in Grand Central Terminal stopped dispensing tickets.

On Central Park Street, those crowds waiting for the bank machines to spew out their contents went home to their apartments none the richer.

On Broadway, Donna stood in the street and waved her arms in the night. Headlights of passing cars swept across her body. The flashing red light of the approaching ambulance strobed her body.

On Broadway, between 72nd and 73rd, I knelt in the slush. Cold hard concrete pushed a chill deep into my knees. My jeans wicked the melting slush with each passing moment.

I compressed Father's chest.

I put my lips to his to blow breath into his lungs.

On Broadway, near the statue of Giuseppe Verdi and between chest compressions, I choked out one phrase over and over again.

"Please don't die, Dad."

CHAPTER 14

We Have Started Our Descent

"Ladies and gentlemen, this is your captain speaking. We have started our descent..."

Truer words had never been spoken. At twenty-five years old, I was still too young to recognize the captain was talking about more than the airplane I was strapped into.

"The ground temperature is a lovely 82 degrees and sunny. We'll be landing in twenty minutes and will have you to the terminal shortly after that. Right now though, please ensure your seat belt is fastened and your seat back and tray table have been returned to their upright and locked positions..."

Landing is the most dangerous part of flying. It is the only difference between having flown and having crashed. One pilot, one co-pilot, a crew of eight, four hundred passengers, 400,000 kilograms of people, luggage, machinery and the occasional Shih Tzu plummeting toward a very solid tarmac at 450 kilometres per hour, I guessed things should be as tidy as possible in the event of something going wrong. It was only civilized.

I watch my seatmate wrap his earphones around a tiny device he had been listening to.

"It's an iPod," he said and looked at me as if he suspected I was a bit simple.

I nodded and smiled vacantly which seemed to confirm his suspicion.

It was August 2001, a month before those guys flew those planes into those towers. The world didn't know anything in August. After September, we would know the span of time it took a building to fall was the exact time it took to judge an entire people, how long it took for someone to fall in love and how long it took to change the world. Twenty seconds. In twenty seconds, judgments are made. I have said it before. It's all about math and it happens faster than our conscious mind works. We don't even know we do it, but we do.

But then, one month earlier, in a more naive world, the plane I was on bumped into the earth and screamed to a halt. A few people clapped, as if they weren't expecting to make it but somehow survived and thought that subdued clapping was a sufficient celebration of life.

Since New Year's Eve, I'd floated. I had spent most of my life savings. I had turned down shows and effectively snuffed out my career. I said goodbye to my friends and family. I had been ready to die and had been at peace with the fact, maybe I had even secretly looked forward to it.

Then, I lived.

It wasn't the worst thing that ever happened but it took some adjustment. I realized, over my career, I had worked everywhere but had never really been anywhere. So with what little money I hadn't given away or spent, I travelled. I bought a ticket to Southeast Asia.

I started writing strange sentences on errant pieces of paper.

I have packed my suitcase with a million of your tears.

On napkins and boarding passes.

On the loneliest night, even the dogs don't howl.
And on menus and receipts.
My heart is held captive in the prison of these ribs.
I littered the world with words as I travelled. My accommodations degenerated from hotel to hostel to tent to street. My mode of travel went from airplane to train to bus to hitchhiking and walking.
I got the runs in Delhi.
I got crabs in Thailand.
On a prescription for medicated shampoo, *Love is a sexually transmitted disease.*
I got drunk in Greece.
I got lost in Belgrade.
On a city map on which all the street names were written in Cyrillic, *I am lost in a city full of people who know exactly where they are.*
I went hiking in South Africa.
I saw some old ruins in Zimbabwe.
On a tourist brochure, *Everything we are has been before and failed.*
I made friends, then left them behind.
I left my family behind.
I left my bags behind.
In the end, I was left with nothing but the feeling of being a small man in a gigantic world and anything that I did in life mattered, but only for a short while and only to a few people.
Dad didn't die on New Year's. Donna rode in the ambulance with him to the hospital. I called Mother and Dr. Sloane and we made our way to join them, together but in silence. When we arrived, a doctor pulled us all aside, took us to a private room. He flipped a switch and fluorescent lights tick-tick-hummed to life.
"Jack is doing well. He suffered a heart attack but we think we got to him in time. A full recovery is expected," the doctor said.
"It sounds like there's more," Mother said.
"There is. In the course of our tests, we saw something that pushed

us in a different direction. There is no gentle way to say this ... Jack has cancer."

Donna held a hand over her mouth and started to cry.

"And," the doctor continued, "well, there's a lot of it and it's spread. We've located several metastatic tumours."

After a week of observation, they released Dad into a different world than he had known previously. I had left shortly after.

On my last call to Mother, I was somewhere on the northern coast of Africa, at a dusty phone booth in Tripoli, I think. She said I should come home right away. She wired me money for the next available flight. The airplane home seemed too clean and modern. I had become unaccustomed to soft chairs and fabrics that didn't smell of sweat. The television in the seat back in front of me was a magical mesmerist.

I handed over the last forty dollars of Mother's money to the taxi driver when he dropped me off in front of the hospital. It was early evening and the heat of the day lingered in wavering ghosts escaping from the asphalt and concrete. It coated me with a tactile embrace.

I stood on the curb as the taxi drove away, its crown light glowing a thin yellow in the fleeting light of the day. I inhaled and concentrated on the air held in my lungs.

I stood as people came and went through the automatic door, it sliding open and shut under the backlit *Entrance* sign. The motor hummed as it worked. Watching those people, I focused on consciously experiencing their presence, seeing them move through this world and then seeing them no more.

I stood until the streetlights flickered on overhead and then, I went into the hospital.

I was struck by the antiseptic smell in the air. It took me back to the last time I had been in a hospital and the immediate association I made with the smell was Mother.

I approached the information desk.

"I'm here to see Jack Trench," I said.

The man behind the counter removed his hands from where they had been resting, fingers interlaced on his belly. "Are you family?" he asked. His sausage fingers poked at a keyboard.

"He's my dad."

"Six fourteen," the man said. He jabbed a thumb over his shoulder. "Bank of elevators. Sixth floor. Take a left once you get there."

His chair creaked as he leaned back and wove his fingers together over top of his belly again. He looked over my shoulder, into the night outside.

Bank of elevators. Sixth floor. Took a left. Six fourteen.

I surveyed the room from the door. Mother was looking out the window. Dr. Sloane sat in one of the two chairs in the room, his fingers templed in front of his mouth and a blissful look on his face. Donna was in the other chair, which was pulled up to Dad's side. She held his hand.

Dad was pale and gaunt. I didn't recognize him from when I left seven months ago. He had come to the airport to see me off. He had still been a bit unsteady. When I glanced back from the far side of the security scanners, he stood, the only stationary person in the bustling airport, and waved goodbye to me. He had been a mountain of a man then.

Now, his hand seemed frail in Donna's. His skin was slack, draped like a shroud over his bones. His eyes were sunken, his lips thin. What hair he had left was a baby's wisp, but grey.

Then, surveying the room, I knew why I had left. I couldn't watch him turn into this. I couldn't watch him fade away. Even so, I came back because I needed to watch him die. I owed it to him.

What I had learned about myself over the past months was that I was afraid of this. More than anything, I was afraid of drifting away in time without a trace. That was why I needed to watch Dad die. I wanted him to know he wouldn't just disappear, that he would be remembered; that as his son I would do my duty and carry him on in the world after he was gone. Regardless of what had happened over the past twenty-five years, I owed him.

I cleared my throat.

Mother spun on her heel.

"Richard, you made it." In a blink she crossed the room and wrapped her arms around me. I squeezed her back. Over her shoulder, my eyes locked with Donna's and I saw pain and something else I had never seen before in those eyes. Awareness.

"What's wrong with Dr. Sloane?" I asked. Sloane hadn't moved a titch.

Mother released me. "He's conversing with the universal flow. Trying to ease Jack's passing."

I wanted to cross the room and stick my foot through his chest, pushing his heart under my heel until it was impaled on the shards of his broken ribs. Then, as he bled out into his chest cavity, I wanted to watch the last painful moments of his life fade from his eyes. I wished it were he who was rotting from the inside, not Dad.

Mother went to Dr. Sloane and rubbed his shoulders. He didn't move.

I joined Donna by Dad's side.

She stood and I embraced her.

"How're you holding up?" I asked.

"He's sleeping," she said, fear and sadness wavering in her voice. "I'm so scared for him." She whispered, her breath warm in my ear. Her cheek, wet with tears, pressed against mine.

"I know," I said and held her out at arm's length. "When the time comes, you and I have one job."

"I don't want him to go. It's not fair," she said. "I don't want to be alone again, not like I was with you."

If we were still together that comment would have festered in me, one more thorn among many. I let the slight slide. I knew what she meant. Since we parted years ago, I had grown to understand her.

"I know," I said. "But that's our job, Donna. Don't let him leave you. Remember him well."

Donna's body shook in my arms. I had never given Donna credit to be able to feel such true emotion. I wondered when she had learned it, or was it always there and I had just chalked it up to drama.

"You're small," a croak came from the bed. "You should hit the gym." While Dad's face was pained, his eyes sparkled.

"You're one to talk," I said and released Donna.

"Harsh," Dad's chuckle sounded more like a series of breathless coughs. He grimaced. His lips looked blue set against his ashen skin. "I'm glad you're here, Richard."

Donna sat back in her chair. She fought her tears, wiping them from her face with an open hand.

"You don't have to be so brave, Donna," Dad said, reaching out an IV-tentacled arm to her. "It's okay to be sad."

"I know," Donna said. "It's not easy though."

"Richard." Dad held out his hand.

I took it and tried not to flinch at how frail and clammy it felt in mine. I remembered how strong his hand used to be from those foggy childhood memories of him holding me, to the crushing hug I had received when I introduced Donna as my fiancée to the family, to the tens of nearly forgotten handshakes and hearty backslaps we had shared.

Dad had waved goodbye at the airport and then faded to this.

I finally understood why Donna and Dad worked so well together. Dad could see through Donna's facade. He saw who she was after the catwalk show was over and the venue was dark and empty. He deciphered Donna's language and translated it into something he could love. Donna knew this and, in a world where she was always eyed and known whisperingly as Prima Donna, she had found someone who finally knew her. In her eyes, he was the only person in the world who could comprehend the words she said and the things she did.

I squeezed Dad's hand and felt a weak contraction in response and then it went limp again.

I had nearly forgotten Dr. Sloane was in the room, he had been sitting in his trance for so long. Then he said, "He's gone."

"He's fine," I shot over my shoulder, through gritted teeth.

"He is fine, but he's also gone," Dr. Sloane said.

I looked down at Dad. The blanket covering him no longer stretched and crinkled with his breathing. His hand, which had been so weak in mine, was still.

Donna wept openly and with abandon. I leaned forward, kissed Dad's forehead and said, "You did well."

I tucked his hand under the blanket and stepped back from the bed to make room for Donna to fling herself on it. I left her there, raw and undignified. It was what she needed.

I joined Mother and Dr. Sloane who were in a quiet embrace near the window. I stood for a minute, looking into the dark night, until they released each other.

"I miss him," Mother said to me.

"I know. I want you to know something though. I wanted to say..."

"You still loved him a little bit," Dr. Sloane interrupted. "We carry little pieces of the people we know, inside us. Some people leave bigger pieces behind and those tug to rejoin the universal flow, to be with the rest of him. That's what we're feeling now. Little pieces of Jack left embedded in each of us, trying to rejoin him."

I punched Dr. Sloane in the mouth. It was lightning quick and carried as much might as I could muster. I had never punched anyone before. I felt his lip split and warm blood pour over my fist. I felt two of his teeth fold, sliding neatly from their sockets. My fist met bone.

There was some give in his jaw as it strained against tendon and muscle. It kept its form though, and that was where my fist stopped.

Dr. Sloane dropped to the floor.

I kissed Mother's cheek, which was taut because her mouth hung open.

"I wanted to say I love you, Mom. I wanted to say that because we never know when we'll get another chance to," I said.

"I love you too, honey," Mom stammered.

I left the room. I don't remember anything until I was going down in the elevator, picking at the torn skin on my knuckles. The elevator door dinged and slid open. I shuffled to one side, making room for whoever was getting on.

"Richard."

Without looking up I said, "I think there's some tooth lodged in my knuckle."

"Richard."

My name snapped me back to reality. Leonard stood in front of me, his foot wedging the door open, which chimed from being held ajar for too long.

"Leonard?"

"Yeah. Are you okay?"

I staggered out of the elevator and it took me a moment to register the question. I looked down a bustling corridor over Leonard's shoulder. Nurses in pale green uniforms flitted like leaves in rapid water, in and out of rooms. Doctors in white coats and stethoscopes draped across their shoulders moved like icebergs, examining charts and chewing on the ends of pens. Patients and visitors moved in and out of the bustle, flotsam drifting around in an eddy.

Life went on.

"Dad just died," I blurted out.

My cheeks burned. I cried. Relief spilled out of me in big waves. I hadn't realized I had been carrying so much.

Over the past year's travels I thought I had grown strong and gained control. I had convinced myself I was ready for anything and, suddenly, that was gone. But maybe, I thought, maybe this was strength. Maybe strength is reaction and is allowing control to be lost. Without control, without a filter, blubbering incoherently like a child with a gelatinous pendulum of spit quivering from the corner of my gaping mouth, maybe this was strength.

Leonard embraced me. He wrapped his arms around me, his open palms on my back. He held on tightly.

"I knew he was here," he said. "I was just on my way up."

Leonard smelled. I could smell his armpits and the nutty scent of his unwashed hair and skin. I wrapped my arms around him, returning his embrace. After a while, my breathing became regular, matching Leonard's. His chest slowly, smoothly expanded and contracted against mine. My breathing grew calm.

Through his open palms on my back, the embrace of his arms, the pulse of the crook where his shoulder met his neck, that same spot I had inadvertently deposited my stringy spit to form a dark, damp spot, I felt my heartbeat align with his.

I released Leonard. "Can you write something about him for me, for your paper?"

"Of course," Leonard replied. "Of course, I will."

"I don't know if I remember him right now, anything about him," I said. I had always thought Leonard's job was obscure curio but I started to realize the importance of what he did.

"That's okay. You'll remember. You don't realize how little you know until you start exploring people's pasts. Their lives, after they have been lived, move from things that are works in progress to complete stories with a beginning, middle and an end. Once we know the dead like a friend, once we've explored their life lived, then we know what we've lost," Leonard said. "Obituaries don't just serve the memory of a person, they testify to what we've all lost."

"It could've been me," I said. "It should've been me on New Year's Eve. You said it would be me."

"I made a mistake," Leonard said. "But I've figured it out."

"When do I go?" I asked. I had to know. My tone must have conveyed my need.

"You remember when I told you about my theory. Paul Winchell and John Fiedler?"

I thought for a moment. It had been the night I introduced Dad to Donna. Leonard and I had been standing in the backyard at Dad's house, watching Donna wander "the gardens."

"Tigger and Piglet," I said.

"Yeah. And the Pope and Prince Rainier. You're tied to all of them."

I thought back to that night. The Chinese takeout. Dr. Sloane grinning across the table from me and the feeling of wanting to push my fist through his face.

What was it Leonard had said?

"2005," I said.

"Yes."

"Four years left," I said flatly.

Leonard nodded. "Sorry."

"It's all good." I shrugged. "You were wrong last time."

"Yeah," Leonard said, though his face told me that this time he knew he had it.

I felt tired suddenly. I was jet-lagged. I tried to remember the last time I slept. How long had the flight been? Eighteen hours? Half the time I didn't know where I was sitting—on an airplane, in an airport waiting room? Where had I been and where did I end up?

Leonard looked as terrible as I felt. His hair was a greasy bird's nest. He had a shadow of a beard and his clothes were wrinkled and sported many stains, only one of which was courtesy of me.

"Why are you here?" I asked.

"Come on." He grinned. "I'll show you."

Leonard led me through one corridor and down a second. He stopped outside a yellow door and peeked inside.

"Come on," he whispered. "Quietly though."

The room was still. Leonard eased the door closed behind us, locking out the bustle of the hallway.

Rachel lay in a hospital bed. It was the same type of bed I had left Dad in a short while ago, the kind that could be made to sit up, the kind with side rails. My heart jumped, then I saw she was breathing. In her arms, she held a bundle of blanket. Her eyes opened slowly and she smiled.

"Were you sleeping?" Leonard asked, sidling up beside her on the bed. The pair of them looked so pale and exhausted.

"Just resting my eyes. Maggie and Tony stepped out to get something to eat." She beamed at me. "Richard, my God, I haven't seen you in forever."

I made my way to the bedside. "It's been way too long," I said.

Leonard gently took the bundle from Rachel's arms. "I want you to meet our daughter. Here," he held the bundle out to me, "hold her."

"Congratulations," I said. I hesitated. I had never held a baby and didn't know where to start.

"Here," Leonard said. "Like this," he manoeuvred the bundle into my arms. "Just support her head."

Leonard was suddenly an adult in my eyes. Until that moment, I had never thought of us growing older, growing up. Leonard had always been my childhood friend but now, with the responsibility of another life weighing in my arms, all I could think about was how we were becoming our parents. Auntie Maggie and Uncle Tony had been our age when they had Leonard. Mom and Dad had been twenty-five when they had me. Now, I held Leonard and Rachel's daughter.

"Uncle Richard," Leonard said. "Meet Aaliyah."

I folded back a flap of soft blanket and revealed Aaliyah's face. She had chubby cheeks, a cute button nose and she was perfect.

"She's gorgeous," I whispered.

CHAPTER 15

The Evolution of Beauty

What the hell is this? I thought.

      French Rococo?

      Boca Raton?

"What would you call this?" I asked the woman sitting next to me.

She raised an eyebrow and gave me an annoyed sidelong glance.

"This," I continued, oscillating my arm in front of me like I was dealing cards. "The decor. Is it Frank Lloyd Wright-inspired West Coast?"

"I … I don't know." She looked around as if noticing the waiting room for the first time. Then she gave me a noncommittal "Contemporary Gothic?" Her eyes drifted back to the fashion magazine she was flipping through.

What was this room meant to inspire, exactly? I wondered. *A calm, comfortable excitement with a modern edge in a traditional sort of way?* All those things thrown together made something entirely new. Everything was familiar yet arranged in such a way that there was nothing real about it. Each piece—the furniture, the fixtures, the art—was nothing on its own but together they made something entirely new.

The woman next to me focused on flipping past glossy photos of models and celebrities. A spread on Paige Green's 2003 spring line flashed by before a flickering light caught my eye. Behind the receptionist on a television—volume down, beautifully flat-screened—a new advertisement glimmered every thirty seconds. This one was for the Capital One Health Care Finance Credit Card. With 25 percent interest and a limit up to $40,000, it was the only card I knew that was tailored to finance cosmetic procedures. I knew this because I had one in my wallet.

The woman beside me leaned forward. Her toned ass, gift-wrapped in tight jeans, slid across the taut leather chair, causing it to emit a friction fart. She dropped her magazine onto the table and started pushing others around. Her hands were a spiderweb of blue-green veins under parchment-paper skin. Her hands, the only part of her that seemed aged, prompted me to wonder how old she really was.

I watched those crone's hands slide magazines around. There were glossy covers about breasts, noses and liposuction. There were titles like New Beauty, Elevate and Only Skin Deep.

I admit: everything in the room made me nervous and more than a little bit anxious. How I got to be in this seat, in this particular waiting room, had been even more nerve-racking.

Two months ago, Chester signed me for my first show in almost five months. It was a Deacon Grande show but I was so desperate for the money and the camera time that I agreed. A long story short, Deacon exploded in one of his legendary tirades and, with Chester on speakerphone, fired us all because we were, "too fat and made his clothes look like shit."

With six hours to showtime, the venue buzzed with the hairy butt-cracks of contractors. With two hours to showtime, the installation of a Planiform Multi-Plan V garment conveyor—just like the ones dry cleaners use—was complete. The models from the Agency clustered around the device, murmuring and poking at it like a clan of fabulous-looking cave people at an obelisk. Deacon strode out, put one hand on a hip and draped the other on the conveyor.

"All of you," he announced, waving an arm magnanimously over our heads, "can attend the show." He spun on his heel and made his way backstage. "But you have to stand at the back."

We did attend the show. The Planiform Multi-Plan V ground a clattering path, the chain driving the whole mechanism churning its way from the back of the stage to the front. At regular intervals, it dragged captive coat hangers. Each draped in a Deacon Grande creation that shimmered in the spotlights because of the quivering vibrations of the motor. I pictured Mitsi and her team of dressers grumbling and toiling backstage, stripping and redressing coat hangers with frenzied fingers.

I stood next to Donna at the back of the room, in the dark, watching Deacon's clothes quiver by like a parade of the world's most elegant jellyfish. Donna let out the occasional gasp or sigh of appreciation as the clothes passed. To Deacon's credit, his clothes had come a long way in the past three years. Gone were the cringe-worthy millennium frocks, here were the Grand Palais-worthy ones.

Doug had done Estevan—no, all of Saskatchewan—proud.

After the show, the Agency models gathered for drinks in the hotel lobby. It was a sparkling cavern filled with the noise of chatter, piano music and clinking glasses.

"I thought they did an awesome job," Donna said. She fished a pickled onion from her Reverend Mordant Toehold and flicked it into the dark in disgust, muttering that she didn't know when they "started sticking fucking salad in her fucking drinks, fuck."

"Yeah, his clothes have really improved," I agreed.

"No, Richard. The *coat hangers*," Donna said. "They made those clothes look amazing. Something to inspire to."

I checked my watch and saw I was running late. If Donna wanted to aspire to be a coat hanger, I would have to leave her alone with her dreams. I excused myself.

After the Deacon Grande show I had run into Paige Green. I knew she was part of the weekend's events; her name was on all the marketing material, though this was the first I saw of her. Things had been awkward since she confessed her love for me at our last meeting. We hadn't really talked since the morning after the orgy. How long had it been, five years? Anyway, Paige called to me as she was swept by, caught up in a crowd. She just blurted a request as she passed.

"Richard. Room 2317. 9:30. I need you. I'll pay."

I nodded though she was already gone. It sounded like honest, paid work to me and everyone seemed to know that I was desperate for any opportunity. Somehow, I had become charity. Somehow, it had become necessary.

I left Donna and the others and wove my way through a forest of martini waitresses to the hotel lobby where I pushed a button and waited for the elevator. As I watched the numbers above the door tick down, I began to feel a mounting panic, as if the countdown signified something more than a descending elevator. The number reached zero and the door opened.

Room 2317. Brass numbers above a spy hole. Between the numbers and the hole, there was a knocker in the shape of a bull's head with a ring through its nose. From behind the door I heard voices, music and a less-defined clatter. I grabbed the nose ring and knocked it against the door.

"Can you get that?" a voice said.

Promptly, the door swung open and Stella stood before me, a teacup in one hand and the other on the doorknob.

"Richard," she said. "When Paige told me you would be joining us, I was ecstatic. Do come in."

The room was large and smelled of cigarette smoke and body odour. There was a small table in the corner with a carafe of coffee on it and a constellation of lipstick-kissed cups. A vase of roses sat as a lonely reminder of beauty and glamour. Champagne flutes were scattered around a stack of something-salad sandwiches. Could I smell egg? Or perhaps it was tuna.

A large window framed the table. Far below, through dusty streaks, the city lights shone a brighter reflection of the stars above.

There were three people in the room. I recognized Stella and Sienna, who was standing in the corner looking out the window at the city lights stretching to the horizon. The last time I saw Sienna, she was talking to Donna at Charles de Gaulle airport, just before the Heavenly Show.

"Paige has stepped out for a moment," Stella told me as she shut the door. "Room service was supposed to deliver more champagne but they haven't been seen for ten minutes now. She's gone to emasculate them, the lovable little gynocrat she is."

Meetings like this are called "sales calls." They are common though I had never attended one before. I never felt the need. The purpose of tonight's visit was to sell very expensive garments to the richest fashionistas and most exclusive boutiques in the world. Clients booked an hour to review Paige's season. Boutique owners placed their orders and billionaires drank warm champagne, ate bad food and bought their family wardrobe.

"That man…" Stella whispered, pointing to a fifty-something balding fellow sporting a ponytail and earring. He leaned against the table, flipping through the line sheet, looking at Paige's sketches, sizes, colours and the list of prices. "He's a prince of some tiny country in some desert place that has more oil than water. Can't remember where but it's apparent there are some cultural differences with regards to manners and social interaction."

Stella led me across the room. I nodded and smiled at the man. He glanced at me, and then went back to the line sheets.

"Charming, isn't he?" Stella said, loud enough I was sure the man could hear. "But not as charming as his wife, the woman we're all here to entertain and dress up for."

"And where is she?" I asked as we arrived at the table. I poked around for a clean coffee cup but couldn't find one so I filled a champagne flute with coffee. I grabbed a sandwich—the bread felt stale and crusty between my fingers and thumb.

Stella pointed at a door and, as if on cue, a toilet flushed.

"Poor dear," Stella said. "She suffers from a constitution which could handle neither the champagne nor the salade de poulet."

I put my sandwich back on the table and took a gulp of coffee, holding the flute by the stem because the bell of the glass was too hot.

"Yes, she's actually very nice, very appreciative of our efforts. Doesn't speak a word of English but seems wonderful. She's only twenty-two, blessed with the body of a goddess but cursed by a face that far from matches."

"Twenty-two? A bit of a trophy wife…" I commented, glancing at the man leaning against the table and inadvertently pictured him naked.

An unfortunate-looking woman with a body to match Sienna's exploded from the now-fragrant bathroom, chattering in a language I didn't understand. She sounded like machine-gun fire.

"A trophy wife, yes," Stella said moving to the woman's side and gently rubbing her back. "I should guess third or fourth place, but a trophy wife nonetheless."

The man barked something at her. She flipped through the "look book," a similar book to what the man held but this one was full-colour, glossy, with Paige's garments in action, on models. No prices.

There was a clamour at the door. Paige returned, champagne bottle in one hand and a bouquet of fresh flutes in the other. She smiled when she saw me, which was a relief. I had been expecting the worst but hoping for more. I was happy Paige fulfilled my hopes.

Paige had put on a little weight. No, I thought, that wasn't fair, she had filled out. There was a premature frost of grey in her hair and her face seemed older, warmer and a bit more refined. She was no longer a girl; time had transformed her into a woman.

I admired her aging as she apologized at length to the old man and his wife. I thought of how I hadn't really noticed people around me aging before. In fact, most people around me didn't age. Whether it was from the perennial nips and tucks, as with Donna, or from some other indefinable grander beauty, as with Stella, for some reason my eyes didn't see people age. And here was Paige, five years older, expertly popping a champagne cork, apologizing so profusely she was almost bowing as she filled Prince What's-his-name's flute.

Paige smiled when she caught my gaze, said a few words to the prince and made her way to me.

"Richard." She embraced me. She was soft, warm and smelled of an oddly comforting blend of champagne, cigarettes and stale perfume.

When our embrace broke, she slapped me. The smack sounded the room to silence. As if by the same strike, all faces in the room snapped toward us.

"You could've at least called," she said.

I rubbed my cheek, feeling the phantom burn of a hand strongly applied and shortly passed.

Paige leaned in. I flinched. She kissed my cheek, her lips sensually electric against the heat of my insulted skin. I had to admit, it felt amazing and it excited me. I shifted and crossed my hands in front of my groin, feeling embarrassingly adolescent at its creeping growth.

"I missed you," she said. "Thank you for coming."

I had forgotten how arousing our past encounters had been. Paige and I had always connected physically and, on some subconscious plane, mentally since our first meeting. My memories tripped back to the first time we made love, mere children in hindsight, clumsily rolling around in front of the campfire. I remembered the terrible void in my chest as Paige walked back to camp, ahead of me through the dark forest. I remembered the profound loneliness when Leonard and I stood on that abandoned highway under a solitary light, sharing a cigarette. Those feelings I had felt often in Paige's absence. I knew them well.

"I'm sorry," I said. "You're right, I should've called." As I said it I knew I meant it. I don't know why I didn't see the connection we had, as clearly as Paige saw it, until that point. Paige had never been bad to me, never been cruel and she had always been an interesting puzzle. She was intriguing to me, a little scary, and totally exhilarating. She always had been. Like that time we fucked on the airplane, I never knew what she was going to do or say but everything she ever said to me had been true and honest and sincere. And, at our last meeting, she said she loved me.

Now, thinking back, I may have always loved her, too. It was just that she was direct with her feelings and thoughts; something I wasn't used to. Paige always displayed a brutal, bare and complete exposure of emotion that I had encountered only in her.

I also liked the way she had used my body. There was honesty there, too. She hadn't slept with me because I was a model. She slept with me because it was a way for her to explore a different way to communicate. I liked her sex because it was as true as when she spoke.

When I spoke, I was a show. When I fucked her, well, that word says it all. It was the pursuit of getting off. It was a fashion show. I had never thought of it in another way until that night. Paige's bare feelings, her willing exposure of her emotions, regardless of the potential for rejection and pain, had changed that. I was ashamed that I never returned Paige's honesty that it took me this long to realize.

I needed to be that honest.

I needed to foster the same explorer's quality that endeared Paige to me, the childlike frankness that knew no bounds. I would be honest from then on, I resolved.

"You've put on a little weight," I said. "And it looks great on you. And..."

My vision rocketed sideways and I swear I heard a popping sound from the cartilage between the vertebrae of my neck.

"And?" Paige asked.

I slowly swivelled my head back to centre. She looked at me expectantly.

"And I love you ... I always have," I said. "Well, maybe not always, but for a long time anyway."

Then we kissed.

Later that night, after the sales were done and the clients had gone, I stood in the bathroom, unable to sleep because Paige was snoring and sprawled out over most of the king-sized bed. I examined myself in the mirror, the bite marks recently delivered to my chest. I twisted my body to inspect the claw marks that ran diagonally from my shoulder to the line of my spine. I straightened up and smiled at my reflection. I had made it. I felt that thing that people feel when they find someone. Love.

A bruise had risen on my cheek. I leaned closer to find the web of several tiny burst vessels on my cheekbone. I marvelled at perspective, how what I saw changed with it. From far away, a glowing, purple bruise. From up close, a nebula of colour detailed in pores and vessels. It changed everything.

I spent the rest of the night in the bathroom examining my face and my body. I scrutinized my skin, my features, how they worked together to make a person, how they were beautiful as their own pieces. I looked at them from afar and then a mere fraction of an inch from the mirror. I stretched skin. I flexed and pinched.

Models are necessarily introspective, self-critical and vain. The career requires detailed examination of the features of the face, the musculature of the arms, chest and stomach, the curve of the buttocks and the shape of the legs. All parts, every blemish, every mole, every angle of bone under skin, every ripple of tendon and muscle need inspection. It is the search to admire, to mend the imperfections.

I think it's in all of us, really. It is a necessary meditation. Those elements making up the molecules making up the cells making up our bodies, they are the same elements composing the trees and the air. They all started as particles, floating around, billions of years ago. They all remember each other, long to see each other again.

What had Dr. Sloane said before I punched him? "We carry little pieces of the people we know, inside us. Some people leave bigger pieces behind and those tug to rejoin the universal flow."

I paused for a moment and smiled as Paige's snoring reached a crescendo punctuated by a snort. She mumbled something and then all was quiet again. I turned my attention back to me.

A highly developed sense of self-criticism, of vanity, is the quest to understand the intersection of oneself and the universe. It leads to the realization that the physical interaction between the two is one and the same. Me, picking at my face in the mirror, that is a meditation of the universe looking at itself, interacting with itself, learning about itself, remembering itself from billions of years ago.

I found my pants on the floor, between the toilet and the tub. I rummaged through the pockets for my cellphone and called Chester. He sounded a sleepy grunt from the other end.

"Chester, are you there?" I said quietly into the receiver. "I've been looking in the mirror for the past few hours and I think I get it."

"Trench?" He cleared his throat. "That you?"

"I have come to terms with most of my imperfections. There are just a few that need to be fixed and my body will be free. My body and mind are so close to being united. They have been at war for so long. Get ready for the next phase, perfection."

"There's this thing called 'blind sight,' Richard. Know what that is?"

"Get ready for the next phase," I spoke over Chester. "The evolution of beauty."

Chester didn't stop speaking, so we wound up talking at the same time.

"Your brain sees things that aren't there," Chester muttered. "Or they might be there but your eyes can't see them."

"I'm going to give you a true beauty," I said. "Something so true, you'll be able to see my naked soul."

"Blind sight is said to be the depth of your conscious mind. You're a wading pool right now, Richard. Are you listening to me?" Chester said.

"Once I correct a few things," I was saying, "I won't be bound by any perceptions of imperfection, no more doubt or self-pity. My spirit and body will fuse, becoming the ultimate instrument of free expression. I will truly just *exist*."

"Oh, Richard, do you know what time it is? I'm going back to sleep. We can talk later."

Then Chester called me "quixotic" and hung up.

I had no idea what that meant.

And that's how I wound up at Dr. Bella's office in Burnt Timber Acres Mall, the largest strip mall on the coast, watching the woman who didn't know what Gothic decor looked like, wander over to a mirror and pick at her face. The woman turned and looked at her fanny, lifted the cheeks a bit using both hands, and then let them fall, meaty and thick, with a sigh.

Dr. Bella came highly recommended by Donna.

"I absolutely love her," Donna gushed. "I was looking for a plastic surgeon who understood my emotional needs, you know, and Dr. Bella was the answer. It's like she can look through your skin and see the real you. And then make your looks match."

Paige didn't know I was here. I told her I was going to a talent call for the Agency. When I actually got the surgeries, I would tell her I was off to a show in Tokyo for a week. Then I would hole up in some airport hotel and watch movies on-demand and eat room service while I healed.

When I had poked Paige gently with the idea of me getting plastic surgery, I had brought it up in a sideways, "a friend of mine" kind of way. Paige's response had been definite and negative. She thought plastic surgery was a solution to nothing.

"I've seen enough of it, Richard," she'd said. "I can't look at a beautiful woman without wondering, without looking for the work she's had done. Plastic surgeons are making a new species of plastic people when it's really just sticking peacock feathers in a chicken's ass. The genes don't change, it's just a mask." She paused for a moment to inspect me. I thought she had seen through my clever ruse. "There's no beauty in what's not real. Fuck the plastic people and you still get beautifully ugly babies who'll never grow up to look like their parents. They'll have anomalous hairy patches and bumps on their heads that challenge their mother's love. Plastic surgeons can mess around all they want—nature gets the last word."

The next morning, having coffee in the white sunlight of our apartment's breakfast nook, she read to me from a "special section" in the paper about beauty and style. It was as if she was explaining to me why she was so opposed.

"You know," Paige said from behind the newspaper. She used a finger to fold one corner toward herself and looked at me over the edge. There were toast crumbs at the corner of her mouth. "This year, 2003, Defence spending in our fine United States will hit $115 billion," Paige paused for effect. "That's the same as the projected revenue of the cosmetics industry."

All I could think was, does she know about my appointment to see Dr. Bella?

"Richard Trench," the receptionist called. "Dr. Bella is ready for your consultation."

I glanced once more at the woman inspecting herself in the mirror. She pinched her cheeks and pulled the flesh back toward her ears. She smiled a wind-tunnel smile and opened her eyes wide as if she had just been goosed. The combined efforts gave a deceptively youthful visage of innocent surprise. Deeper, in her eyes, she looked unhappy. She was trapped in an aging prison.

Dr. Bella's office was dimly lit and furnished in dark wood and heavy leather chairs. Chocolate brown, velvety drapes were drawn across the windows.

The receptionist closed the door with a quiet click and it was only then I could hear violins playing from somewhere in the room.

Dr. Bella sat in shadow, backlit by soft glow that diffused around the drapes. Her silhouette was thin and graceful. Her slender limbs worked at something on the desk in front of her, though I couldn't tell what. My eyes were slow to adjust to the light.

I stood, with my hands in my pockets, exactly where the receptionist had deposited me. Unsure what to do, and feeling like I had intruded into someone's private residence, I waited. Dr. Bella gave me no acknowledgement and for a moment my mind tripped and wondered if I really was there—or was I indeed invisible and observing this woman's private reverie without her knowing?

As I stood, my eyes grew accustomed to the light. The violin strings emanated from a small stereo that sat on a bookcase lining one side of the room. The stereo sat next to a bust of some stern-looking patriarch, scowling over the room as if with great concern over the loss of his limbs and half his torso.

I shifted my attention to Dr. Bella. Her slender fingers worked tweezers in one hand and a small eyedropper in the other. She was working with such focus yet her brow remained unfurrowed, her face remained an impassive kabuki mask. And, before her, she was building a rose. The tweezers delicately pinched a petal. The eyedropper dabbed what must have been glue, and painstakingly the two came together.

"It's real," she said. Her voice was smooth and strong. "The petals are imported and I put them together. I build roses because nature can't seem to do it right." Her eyes remained on the flower as she spoke. "She always has one petal with a cleft in the wrong place or veins that are too prominent or, mostly, just a few petals that are wilting so slightly—a minor discoloration and curling at the edge. So, I do it myself. I take beautifully flawed things apart and put them back together properly. I fix Mother Nature's mistakes."

She looked up at me. Twenty seconds passed before she spoke.

"Richard Trench. I've seen your work. I'm a big fan." Her teeth shone bleached white in the half-light. "Now, sit."

I did as I was told. The strength of her presence left me with little choice really.

Her eyes roamed about, taking in every part of me yet settling on none. Even as she spoke, her eyes moved.

"You're lucky," she said. "In the old days, I was forced to work my craft in a hospital. Now it's easy. You can come to the mall to have a procedure. In the old days, it was a stigma to have improvements made. Now, it's a badge of courage. People talk openly about the work they've had done. It's a statement of financial fecundity. It's bold. It's daring." Her voice grew louder and more excited. "You can go on vacation to Costa del Sol for a month and come back twenty years younger. Why? How did this fabulous transformation happen?"

I opened my mouth and said, "Plastic surgery…" and was promptly silenced by a finger.

"My questions are not for answering. Not by you," Dr. Bella said. "This is your consult. You are not to speak." There was an awkward length of silence. "That's a horrible thing you said but I forgive you, you're new. There's no such thing as plastic surgery, there's only aesthetic activism."

Dr. Bella leaned forward. Her chair creaked luxuriously and the sound took me back to breakfast.

Paige had shifted in her chair, it creaked. She slurped some coffee and said, "What if everyone was pretty? I mean, the same kind of outrageous pretty that these people are gunning for?" She slapped the newspaper with the back of her hand.

"Never thought of it," I said.

"Well, if everyone were the same level of beautiful, you would need to become a more extreme vision to stand out," she said. "In the end, we really have the ugly to thank for beauty. It's this thing called the contrast effect. If everything's the same and there's no gradation from one to the next, any kind of judgments—say beauty and ugliness—don't exist. There would be no thin or fat. The pretty war is not going to stop, it's going to escalate. We have been moving away from the beauty that can happen naturally and into something that only humans can make because we're pushed to make the differences between the two things, beauty and ugly, even greater so we can stand out even more."

I looked at Dr. Bella. She leaned closer now and I wondered how old she really was.

"Some of the first procedures were restructuring the noses of syphilitics over one hundred years ago," she said.

Could she have been there? I wondered.

"Their disease ate the cartilage of their noses, announcing them publicly. Their disease, their immoral sexual antics, were out in the open for all to see. Their faces betrayed them and they suffered economic and social harm because of it. They couldn't get jobs, they lost their friends. Their physical appearance hampered their lives and their livelihood. They were a sad, sad miserable lot. Aesthetic activism changed these patients' lives. It cured them by altering their displeasing forms into passable visages once more, allowing them to re-enter everyday society and lead happy, fruitful lives."

"But they still had syphilis, right?"

Dr. Bella sighed. "If you insist on speaking," she said, "please do so silently," she tapped her temple with her finger, "in your head."

Again, an awkward hush settled between us.

I thought back to Paige, the sunlight streaming through the nook window. Her housecoat was loose around her neck. She caught me staring at the swell of her breast and she smiled.

"Did you know," Paige said, holding up a knife crusted with a peanut butter skid mark, "that hair transplants are the most common plastic surgery for men? There is this book, the International Statistical Classification of Diseases, in which hair loss is identified as a disease in section L65.0." She smirked.

Since moving in with Paige, I noticed my hair was thinning. I tried to chalk it up to the penetrating nature of the harsh fluorescent tubes lighting Paige's bathroom, but the more I stared, preened and fluffed, the more I saw a larger volume of scalp. Each time I found one of my hairs resting on the sink or in the shower, I felt a little stab of loss. Every time I splashed water against the errant hair, I watched a tiny bit of me slither down the drain.

"Balding is linked to the secretion of androgen and dihydrotestosterone which is partially genetic and partially triggered by psychological stress. Your testicles secrete these hormones," she read and smacked her lips.

I shot an accusing look at my lap. At the sight of the bulge in the fabric of my pyjamas, I suddenly and fully understood the meaning of "love/hate" relationship.

"Eunuchs castrated before puberty, they never go bald," Paige read. "And in ancient times, a poultice of dates, dog paws and donkey hooves, fat and grease was cooked up and applied as a paste to stimulate hair growth." She scrunched up her face.

I wondered what was in Rogaine and minoxidil. I thought to ask Dr. Bella.

Dr. Bella leaned back in her chair and finally spoke. "There's a disease, one that affects millions of people and one that I can cure … R46.1: *bizarre personal appearance*. If the body can't be corrected, the mind remains tormented. I can remould the body and remake the character. I can alleviate suffering. The new character that I forge is one driven by the ideology of the pursuit of happiness. I just have to cure the disease that genetics has wrought upon you." Dr. Bella paused. "I'm going to start you on a bit of nose and eye work."

The finality of her statement was shocking. It was as if personal choice had been removed from the equation.

"You would do well to start with many small prunings at an early age," she said. "The body's more vibrant and vital. It can recover easily from insults, which will mean fewer procedures when you're older. It'll be quick. It'll be painless."

Paige. I thought of Paige sitting in the sunlight this morning. It was so different than the darkness I sat in with Dr. Bella.

"In plastic surgery," Paige read, "anesthesia complications are the prime cause of death."

"It got Mila," I said.

"I thought she died from bulimia."

"Oh," I said. "I don't really know."

Paige mulled this over for a moment before focusing on the paper again.

"Here's a gruesome section," Paige said. "It's about people who have been assaulted because they're beautiful. Katrina Spiros, she was twenty. Some guy splashed acid on her face, blinding her and scarring her for life." Paige paused, her eyes travelling the lines of text as she took a sip of coffee. "Apparently, the guy was a student obsessed with her beauty. The cops went back through her fan mail and found hundreds of letters from him. Creepy shit, like pages with hair taped to them or stains on them. When her agent announced she was getting married, the guy flipped." Paige shook her head. "Really," she said with disappointment.

Having never understood the obsessive personality, I shook my head along with her. I ran my fingers through my hair in hopes to make it look thicker and I thought about how many sit-ups I would have to do to counter the toast and jam I had for breakfast. I thought about how I'd love to get rid of that half-moon of flesh just below my belly button. It had recently appeared and no number of sit-ups seemed to make it disappear.

"This is sick." Paige's eyes traced a few more lines of print and then she said, "In 1986, this other guy, Steven Roth, he was a TV makeup artist, hired two guys to attack this model named Marla Hanson. They cornered her outside a West Side bar, held her and slowly carved up her face with a razor…"

"Fuck," I grimaced.

"…for two minutes." Paige finished with raised eyebrows. "You don't have any psycho fans do you?"

"None that I know of," I replied.

CHAPTER 16

As With Life, You Knew How This Story Would End

It had been morning when Leonard knocked on the door. Paige and I were still in bed. Our limbs casually intertwined, we drifted awake to plant a soft kiss on a sleepy eyelid or cheek, only to drift away again. It was bright in the room; the spring sun wove through the cracks between the blinds. The air coming in the open bedroom window was alive with the whisper of traffic and fresh with birdsong.

I had answered the door wearing a towel.

"You're not supposed to see each other today," Leonard said. He held a coffee in each hand. "It's bad luck. We have to get you away from here or we'll both face the wrath of Rachel because you've willingly cursed your marriage." He handed me a paper cup and an elastic band-bound newspaper before brushing past into the hallway. "You got some gooby in the corner of your eye," he said. "Get dressed."

"Morning, Leonard." Paige came from the bedroom wearing a nightshirt that went to her knees. She pointed at the coffee. "That for me?"

"Good morning, Paige." Leonard pecked her on the cheek. He contemplated the coffee for a moment before handing it over.

Paige took Leonard to the kitchen while I went to shower and get dressed. Wearing my dress pants and a pressed white shirt, I grabbed the remainder of my tuxedo from the closet and hung it on the front doorknob on my way back to the kitchen.

Leonard and Paige were sitting in the breakfast nook and smirking about something when I joined them. I kissed Paige on the forehead before sitting down at the table. Sunlight streamed in the window and the room was filled with the warm smell of coffee.

"What are you two up to?" I asked.

"Leonard was showing me this picture of you, when you were kids."

Paige handed me a small square, a picture of Leonard and me in a photo booth. It was the one taken at my tenth birthday party, the one where no kids showed up except Leonard.

I paused for a moment as I recalled the incident and then said, "That's not funny. That's a horrible memory."

Leonard and Paige laughed.

"You both looked terrified. What kind of birthday was it?" Paige reached across the table and gave my forearm a reassuring rub.

I smiled for Paige's benefit, even though I was serious. It really wasn't funny.

"Hand me the paper," I said and pointed.

"Really?" Paige raised an eyebrow and then passed the paper across. "He's been doing this for months," she said to Leonard. "We actually got a subscription because he needs to read the obituaries every morning. I don't get it."

"Hey," Leonard said. "They're works of art."

"Yeah, they're works of art." I sided with him as I slid the rubber band from the paper. I flipped though the sections. "Just give me a second and we'll be out of here."

"Looking for someone in particular?" Paige asked.

Leonard and I glanced at each other before I answered, "No. No one in particular."

"Oh, you guys suck." Paige shook her head. "You're such bad liars. What's with the look, did you guys kill someone? Are you waiting to see if the body was found or something?" Paige laughed.

I looked at Leonard and he looked at me.

"Man…" Leonard said. "After today she's your wife. You should tell her."

I sighed, unsure how to explain that I was going to die this year. Paige's smile inched from her face, ticking the seconds by.

"You idiots didn't kill anyone, did you?" Paige asked.

"No," I told her. "Leonard can predict the future by people dying."

Leonard nodded solemnly.

"It's true," he said.

"A few months back, the Pope and Prince Rainier died. Now, I'm watching for Tigger and Piglet to die, then it's my turn," I said. "I'm sorry. I should have told you earlier. It's just that I love you and I wanted to protect you."

Paige contemplated this for a moment.

"So you're going to die later this year?"

I nodded.

"2005?"

I nodded.

"After some cartoon characters die?"

"The voice actors that played them," Leonard corrected.

I was still nodding. "Our fates are tied," I said. "It's true."

"Say I believe this," she said, though the tone of her voice turned serious and told the opposite. "Say Leonard can predict when you're going to die…"

"I can…"

Paige silenced him with a finger in the air and a look that made my blood cool a few degrees.

"Richard," she said. "Do you believe this?"

I dropped my gaze to the tabletop and fiddled with the rubber band.

"Yes."

"Say you are going to die this year," she said. "Why are we even getting married? I don't want to be a widow in six months. Why would you do that?"

The pause that followed was not because I didn't know the answer—I was all too aware of why we were getting married. It just took me a moment to put the words together in the right way.

"As with life, I know how my story will end. We all know how our stories will end, every time. We all wind up in the same spot yet we all try. We learn, we love. It's when we live that makes the difference, not when we die."

The breakfast nook was silent. Our coffees steamed lazy opalescent spirals above the cup rims.

"I'm no different because of what I know," I continued. "I don't know that much more than anyone else does, the ending is always the same. Whether it's tomorrow or forty years from now, we all deserve that time. Paige, I'll love you until tomorrow or I'll love you until forty years from now, it doesn't matter."

I raised my gaze. Both Paige and Leonard were staring at me. Leonard wore a smile and Paige's eyes had melted from stern to mildly perturbed within a few seconds.

Paige took my coffee, sniffed it, then said to Leonard, "Have him at the gardens by two for the ceremony. No excuses. I'm going to have a shower." Paige put my coffee back on the table. "Rachel's supposed to be here in an hour to help me get ready."

"She'll be here," Leonard said.

Paige kissed me on the forehead and left the room. A few silent moments passed. Neither of us spoke until we heard the shower running.

"You think she's worried about me dying?" I asked.

"I think she thinks we're nuts and she's probably questioning the wisdom of marrying you right now," Leonard said. "Did I ever explain to you the power of testimonials?"

My blank look must have sufficed for an answer because he kept talking.

"Think about it. Next time you try to explain this, you may want to break her in with a few examples of my correct predictions. It'll make it seem less crazy."

"But you've never been right," I said.

"I was right about the Prince and the Pope," Leonard said.

"That's the first time though."

"I've been close on many occasions and a few examples might have helped convince her."

"Oh, I see."

"Now she thinks we're nuts. This is why you aren't supposed to see each other on your wedding day," Leonard said. "Because any shit you say today actually gets heard and means something. That's why you're not supposed to talk to each other until after you're married."

The shower stopped running.

"Let's get out of here before she comes back," Leonard said. We grabbed our stuff and ducked out of the apartment.

We spun around one descending flight of stairs and dashed down the next. Within moments, we broke onto the street. Leonard had found a rare parking spot right in front of the building and all I could think was that it really was a perfect day. I hung my tuxedo jacket from the clothes hook in the back of his car and got into the passenger seat.

I took a sip of coffee as Leonard nosed the car into downtown traffic. With a sharp horn-blast we merged into the line of cars coursing through the street.

I thought of the picture Leonard had shown Paige.

Auntie Maggie had said, "Come on, you will look back at this picture in twenty years and laugh." If Leonard was right this time, I would die a year short.

Those little boys trapped in the chemicals of that creased and faded photograph were now full-grown men. The little boys in that picture now bore the marks of nineteen years past and I marvelled that we sat here, in the same positions; Leonard on the left and me on the right. The windshield replaced the camera and this time, unlike in the picture, I smiled.

I turned to Leonard, raised my coffee cup to him and said, "Thank you. You couldn't have been a better friend."

"No need," Leonard replied and looked my way. "I couldn't imagine not being a part of your wedding."

I had meant "a better friend in life," but let Leonard think I was talking about the wedding. It didn't matter. I glanced forward, gasped and braced my arm against the dashboard.

Leonard's eyes shot to the road and his foot stomped on the brake. The tires locked and laid a solid, greasy black line on the asphalt. We slid to a halt a mere hairbreadth from the bumper of a garbage truck that had veered into our lane.

The lid flew from my cup as I grasped it tightly and what was left of its contents splashed forward with the application of the brake and then backward as we rebounded from our inertia. My white dress shirt received the brunt of its tarnishings. We, of course, hadn't registered the coffee spill yet. Our focus was on how close we had come to being in an accident.

Leonard gripped the wheel and his leg was tensed, pinning the brake pedal to the floor. My heart pounded. A look of relief eased itself onto Leonard's face as he let out a slow breath that sounded like he was hissing a drawn out version of the word "shit."

I glanced in the rear-view mirror at the rusty maroon '82 Monte Carlo that sat mere inches from the rear bumper.

As traffic began to move again, I felt the warm wetness of my shirt.

"Fuck."

"What?"

"Got coffee on my shirt."

"I think we got off pretty easy then," Leonard said, glancing my way.

"Keep your eyes on the road," I said. I patted and rubbed the coffee spill, only succeeding in smearing it around a bit. "I can't get married in this."

"We still have a few hours." Leonard signalled his way around a corner. "There's a department store on the way. Let's go get another shirt."

As we drove, the tall buildings gave way to rows of houses and the occasional strip mall. Within fifteen minutes of leaving downtown, Leonard eased the car into a spot near the entrance of a department store. The parking lot was largely empty, a broad expanse of lonely asphalt dotted by the occasional weed that found a crack to poke through. A warm breeze blew, unhindered across the flat expanse. We made our way into the department store and took a rattling escalator up to the menswear department.

"Over there." Leonard touched my elbow and pointed. "The shirts. I've got to go take a leak. I'll meet you there."

I nodded and made my way past the Diesel to the Deacon Grande display. I didn't know when department stores started carrying his line but I relished the fact that he had a sale rack in a suburban shopping mall.

I absent-mindedly rubbed the coffee smear as I fingered my way through the rack. My head bounced along to the tinny, muzak version of ABBA's "Gimme! Gimme! Gimme!" I thought about how the past constantly reinvented itself, as if it has all happened before in one way or another. I found my size and pulled the shirt from the rack.

Done, I nodded to myself, 20-percent-off Deacon Grande, white shirt, French cuffs. All I needed.

I glanced over to catch a clerk fiddling with a mannequin. She pulled off one of the arms, adjusted the position of the peg that held the arm to the torso, and then reattached it. The newly positioned limb was now held out, as if in a sweeping motion over a kingdom, saying, *One day, all this will be yours.*

I chuckled and shook my head. I had been the model for that mannequin twelve years ago. It had been early in my career, when everything was amazing, when I still had amazing abs. I was eighteen. It took only an afternoon for them to make the cast for the mannequin and here I stood in my old body looking at my young body. Only one of us was unchanged by time.

"Hey."

Someone had been trying to get my attention. I didn't know how many times it had been said or how long he had been trying to get me to notice, so I apologized.

"Sorry, hi." I looked at the man, trying to place his face. It was a face that would have been easy to remember, yellowed teeth worn to pegs in the front, pockmarked skin and a ruddy complexion that came with excessive drinking.

"Ain't I seen you somewhere before?" he asked, his voice a chunky growl of a long-time, heavy smoker.

It was wonderful, being singled out, being recognized. It was a warm feeling I hadn't felt in so long. I wanted to hear it again, it didn't matter from where or whom. I wanted to bathe in it just once more, so I feigned distraction and said, "What's that?" Like I had been thinking about something else. I wiggled the shirt I had chosen to make the point.

"You look familiar." He smiled his broken smile. I could see little chunks of food between his teeth.

"I've done some modelling," I said.

"No kiddin'." A searching look passed over the man's face, his head cocked to one side in examination. "Yer the tank-top guy, right?" he asked. "The one on the boat."

Wow, good call, I thought with surprise. Jungo undergarment shoot. The boat on a trailer in the middle of a parking lot downtown. Man, I marvelled, that was back in 1994. Eleven years ago. I had been eighteen.

"That's me all right," I said. "That was a while ago though."

"Yeah, I remember that." The man's voice rolled like gravel. "Musta been early nineties." The man stood for a moment and then continued his rummage through a sale pile of singlet shirts.

I couldn't let the moment go, I wasn't ready to be forgotten quite then. The warm rush of recognition cooled slightly. I glanced around to see if Leonard was coming back but didn't see him. In fact, there was nobody in the store but me, the man, and the woman changing the mannequin.

"You see that mannequin?" I asked. "That one over there?"

"Yeah?"

"That's me."

The man's eyes flashed from the woman stripping the mannequin to me, from plastic to flesh.

"Really?" he said. "The face ain't yours."

"It's my face."

"I don't know." He scratched the bristle on his chin, making a sandpaper sound. "It don't really look like you."

"It is my face," I insisted. "It's just…stylized. You know? They made the nose sharper."

The clerk stood in front of the naked mannequin, hands on hips contemplating something, before walking away.

"Yer nipples that pointy?"

"No. That's stylized too. My nipples are normal."

"Oh." The man nodded. "So, what you been doing lately?"

That hurt. It prompted the words "nothing" and "looking for work."

Lately, I've had a feeling of panic.

"Things are moving along nicely," I said. "I've decided to do less modelling and take more of a management role. You can't stay beautiful forever, right?" My laugh sounded more desperate than I thought it would.

Lately, I've had this tightness in my chest that made it hard to breathe.

"No…you can't stay beautiful forever. It ain't like there's a fountain of youth or nothing to make you immortal, right?" The man chuckled and moved closer. He started fingering the Deacon Grande shirts but I could tell he wasn't really looking. He had a distinct odour, a mix of earth and whiskey sweat.

"True." I smiled uncertainly and took an instinctive step backwards.

He matched my retreat with a step's advance and said, "The body of work you left behind's admirable, though. In itself it kinda preserves an immortal youth, right? Kinda like a time capsule."

"Oh, you know my work," I said.

"I do, Richard." The man glanced around. I did too. We were horribly alone. The clerk was nowhere to be seen. Leonard was still absent and the store was as expectedly deserted as a failing midday suburban department store should be. "I'm very familiar with your work."

I felt the overwhelming urge to run. The feeling sprouted from deep in my primordial mind and the flight instinct came through louder than any other thought. It may have been the hunger in the man's eyes, it may have been that terrible predatory grin, it may have been the way his wiry, insectile arms shot out to grab me—and it was likely all of the above that compelled me to push off from one planted heel like a sprinter out of the blocks. The man's arms closed on air.

The best I can figure, it was one of the shorter escape attempts in history. I slammed facedown on the linoleum, hard and fast. The best that I can figure, I made it two steps before he knocked my feet from under me. My landing thumped the wind from my body so hard it hurt deep in my chest.

My hands and elbows squeaked across the linoleum as the man crawled on top of me, both of us moving together but in opposite directions; I slid backwards along the floor as he scrambled his way onto my back.

I couldn't scream. I tried. I couldn't breathe. His weight on my back. I felt his arm wrap a vice-like chokehold around my throat. My face was pushed into the floor as he wedged my neck into the crook of his arm and levered it like a nutcracker with his free arm. The man's breath blasted a rhythm against the back of my head.

At first, I lay still: initially from shock and then from the thought that he would release me if I didn't resist. There was no air going in or out. Pressure built in my head as the need for oxygen grew desperate. I couldn't swallow so a string of saliva pooled on the floor from the corner of my gaping mouth. As the seconds passed, my lungs—emptied from my fall to the floor—demanded more than basic submission.

My body started to convulse and buck. It was an autonomic panic reaction. I heard flesh squeak against linoleum and the man's breath in my ear. I heard the steady *whoosh whoosh* of my pulse grow louder. With a strength I normally lacked, I pushed up and flipped us onto our backs. The man grunted and wrapped his legs around my waist to reinforce the fact that he was immovable. I pushed backwards, crab-walking us into a display rack. The hanging shirts enveloped us. I reached out an arm, feebly grabbing at the rack. It slid sideways a few inches and then stopped. With every passing moment, I lost strength. My struggles became pathetic spasms.

"Hush, hush, hush. There, there," the man whispered in my ear. He rocked me gently back and forth. He tightened his grip on my throat.

"Hush, hush, hush." His fetid breath in my ear was the last thing I felt.

"There, there." His harsh voice in my ear was the last thing I heard.

There's nothing I remember clearly after that point. It's hard to separate my unconscious dreams from the hazy reality of anesthesia-induced visions.

I remember Leonard walked, tall under the fluorescent lights, across the scuffed linoleum in the menswear section of the department store. His head swivelled back and forth looking for me. His black patent leather shoes stopped at the Deacon Grande display. He didn't distinguish between the fresh scuffmarks of my struggle and the old ones from past traffic. He didn't see the puddle of saliva from where I deposited a stringy slime.

Leonard stopped to pick up the shirt I had dropped when I turned to run. He looked around, trying to piece together my vanishing, trying to figure out what to do next.

He continued his slow search, the shirt hanging limp in his hand. He walked past the mannequin and stopped at the watch counter. The woman behind the display counter smiled at him. Every watch displayed a different time but each reminded him that we were mere hours from my wedding.

I remember waking again with a headache and a deep soreness in my neck. I stared up at exposed wooden beams of some dimly lit space. The musty smell in the air was of an underground, basement space. I heard voices.

"He's coming to." The rusty voice of the man who attacked me.

"I'll put him under in a second." A woman's voice. "He's wonderful," she admired.

The voice was familiar but I couldn't place it.

"He'll do," the man said.

"He'll more than do."

I turned my head, my neck screaming in protest. I winced and tried to swallow but it hurt too much.

An IV tube was attached to my arm. A bright light flared on, blinding me but not before I caught a glimpse of Dr. Bella and the man. The IV tube tugged gently. Shortly after, the pain in my neck subsided and my head no longer throbbed. I smiled thankfully and closed my eyes.

I remember Leonard and Paige talking. He was wearing a tuxedo and Paige looked stunning. She had designed her own wedding gown.

"What do you mean," she asked, "disappeared?"

"Um…" Leonard stammered. "He was looking for a shirt. I went to the can and, when I came back, all I found was the shirt."

"Seriously, I'm going to kill him." Her voice wavered with emotion. "I'm going to kill him and then I'm going to kill you for losing him." Then her face crumpled and her composure was destroyed by wracking sobs. "We were happy. He was happy. Why would he leave me?"

Leonard embraced her. He stroked her back and she wept on his shoulder.

I remember opening my eyes. The exposed beams overhead were set as a series of black and white lines from a severe light source. My body was numb and I felt nothing but a rapid, repetitive tugging on my leg that reminded me of a documentary I once saw, one where a feral dog tugged to rip a meaty chunk from a carcass. My body felt so heavy and the tugging made my vision oscillate, the beams above shifted back and forth rapidly.

"Come on," someone encouraged generically.

A power tool whined briefly, deafeningly, and then whirred to a stop. There was a wet crunch and a pop. The sound reminded me of dad chewing on the gristle from a steak. The tugging stopped.

"Shit," someone else gasped. There was a retching sound and a liquid splash. The sharp stench of vomit wafted over me.

"Christ," Dr. Bella's voice said. "Get out. His chances are slim as is. Forget blood loss and infection, I don't need you puking all over him."

"He's awake," the first voice groaned.

"If I give him much more anesthesia, it'll kill him."

"He's looking at me."

"He's not really all there. Wait a sec..."

I grew drowsy again and, as I closed my eyes, I heard Dr. Bella say, "We're almost done."

I remember Paige, sitting in a room, on a bench near a window. She looked outside, into the evening light bathing the gardens where we were supposed to get married. Out there, amidst the flowers, one hundred empty white chairs sat, laid out fifty per side, with an aisle bisecting them. They looked like tombstones spaced out in the failing light. The hanging tendrils of the weeping willow framing the altar swayed in a gentle breeze.

I remember the breeze. I couldn't feel it but I could smell it. It was fragrant with vegetation of a summer's evening. It was dark and I was being carried on a sling of some old blanket. One shadowed man grunted, holding the corners of the blanket near my head. Another, similarly burdened, struggled with the edge of the blanket at the opposite end. He stumbled as he walked backwards.

Above us, the black and white leaves of trees flickered on and off, their swinging surfaces reflecting the streetlights. Higher, far above us but below the stars, the gentle breeze blew in the dark, bringing with it the smell of mown grass.

A dog barked in the distance.

In a house across the street, I saw the back of someone's head framed by the blue glow of a television set.

The two men muttered and grumbled. We stopped moving. With

a final straining heave, they deposited me in the trunk of a car with a thud. The springs squeaked once under the weight.

The men stood for a moment, panting. From my perspective, on my back, looking up from the stinking nylon carpet lining the trunk, a streetlamp cast a halo around their heads. The stars were nearly blotted out.

"That's it then?" One of them asked, not looking at the other. His eyes were fixed on me.

"I suppose," the other replied. "I kind of expected more, really."

The first hissed out a laugh and then said, "What did you expect, that he'd be filled with gold or something?"

The other mulled that over before replying, "I don't know. Either that or chocolate."

They leered for a moment longer. Then one of them lifted his arm, rested it on the trunk lid for a second before closing it, plunging me into darkness.

I remember coming out of the anesthesia and regaining consciousness. My black world smelled of exhaust with a sharp tinge of burning antifreeze. We were moving. I heard the chatter of gravel under the wheels. The tailpipe rattled in its bracket as we powered over bumps.

I knew the anesthesia was wearing off because, for the first time, I could feel a painful throbbing itch all over my body.

We drove over another bump and a shovel I had seen in the trunk before everything went dark, batted me in the back of the head. Another bump and there was the gurgle of an oil container.

I don't know how much time passed. I moved in and out of consciousness, waking more and more frequently as the pain in my body mounted to a point I had to concentrate solely on not screaming. Thankfully, it became unbearable and I passed out again.

I remember waking up to the absence of noise. It wasn't so much waking up as it was coming to. It took me a moment to realize the car had stopped. It was hot and stifling and, in the crack around the lid and through a nearby rust hole, daylight fought its way into the darkness.

The car shook. I heard one door slam, then another and then a third. There were voices, at first muffled and distant but slowly becoming more coherent as the crackle of walking feet on gravel grew more distinct. I could make out the voice of the man who had attacked me.

"Doc says we gotta give him three shots of this a day to fight off the rot. Doc says he needs painkillers for a good while. One shot of this every six hours." There was a pause. "Looks like we're about a half-day late on both shots."

They laughed and I started at a loud bang on the trunk.

"Seriously though," the voice ground on, "I've invested a lot in getting this guy. Won't do us no good to let him get dead on us. So, you," a pause, "take care of these shots. And you," a pause, "can babysit his pain."

There was some scratching at the trunk, what I assumed to be a key navigating the lock, and then I was awash in a painful burst of light that almost outdid the burning stabs of my body.

I clamped my eyes shut, seeing only the red burning through my eyelids—and even that was too brilliant to bear. I snuggled my face into the stinking nylon until I could stomach the light.

"There now," the gravel voice rolled. "The next attraction."

I cracked my eyelid and looked up to see several looming shadows and a brilliant blue sky above. I looked at my body. My beautiful body, that was admired, that carried me, that fed me, pleased me, sustained me. My body that was envied, gazed upon, used for expression and motion and sex, for everything, my everything was nothing but a torso. The finality and permanence of it, my missing arms and legs. The irreversibility of what they had done shattered my mind.

I tried to howl but my vocal chords were dry and crusted from dehydration and the drugs they had pumped through me. So, I lay there, my only expression a dry wheeze and a mouth that could open no wider to express my sorrow.

"Ladies and gentlemen," the man said, "please welcome our latest addition, the next great attraction. Allow me to present, for your viewing pleasure, Turtle Boy."

As my eyes adjusted, I could make out the assortment of bodies gathered around. The fat man, the Mighty Mite, the carnie with a rusty nail hanging out of the corner of his mouth, Esteban the wolfman, all staring, all smiling.

"Everyone's gonna want to see you," the carnie said. "Yer gonna make us heaps of cash, Turtle Boy."

He leaned forward, jabbed a needle into me and depressed the plunger. My pain subsided almost immediately.

"Welcome to Mexico, boy."

CHAPTER 17

Thank You, Good Night

It may seem like there are moments where nothing is happening but don't be fooled. Every heartbeat leads to the next event and every seemingly mindless conversation will culminate in something. The funny thing is, the story never truly ends. The narrators just change as if life is some endless relay.

The track is circular.

You run and pass the baton.

You run and pass the baton.

You run and pass the baton.

Repeat and repeat and repeat.

The baton is nothing more than existence, a faded collective memory. Between each hand-off, that's where it all happens, life's lived. Once it's passed, once life has a beginning, middle and an end, once we know the dead like a friend, we know what we have truly lost. And that's our job for our time here, that's the baton—don't let them leave you. Remember them well.

But there's a little left to this story yet.

That's me in the rusty li'l Red Rocket wagon, the one with the wobbly wheel like so many kids have toted their stuff around in. That's me lying on my back, looking up at the sky, being jostled across the gravel lot, along the dusty corridors between faded red canvas tent walls. Everything about the wagon rattles, bumps and squeaks.

The wheels raise little trails of dust. Esteban pulls me like he does every morning and this one, this bright blue morning, is no different. He struggles to pull my wagon up a rutted and potholed hill. His feet kick dust from the dry stubble grass, which causes me to cough.

We do this in the mornings, find a hill to climb and look down over the carnival. If the terrain is flat, we just wheel out until the tents are small on the horizon and we watch from the distance. We sit and talk. Some days, when a newspaper can be found, Esteban reads to me. He swats flies from my torso. Lately, my left leg stump has been attracting more flies and smelling a bit like blue cheese.

Today, the wagon rattles to a stop under a scraggly tree at the top of the hill. Its branches click together in the breeze. The tents sit like pimples below, in a valley at the edge of some small Mexican village. To the horizon, whaleback hills make for a soft, scrubby, rolling vista.

"Where are we?" I ask.

Esteban flops down beside me, puffing, his fur matted with sweat. He hasn't complained once about the effort of hauling my torso around. He smells pungent, like a wet dog.

"This town is called La Concepción. In Guanajuato," he says. "Not much happens here."

We sit for a span. Esteban's breathing calms.

"I've been wondering," I say. "What do you think they did with my arms and legs?"

"Don't even worry yourself with it," Esteban says. "When the médico made me, the months of transplants and hormones, man, I don't even want to know whose hair this is or how she got it." He smoothed out his fur with a hand. "When she made the fat man? She must have saved the fat from hundreds of rich folks getting it sucked out, then injected it into him. And you don't even want to talk to the Mighty Mite about it. They had him bound like a mummy, wrapped up tight for years to keep him small. He was…"—Esteban made a scissor sign with his fingers—"…so he wouldn't get big. They starved him and gave him some kind of injections. Took his whole youth—years—you don't want to even know."

Esteban shakes his head and squints at the valley. "Somethings, once they're done, they can't be undone. Sometimes, you have to accept things the way they are."

I nod a bit and look out over the rolling, sunburnt land.

Dr. Bella had said, "If the body can't be corrected, the mind remains tormented."

As we sit on the hill, a gentle morning breeze caresses us and my wolf-man buddy scratches my leg stump. The branches tick overhead and the peace I feel makes me wonder if Dr. Bella was right. Or was she just close? Should she have said, if the mind can't be corrected, the body remains tormented? The soul is the tangible intersection of the body and the mind and the world. It is the harmony of these parts, not simply our physical parts, that creates beauty. When I stopped taking the three apart and started putting them back together, I felt whole again and I could see beauty.

Dr. Bella could treat her patients' unhappiness but, in creating their new bodies, she only created the need for more. She created addicts. With each procedure, she made everyone look more the same. The need to stay young and fabulous creates the need for a more extreme vision of beauty just to stand out. It creates a whole new disorder of pretty ugliness.

Chester taught me about blind sight, where the eyes don't see reality, they see the fantasy of what the brain wants to see. But, from what I can tell, the line between this reality and fantasy doesn't exist. The mind makes its own reality.

"You okay, Richard?"

"Yeah, Esteban," I say. "I'm fine. I was just thinking, looking at the tents."

"Thinking about what?" Esteban shoos a fly away from my leg stump.

"Someone once told me that if everyone looked the same then no one would be beautiful or ugly. No judgments would exist. No one would stare."

"Yeah, but we'd all be the same, nobody different. Man, I don't know about beautiful. I don't know about judgments. I never had a chance." Esteban smiles. "But I like you and the other guys. I like the Mighty Mite. Fat man's my buddy. The people here make me a home."

"I know. You've figured out what I wanted my whole life, not through the quest for perfection but by the acceptance of imperfection. You've subverted the pretty war."

"I don't know nothing about no war. This place, these people, is what I know." Esteban plucks the newspaper from my wagon. He shuffles the papers and starts reading to himself with a sigh.

I squint at the valley. The sun blazing overhead works to wash out all colours save for a few brave shades of yellow and brown. My stump itches.

I thought hard over the past while and I should have known all this would happen. Looking back, I can see the flow of events that brought me to this. Mind you, even now, I can't see what's to come. Leonard's the one who could see all the connections, not me.

Leonard. It was like a lifetime ago.

Paige. I don't even remember how long.

I won't die. It's all a matter of perspective really. The world will just cease to exist to me. It's about the anatomy of any given moment. Without a witness to life, the other building blocks of the moment don't matter. I witness time push seasons from one to the next and each day slip from one into the other, all heading toward an end that becomes clearer to me.

Esteban chuckles. "Someone bought an eleven-year-old grilled cheese sandwich on eBay for almost $30,000. It had the Virgin Mary's face cooked on it. This lady, Duyser, said it brought her years of good luck at bingo."

I grunt. "Can you scratch my left leg stump? It's itchy like crazy."

Esteban reaches over and rubs the stump. His eyes stay fixed on the paper.

"Thanks," I say.

A trail of dust rises between two hills in the distance. It hangs like lazy laundry drying on a clothesline. The air is quiet, the valley below is silent. Esteban reads the paper while I watch the plume migrate closer to the camp below.

Esteban looks up as the Monte Carlo comes into the clearing on the south side of camp. The distant engine noise stops and it takes a moment for the sound of a car door slamming to travel up the hill to our ears. For some reason, the disconnect makes me frown.

"Carnie's home," Esteban says.

"Yep."

"Brought that new attraction he was talking about, I bet," Esteban says.

"I bet so."

Bodies of every shape, size and colour emerge from the tents and migrate to the car. Their differences are muted by the distance from which we view the scene.

"You want to go see?" Esteban asks. "It's the spider man in the trunk. Carnie says he has four arms and four legs."

"No. I don't need to see." I shake my head.

I watch the figures gather around the trunk. Fascinated eyes they have. This is a human zoo. We're all watched. It's why we're here.

After a while, they pull someone from the trunk and carry him into a nearby tent.

"Can you scratch my leg stump again?"

Esteban complies. "Your stump don't smell too good." He waves away some flies and peers at it. "It's turning black." He sniffs his fingers and then wipes his hand in the dirt.

Esteban goes back to the paper.

There are many moments in life that conspire toward making you the person you turn out to be on your deathbed. All of the events, the people you meet, the places you go, the things you do and have done to you, everything foreshadows the person you are in the end. Final hindsight is like the cover of the puzzle box: it shows you the big picture but during life all you get are the pieces.

"Weird," Esteban says, tracing the text with a furry finger. "It says here the guys who gave their voices to Tigger and Piglet died on the exact same day."

"Paul Winchell and John Fiedler," I say.

"You know them?"

"I feel like I do. I feel like I have known them forever," I say. "How old is that paper?"

Esteban scans the page. "It's a week and a half old."

I'd been ready to die several times in my life and had made peace with the fact. Maybe I'd even looked forward to it. I could stop fumbling, stop trying. I didn't want to give up but I was unsure how to keep going.

I'm happy with how it all went though. Everything I've done in my life matters. Even if it only matters for a short while and only to a few people, it's more than enough.

If Leonard's predictions come true, well, I guess I'll know soon.

But then again, Leonard has been wrong before.

I can't wait to see what happens next.

On June 24, 2005, we mourned the untimely passing of Richard Trench. A dear childhood friend of mine and a beloved member of the fashion industry, Richard will be remembered fondly by his mother Debbie, his friends, family and fellow industry members.

Richard was often described as beautiful, stylish, compassionate, and approachable by fans and fashionistas. I personally know these traits applied as truly to the deeper levels of his being as they did on the surface. The words written here, read by you, can't plumb the drive and depth of a man I am proud to have called my best friend.

Like in the 1998 "Heavenly Show," Richard has been promoted to the position of Angel. He now dons an Ozone™ halo and looks upon us all from a higher catwalk.

Twenty-nine years is too short a time for someone like Richard to walk among us. You are missed. You are remembered.

–Leonard Fenton
Obituary from the *Times*
June 24, 2005

Gary Jan Fairway passed peacefully on the evening of June 24, 2005 at the age of 73. Gary, 6'3" and 245 lbs., is described by Sophie Fairway, his loving wife, as a man who had as much caring to give as space to take up.

His brothers at the #713 Fire Hall knew Gary to be a heroic member of the force and, in retirement, he was an active volunteer at all the #713's fundraising activities. During his career, Gary fought fires bravely and saved countless lives. He lives on in the people he saved as well as through his son and three grandchildren.

Memorial services are open to the public and will be held at the Alliance Church on Plainview.

—Leonard Fenton
Obituary from the *Times*
June 24, 2005

Mr. Gary Jan Fairway has called to ensure me that he is very much alive. He thanks me for the kind words written in yesterday's edition. Mr. Fairway also thanks his friends, family, and his brothers at the 713 Fire Hall, for all the lovely flowers and phone calls of condolence.

Mr. Fairway says it fills him with such pride and comfort to know that he will be well remembered when his time finally comes.

He says, "We should all live our lives to be so loved."

This writer and his editor, on behalf of this newspaper, apologize for any undue anguish or confusion caused by this regrettable mix-up.

—Leonard Fenton
Obituary retraction from the *Times*
June 25, 2005

Acknowledgements

This book could not have become what it is without the trust, caring, help and love of a gaggle of people.

First off, I'd like to thank my husband, Nenad, for being the kind of person I strive to be every day and for giving me quiet mornings to scratch away at the paper or peck away at the keyboard.

Hats off to the folks who have slaved and toiled and struggled with me through the early drafts of *Imperfections*. This includes the constructive direction from the ladies of the polycognomenal critique group I attend: Elena Aitken (any continuity errors are entirely my own), Nancy Hayes (apologies for all of the foul language in the book), Susan Lorimar (thanks to you, I now know what a nonrestrictive participle phrase is), Trish Loye Elliott (for bitchin' direction on hand to hand combat ... shit, sorry Nancy, I swore again) and Leanne Shirtliffe (for calling offside when I went too far)! A big thanks to my good friend Amanda Dow who has read and edited pretty much every word I have written so far. Also, good thoughts on derek beaulieu for the always stimulating conversations on writing, publishing and the sound that one hand clapping makes. To you all, my deepest appreciation.

A huge hug and a kiss to Nightwood Editions. To Silas White for seeing the potential in *Imperfections* and for bringing my first novel to print. I recognize the risk in the work you do, the time and effort you put in and I thank you for accepting that role. To Lizette Fischer for keeping me in line, on time and under control.

Like anyone reading this, we have to thank our parents. Mine are good and without them, nothing would happen. Any resemblance to Richard's parents is purely coincidental.

And thank you for reading this book and supporting the literary arts with your patronage. If you liked it, tell a friend to read it too because without someone to read it, a book is a lonely and useless object.

—BRADLEY SOMER

For more reading on nifty deaths, happy pills, pretty dresses and plastic skins, the following books fit the bill. *The Dead Beat* by Marilyn Johnson. *Beauty Junkies* by Alex Kuczynski. *Fame Junkies* by Jake Halpern. *Eccentric Glamour* by Simon Donnan. *Making the Body Beautiful* by Sander Gilman. *Artificial Happiness* by Ronald Dworkin. *The Revolution Will be Accessorized* by Aaron Hicklin, Ed. and *Survival of the Prettiest* by Nancy Etcoff.